A Riot MC Biloxi Novel

KAREN RENEE

Copyright © 2024 by Karen Renee

All rights reserved.

No part of this publication may be reproduced, distributed, or transmitted in any form or by any means, including photocopying, recording, or other electronic or mechanical methods, without the prior written permission of the publisher, except as permitted by U.S. copyright law. For permission requests, contact Karen Renee.

The story, all names, characters, and incidents portrayed in this production are fictitious. No identification with actual persons (living or deceased), places, buildings, and products is intended or should be inferred.

Without in any way limiting the author's and publisher's exclusive rights under copyright, any use of this publication to "train" generative artificial intelligence (AI) technologies to generate text is expressly prohibited. The author reserves all rights to license uses of this work for generative AI training and development of machine learning language models.

No artificial intelligence (A.I.) or predictive language software was used in any part of the creation of this book.

Paperback ISBN: 978-1-957194-33-2

eBook ISBN: 978-1-957194-22-6

Cover Model: Shane MacKinnon

Photographer: Golden Czermak/Furious Fotog

Design: Karen Renee

Editor: Barbara J. Bailey

To all the people who fight against domestic violence

Author's Note

This book is intended for mature readers 18+. It contains scenes of domestic violence and situations which may trigger or upset some readers. Please do not read if you are uncomfortable with those types of scenes. Thank you.

Playlist

A MURDER OF ONE by Counting Crows
ZERO by Imagine Dragons
SAVE YOURSELF by KALEO
RESCUED by Foo Fighters
WHERE THE DEVIL DON'T GO by Elle King
COLD COLD MAN by Saint Motel
LIKE A RIVER RUNS by Bleachers with Sia
WOMAN WOMAN by AWOLNATION
LOST BUT NOT ALONE by Michael Franti & Spearhead
PROMISCUOUS by Nelly Furtado with Timbaland
BRING ME TO LIFE by Evanescence
I JUST WANNA SHINE by Fitz and The Tantrums
MAGIC by Coldplay

Chapter 1

Someone's Old Lady

Riley

The back door snicked shut and I lifted a slat of my blinds half a centimeter. Dad trudged through the backyard to the fenceline. Every week he inspected the fence for signs of neighbor dogs trying to dig under it. The bizarre thing was that he could have paid someone to do this, but he insisted on doing it himself.

Then again, he believed the adage that if you wanted something done right, you had to do it yourself. Particularly when it came to dirty work.

I grabbed my phone and wallet, hurried to the fridge, grabbed a water, opened the freezer door, and made sure his frozen dinner was exactly lined up at the front of the shelf. He'd moved the bag of frozen peas. If I took the time to search, I'd probably find that he threw the bag away. At this point, though, I didn't need them any longer.

I closed the freezer and raced out the front. My cousin had sent a text I couldn't ignore, and it didn't give me time to dawdle. Still, I couldn't let Dad know I was leaving. He'd raise holy hell and I didn't need that today.

It took Dad at least half an hour to inspect the fence. I *should* only need five minutes to jump in my car and drive away, but that assumed I had a normal vehicle or a father who cared about my health and safety. Instead, I needed at least ten to get out of the drive.

First, I popped the hood to make sure he hadn't disconnected my battery. Then I ran through a few other checks to make sure I could drive away. I lowered the hood, slow and gentle, not latching it. Once I got out of the drive and down the road, I would stop at a convenience store to close it completely.

I lived with an overbearing and super-controlling man. It wasn't easy, and I desperately wanted out... but that was much easier said than done.

The moment I pulled into the lot for the convenience store, I heard my cell ding with a text message. It was most likely Aurora, the only person my father approved of me being around because she had attended the same church as us all our lives. Aurora and her family had stopped attending, though. I'd thought that would be the kiss of death for me and I'd have nobody I could count on, but oddly, he'd talked to Aurora's dad, and he approved of their moving on to a different congregation.

I powered off the decrepit Toyota, got out, lifted the hood a few inches and let it fall with a satisfying bang. Inside the car again, I turned the engine over, but the 'check engine' and the oil light came on.

Shit.

This wasn't exactly anything new. Dad had once fucked with my oil in an effort to keep me home. I'd called Aurora and she'd told me to get a quart of oil (there happened to be an extra in the garage). That remedied the situation, but I still had Mensa take it somewhere for service.

I recalled my phone had dinged earlier and I checked it. Aurora wanted me to call her.

"Yo! Your dad just called here looking for you..." she trailed off and sighed. "I don't know how much longer I can cover for you, Riles."

I nodded. "Yeah, just, please tell me you didn't slip —"

"Of course not. I wish you'd let us get the cops involved."

I shook my head. "I wish that too, Rora, but we just can't."

I read my cousin's text for the tenth time. It couldn't be right.

Mensa, a member of the Riot MC, never texted me about when I'd be at the clubhouse... so getting a text telling me I *had* to show up for this afternoon's party hit me funny. For a fleeting moment, I thought about ignoring it because I had a black eye – courtesy of my father.

Yet, I couldn't ignore Mensa this go 'round because for all I knew Block wanted to ream me out for the bad things I'd done to Heidi. It had been over a month since everything came to light, and they'd given me one *last* chance to stick around the MC. Still, things changed. Hell, if I were in Heidi's shoes I'd never have approached Block about giving me another chance. Maybe Heidi wanted to watch the rug get pulled out from under me.

If only this command appearance were two or three days from now. That's typically how long it took for my black eyes to fade enough that my makeup skills could cover up the damage. I spent as much time at the compound as I could because it was the only place I ever felt really safe. Being a sweet-butt was great, but I wanted to be someone's old lady. I wasn't picky... not really. I'd been with nearly all of the brothers, except Mensa for obvious reasons, and I'd never been with Har. I hadn't been confident enough to approach him before he settled down with Stephanie.

Any time Dad hit me though, I steered clear of the compound. Nobody could know what was happening at home. Sadly, I couldn't move out. Tried that once and Dad found me. I imagined the day Dad came here to get me. The brothers would never put up with his vitriol and they'd lose their minds if they saw him lift a finger at me. But, the brothers didn't like sweet-butts hanging around twenty-four seven...so I still called Dad's house home.

I glanced at the blue bubble of words from my cousin. From the tone of Mensa's text, I had no choice.

I'd seen what Har did to a woman who threatened his old lady, Stephanie. Okay, no, that wasn't entirely true. The brothers were careful with what many called their 'wet work.' I hadn't seen it, but I'd *heard* plenty. So, for all I knew, ignoring the brothers might push Block or Har over the edge and they would decide I needed a lesson.

Half an hour later, I drove through the gates to the compound. Instantly, I knew I had to go into the clubhouse through the back door. Gamble, Finn, Tiny, and his new woman were sitting outside the front entrance.

Of all the brothers, *Finn* had to be sitting outside.

Last year, a week before he earned his patch, we'd had two wild and crazy nights. They'd been the best two nights of my life. Then I got stupid because I let myself give in to a desperate hope that he and I had something more.

After he earned his cut, he looked right through me. Even when I cornered him to congratulate him, he'd responded with nothing more than a grunt.

Since then, we'd been around each other plenty, but he redefined the term 'standoffish.' Yeah, so I wasn't that picky, but I didn't want anything to do with Finn.

I hurried out of my car and snuck inside through the back. Mensa's room was on the first floor. I went to his door and knocked.

No response came, and I knocked again, crossing my fingers he wasn't in the common room – or worse, had joined Finn and the others while I'd parked my car.

Then I heard a sound that normally didn't bother me, but when it's your family member having sex... the sound takes on a huge ick-factor.

Mensa yelled out, "Go away! I'm busy!"

I wandered further down the dim hall and pulled up the text string on my phone. Only... Mensa's text from an hour ago was gone. That was really weird. I'd read it so many times, I knew I hadn't imagined it.

It was bizarre, I couldn't count how many times I'd wanted to delete a text and couldn't. How had he... then I remembered he'd bought a new iPhone and the commercials all touted how you could now delete a text.

I shook my head and quickly tapped out a message letting him know I was here.

"Riley, girl! You haven't been by in a long time," Sandy said from the end of the hall.

Shit.

I seriously liked Sandy. She didn't look down her nose at me like so many of the other old ladies. Her caring and giving nature made some people think she was overbearing, but I loved it. Not having a mother made me crave any kind of motherly love. If she caught wind of my injury, she would lose her mind worse than the most protective brother.

In the dimness of the hallway, I prayed she didn't notice my shiner.

I smiled and nodded. "Yeah, been busy. What's goin' on? Have a good time in Daytona?"

With Sandy's huge smile, I knew someone had gotten their cut. "Tiny made Sierra his old lady last week, and her troubles are all over, so we're doubling down on the party tonight, girlfriend. Come out to the common room."

After a deep breath, I nodded. "Sure, I'll be there in a minute. I gotta get something out of my car."

She went into the kitchen, and I hurried outside, my mind focused on getting the hell out of there.

On the concrete patio, I ran smack into a hard body. My eyes had been aimed at the ground, so how I missed the black motorcycle boots, I didn't know.

"Where do you think you're goin'?" Finn asked.

I shook my head, but didn't look up at him. "To my car."

"Look at me, Riles."

Him using that nickname annoyed me, but I powered past it. I tried to side-step him, but he moved with me. I shook my head. "Finn, just let me leave."

"I told you to look at me. A brother tells you to do something, you do it."

That pissed me off, and my head tipped up, anger shining from my eyes. "That isn't true, and you know it. Have fun tonight, Finneas."

For whatever reason, he was the only brother who earned a patch and kept his given name. Maybe it was because of his angular features, but I doubted it. He had thick, tight curls on the top of his head, and I suspected he kept his hair short because otherwise frizz would be a major issue. His steely, gray-blue eyes were normally friendly, but right now they held irritation. His nose was practically perfect compared to other men. No bumps from being broken or anything like that. Normally, I didn't go for beards, but Finn's well-groomed facial hair appealed to me. He had a small soul-patch that led to the rest of his beard and forced my attention back to his full lips.

His large hand came to my face, his index finger stroking my tender cheek. "She was right."

I shook my head, but he didn't drop his hand. "Who was right?"

His voice became gentle. "Sierra. She saw you drive in and thought you had a black eye." He paused and stared at me. "Who the fuck did this to you?" he bit out his question.

His tight tone sounded protective. Hope flared inside me, but I snuffed it out like a bad flame. No, he didn't care about *me* getting hit, he was probably just itching for a fight.

"Nobody. I need to go."

He sucked his lower lip into his mouth. The action forced my attention to his soul patch. "Know it wasn't one of my brothers who did that to you, so who did? You been hanging around another MC or some shit last week while we were at Biketoberfest in Daytona?"

I fought an eye roll. "No. I ran into —"

"If you say a door, I'm tying your ass up until I get the truth out of you."

My eyes darted to the metal shed where they restrained and interrogated people.

With a disbelieving laugh, Finn shook his head. "Not like that, Riles. I'd tie you to my bed until you told me the truth."

My head reared back. "That's just mean. You don't even like me, so I know you don't give a damn about me."

His eyes widened. "Say that shit again?"

I tilted my head. "Seriously, Finn. You got your patch and ghosted me, for all intents and purposes."

He squinted at me. "Hard to ghost someone when you see them every fuckin' week – if not every fuckin' day."

I shook my head. "You grunted at me when I congratulated you on your patch. Obviously you got your two days of getting your rocks off with me and that was it."

There were two wooden picnic tables with built-in benches on the concrete patio. Suddenly Finn's arm wrapped around my waist, and he moved us until my ass was against the edge of a table.

He leaned in and I leaned back. "That wasn't *it*, Riley. Those were the best two nights of my life."

"Right," I drawled.

He leaned in some more, but I couldn't go anywhere. His muscular chest pressed against my tits. The spicy scent of his body wash assaulted my nose.

His voice lowered. "That is right. But, I'm a man who doesn't enjoy watching that woman, day in and day out, throw herself at my brothers. Especially not when I know she's fuckin' those brothers instead of fuckin' me. Now tell me, how am I supposed to talk to you when I know you don't wanna be tied down, which means I gotta *share* you?"

I shook my head. "I never said I didn't want to be tied down. Hell, I want to be someone's old lady so bad, I can taste it."

His brow arched. "Yeah, and that's another damn problem."

I frowned. "What? How is that a problem?"

He leaned back. "You want to be *someone's* old lady. You didn't say you want *me*. You didn't say you want Mensa."

"He's my cousin," I muttered.

His eyes widened. "You get what I'm saying, Riley. Being an old lady is what you want. I want a woman who wants me whether I make her my old lady or not."

I stared at him feeling like such a douche. It hadn't occurred to me that my willingness to be with any of the brothers could be a turn-off.

Chills ran down my spine when he abruptly stepped away from me. I straightened and he crossed his arms.

"Back to my question, Riley. *Who the fuck* did that to you?"

"Jesus! What happened to her?" Two-Times asked, coming up the steps to the patio.

Finn looked at Two-Times. "Trying to figure that shit out, man."

"Did I miss a catfight or something?" Two-Times asked.

He was a patched member, but he didn't live at the clubhouse or hang there quite as frequently as the others did. I often wondered why they kept him on as a member.

"A woman didn't do that to her, a man did," Finn said.

My eyes widened and Finn grinned.

God, I was so stupid. He'd only been guessing, but my expressive face gave me away.

"All right. Now I know it's a man, it wasn't someone with the Riot, so... you gonna tell us who did this? Or should I get Har and the others out here?"

My body went stiff. Mensa couldn't know that his uncle beat me. "No!" I cried.

Two-Times aimed some side-eye at me. "Way you yelled that, I almost think a Riot brother hit you, but Finn's right. None of us would ever do that shit. Who are you protecting?"

I shook my head. "I'll tell Finn who hit me, but nobody else can know."

"Why?" Two-Times asked.

Finn looked at him. "Go inside. If she doesn't want more people knowing, that's her call. She doesn't fess up, I'll bring her to the common room."

While Finn watched Two-Times duck inside the clubhouse, I edged away from the table.

My phone dinged, because making a clean get-away was never in the cards for me.

I caught my cousin's text message before Finn came up behind me.

> Yeah, so? Do you need a gold star?

People in their twenties probably shouldn't feel their blood pressure rising, but with the amount of anger I had coursing through me, that had to be why my ears were ringing.

My fast-flying thumbs started in on a response when Finn snatched my phone out of my hand from behind.

I whirled and luckily yanked my phone back. "Oh, no. The days of the *brothers* taking my phone are over, Finneas!"

His brows went up. "Is that so? Do you have something to hide? Saw Mensa's the contact you got up, what's the deal?"

"That's what I want to know. He's the reason I'm even here. Made it sound like someone demanded I be here, but I don't know why."

He held his hand out for my phone. "Let me see. Mensa doesn't make demands. He isn't like that."

I rolled my eyes. "That's the thing. He went and deleted that text since his new phone can do that shit. Probably just to make me look stupid."

An annoyed expression twisted Finn's lips. "He might have deleted it by mistake, Riley."

I scoffed. "And I might be a runway model."

Finn

She *could* be a runway model, once that infuriating black eye healed, and if she were a foot taller. Why runway models had to be so tall, he'd never know. His mom would say it was a leftover vestige of the patriarchy, but this was no time to think about Mom.

He shook his head to keep his thoughts on track. "Why don't I just get Mensa out here? He can answer that question for us."

"No!" She cried out so fast, Finn heard the same panic that Two-Times had observed. It was as though someone in that clubhouse was the one who hit her.

He cupped her cheek again, watching his thumb trace the edge of the bruise. "Why not? The way you're reacting, I'd think he did this to you, but I damn well know better."

She closed her eyes and took in a very deep breath. In a low pained voice, she said, "He can't know about it."

"Why not?"

"He just can't. I need to know why he demanded I show up here today."

Finn bit his tongue to keep from telling her Mensa didn't send her that text... *Finn* did. And then he'd had to wait a very long hour before he could snag Mensa's cell again to delete the evidence.

Riley slipped past him, again, marching toward the clubhouse. In two strides, he caught up to her, and twisted her around to face him.

"What are you doing?"

"What I should have done a year ago," he muttered, then he dipped down, put his shoulder to her belly and hauled her to her car.

"Oh my God, put me down!" she yelled.

His hand locked on her ass, and he smiled. "You don't want Mensa to know about your shiner, you better keep it down, Riles."

She growled, and it was so damned cute it turned him on. He willed himself not to get hard.

Gently, he set her down. That was a mistake. He forgot how feisty Riley got when she was angry.

She put her hands up to shove him, but pulled back at the last minute. Anger blazed from her eyes. "For the last time, Finn, what are you doing?"

He wanted to say he didn't know, but that was a lie. Six weeks ago, Har had announced that Riley wouldn't be welcome in the Riot MC clubhouse. The lead weight Finn felt in his stomach had been an unwelcome surprise. He'd reasoned that it was a sign. Between her willingness to be with *anybody* and his inability to fight for her attention, things had played out the way they were meant to.

Except, a week later, the decision was reversed with a heavy emphasis that this was her very *last* chance with the club.

He resolved to make the most of it.

In theory, that should have been easy. Nothing with Riley had ever been easy though.

He stared into her dark brown eyes. "I'm driving you home. On the way, you're gonna tell me who did that shit to you, and then I'm gonna kick their fuckin' ass."

Fear flooded her eyes, and she shook her head. "I can't go home. Not tonight. Please."

Shit.

He had to be wrong, but things were adding up. "You're gettin' shoved around at home?"

Her head twisted, then she looked back at him, defiance replacing the earlier fear. "No, that's not it. I just need a night out."

He nodded. "Get in the car."

She dug her keys out of her pocket as he rounded her trunk to the driver's side. He stopped at the rear wheel well and grabbed the magnetic key box that Mensa had mentioned putting on her car.

"What are you doing?" she asked – for the third time, but he wouldn't point that out.

He grinned. "Driving you home."

She scurried around the hood. "You're not driving my car, Finn."

He unlocked her door, and slid halfway into the car and moved the seat back. "Get in, Riles. I'm driving. You better hurry. Mensa's probably looking for you or he will be soon."

She planted her hands on her hips. "Are you listening to me? I can't go home."

He settled into the driver's seat. "Didn't say I was taking you to *your* home. Now get in the car, woman."

Chapter 2

Judge

Riley

How did this happen?

I didn't know what was worse, the fact Finn was right about Mensa coming to find me or Finn driving my beat-up Toyota. Both were embarrassing, but I couldn't afford to run into my cousin.

With a sigh so strong my father would have blackened my other eye, I buckled up in the passenger seat.

Finn started the car, put his hand on the gear shift, and then blew out a breath. "The fuck, Riles?"

"What?"

He glanced at me and back to the dash. "Your check engine light is on and your fuckin' oil light's lit up too. What the fuck are you doing driving this rust bucket in this condition? Are you trying to get stranded?"

"The lights just came on today, Finn. I don't have a service shop on stand-by or something."

He turned to me with wide eyes and a strange sneer on his face. "You kinda do since you're a fixture around here and the president of the club —"

"Does custom work on *bikes*, not Toyotas. I really don't have anyone I can just —"

"Stop. I'm taking you to my place, and we're getting this fuckin' thing taken care of in the morning."

"Morning?" I croaked.

He drove out to Beach Boulevard. "Yeah, it happens about nine to twelve hours after the sun sets."

I rolled my eyes. "I know how sunset and sunrise works, Finneas."

"I had to wonder."

I gritted my teeth. "I have to be somewhere in the morning. Early in the morning."

He stopped at a red light and leveled his gaze on me. "That's going to be difficult with this car in such bad shape. You're gonna have to call in sick."

"There are no sick days with Jonah," I blurted.

Shit.

"That's your boss?"

He didn't deserve to know this. Hell, after the way he'd treated me, I didn't *want* him to know this about me.

"Wait, that name sounds familiar... he's in your family, isn't he? Mensa's mentioned someone named Jonah."

I nodded once. "Yeah, he's family, and I take care of him."

"Everyday?"

"Almost."

Finn made a couple exaggerated sniffing sounds. "Goddamn, is this thing burning oil. If we make it to my place, it'll be a fuckin' miracle."

I shot him a sideways glare. "Where is *your* place?"

"Not quite to Gulfport. That a problem?"

"Yes, not that you give a damn."

He grinned. "Glad you're finally catchin' on there, woman."

Damn him. For most women, they would just order an Uber or something. I could do that, but there would be hell to pay with Dad. He kept a tight grip on my credit cards — if I bought anything online or where the 'card wasn't present' for the transaction, he got a text message. Even when the card *was* present, he'd get a text later in the day. That all meant he'd know I spent twenty or thirty bucks to get back to the house.

The worst part was that I wasn't able to keep jobs long enough to build my own savings. Some days Jonah had rough mornings. If I stuck around for him on those mornings, I became known as an employee who wasn't on-time. Then there was the fact that I didn't go into work when I was all banged up. My erratic employment record made it difficult to apply for my own credit cards, not to mention we didn't have a physical mailbox. All of our mail went to a post office box. While I had a key for it, Dad rejoiced on the day the postal system allowed for online previews of every bill or letter received.

So if I got so much as a credit card offer, he knew it.

Days like today... it sucked not having financial independence.

Maybe I could convince Aurora to come get me. She'd always wanted me to take her to a Riot MC party - or even introduce her to one of the brothers. Swinging by one of their apartments to pick me up would have to give her a small fix instead.

"I'm taking you home in the morning," Finn said.

My head whipped around. "What?"

"I'll take you home on the back of my bike in the morning. Then I'll get your car to the nearest mechanic or a junk yard. It's a toss-up at this point with the way the seat's cutting into my ass."

I couldn't stop my eyes from traveling down his muscular body to his crotch.

He chuckled. "Man. I don't know if that should stroke my ego or if that's just standard procedure with you."

My lips pursed and I turned away before he caught it, though it was unlikely he missed it.

He reached over and grabbed my hand, giving it a squeeze. "I'm joking, Riley. Lighten up."

He wasn't really though, and that was what kept me from lightening up. I didn't like people hiding their true meaning behind 'jokes' or the idea that they were just kidding around.

It might seem like I didn't have a sense of humor, but I did. But after living with a narcissistic abuser for the last twenty-five years, I didn't respond well to derisive humor – especially when it was at my expense.

We turned right onto a side street, and then Finn pulled the car into a small driveway. "Miracles never cease. Your car didn't leave us stranded. This is me. Let's get some ice on your shiner."

My growl was quieter than when he hauled me over his shoulder, but from his smirk I knew he'd heard it. "It's too late for ice packs."

He took the key out of the ignition and leaned toward me, his nose inches from mine. "It can't fuckin' hurt, Riley."

I faced forward and took in his place. I'd expected an apartment, but this was a cute little patio home. Too cute for a biker.

He chuckled and unlatched my seatbelt buckle. "Yeah. It is too cute for a biker," he muttered.

Heat singed my cheeks. "Sorry. I hadn't meant to say that out loud."

His arrogant grin stayed firmly in place, and he shrugged. "Don't sweat it. The house belonged to my grandpa, who passed away the day after we were together. I'm staying here until my family decides what the fuck they're gonna do with it."

"Why can't you keep staying here?" I asked without thinking.

His eyes locked with mine and I had a fleeting glimpse of how much he wanted that, but it was overshadowed by cynicism. "Because only my mom's down with that. Her brother and sister both want to sell, but the house has to come out of probate first. Let's go."

Inside the house, I fought the urge to bolt. It smelled just like my grandma's house, a warm scent from a mixture of home-cooking and older furniture. It surprised me I could even remember that smell, since I was seven years old the last time we visited. I hadn't thought about that house in ages because it was like torture. A mirage in the desert of an abusive life.

"Don't know why you just went tense, but you got nothing to fear from me, Riley," Finn said from behind me.

I took a deep breath. "I know that, Finneas."

His hand settled on the small of my back and he guided me to a large brown leather sofa. Once I was seated, he crossed the living room, and went into the kitchen.

The moment he had a hand on the freezer door, I spoke. "You don't need to get me ice or anything."

He looked to me with a blank expression. "Not... anything? Not even a beer?"

On the one hand I could do with some alcohol right about now, but on the other I needed to keep my wits about me. Finn was slick when he wanted to be. He'd proven that plenty today alone.

It was on the tip of my tongue to say I'd take a beer, but Finn got there first. "Tough, club bunny. I say you need ice on your face and a beer in your hand."

"Not a club bunny," I said through gritted teeth.

His head tilted at a sharp angle. "Really? Pretty sure I can name the brothers who *haven't* had you, and that's roughly three – maybe four. I don't know if you've been with Gamble."

Showing my anger in front of my dad would get me smacked around, but I didn't have to stifle shit around Finn. So, I didn't.

I shot to my feet. "I don't need to stick around here and take this crap from you."

He held two beer bottles by the necks and stalked to me. "I'm not giving you shit, Riles."

My eyes widened. "Then what do you call this?"

Remorse filled his eyes before he blinked and set the beers on the coffee table. "I don't know, but it isn't me giving you shit. I'm sorry, babe. Guess I'm pissed because the past year I've been stewing about the fuckin' wasted time."

My brows crinkled. "Wasted time?"

"We hit this at the clubhouse, woman, but months ago, I noticed how you look at me."

"I don't *look* at you," I lied. He was right, and that embarrassed me. Of all the brothers he was so mellow and with my uber-controlling narcissistic father that appealed to me like nothing else.

He ignored my fib. "Fuckin' hated watching you throw yourself at all the other brothers, but I'm getting over it."

The coffee table prevented me from jutting my foot out with my attitude, but I cocked my hip and crossed my arms under my breasts. "Well, good for you, Finn, but I don't particularly like how you could treat me like I'm invisible until... what? I show up with a bruise on my face and you're taking pity on me? Thanks, but pity is the last thing I need."

His lips twitched as though he fought between a pout and a snarl. He came closer and cupped my jaw with both of his hands. "Riley Tyndale, I swore I wasn't going to share this, but your cousin didn't send you that fuckin' text." He paused and twisted his lips to the side. "More like, he doesn't *know* he sent that text, because I did it and I fuckin' deleted the damned thing."

I closed my eyes for a moment. Finn moved one of his hands to the back of my neck and I opened my eyes. "But, why?"

He stared into my eyes, then his gaze drifted down, and he watched his finger trace the edge of my black-eye. "Because I'm not gonna watch you bide your time in the common room flirting with prospects and other brothers —"

"Most are taken already," I blurted.

He exhaled angrily. "Not the point, Riles."

"Then what is?"

"It's your last chance, and I'm not letting you fuck it up."

My eyes widened. "Believe me, I wasn't going to. The clubhouse is the only place I can go and feel completely safe."

The moment the words were out of my mouth, I wanted to slink out of his house.

"Why?"

I shook my head. "Don't worry about it."

He grabbed my hands and pulled me onto the couch next to him. I made to get up, but his hands went back to my neck and my cheek coaxing me to look at him. "Let's try this again. Asked you earlier, I'm asking for the last time, who is pushing you around at home?"

I said nothing. It was quite possibly the one thing Dad had taught me to do well. That and getting the hell out of the room if things got heated or a fight was about the breakout.

The irritation could be heard in his soft exhale. "Don't pull this shit. Don't you shut down on me now, Riley."

I inhaled. "You can't fix this." I exhaled gentle and soft. "So, like I said, don't worry about it."

He sucked his lower lip into his mouth, only to let it go in the slowest movement. "Can't do that, darlin'. No matter how much you want me to."

Next thing I knew, he lowered his lips to my cheek. The touch made me rear back in surprise and slight pain.

He jerked away. "That hurt you?"

"Not..."

"Don't hide shit with me. My lips grazing your face hurt you."

"It was more surprise, maybe a tiny bit of pain. If I'd known it was coming —"

He tucked a lock of hair behind my ear. "You shouldn't have to *know* a cheek kiss is coming, Riley. And that's why I want to beat the fucking shit out of who did this to you. Hell, I ought to call Cynic and Har, get the —"

"No!" I cried.

His head turned a bit. "And that almost makes me think it's Mensa again, which probably means you want to hide this from him. So, it must be family at home beating you. And, as far as I know, you don't have brothers —"

I interrupted him. "I have a younger brother, Jonah. He's got ...a medical condition and I take care of him."

"Which means it's your dad."

I gave him a hard stare, but I couldn't bring myself to deny anything.

"It doesn't matter, Finn. You can't do anything about it."

His eyes rounded, his jaw dropped, and he struggled to find words for a moment. "Do you hear yourself? 'It doesn't matter.' It's the only fucking thing that matters right now, woman."

"There's nothing you can do, Finn. You can't fix this, and neither can the club."

Skepticism filled his eyes. "The clubhouse is the only place you feel safe, but the club can't fix it? That's bullshit, Riley."

"Dad is a *judge*, Finn. Even if you had hard proof, he'd find a way to bury it or turn it around on you, the Riot, or worst-case scenario, both."

Finn

Acid churned in his gut. Of all the professions, her dad had to be a fuckin' judge. That explained a lot, but it damn sure didn't explain why the fucker would beat his daughter. Finn still wanted to find him and pummel the asshole.

"Wait. Does your daddy know that you've been hanging at the clubhouse for the past four years?"

Her eyes darted to the side. "Not really. I outright told him once after the third or fourth time I'd gone to a bash."

Finn scoffed. "You told him?"

She wouldn't look him in the eyes. "I didn't think he'd react the way he did."

The churning acid became more of a roil. "How'd he react?"

She waved her hand toward her eye. "This is nothing compared to that morning. He only stopped because he can't afford for me to be in the hospital. Bad for his public image."

He clenched his jaw, not caring how hard he ground his molars together. After a deep breath, he thought he had it together, but the question wouldn't leave him alone and it only angered him more. "Are you saying he cares more about his public image than your health?"

She stared at the wall for a moment. "Honestly, if he weren't in an elected position, he'd probably have killed me with his bare hands by now and covered it up." She locked eyes with him. "He's a master at covering his tracks and spinning things so he looks good. That's why the club can't fix it."

In an effort to get a grip on his anger, he paced the length of the living room. Things still didn't make sense to him.

"Why do you still live there? You're in your twenties, surely you can move out," he said as he settled on the couch again.

A small, humorless smile tugged at her lips. "I moved out first thing when I turned eighteen. Thought I was so damned smart. Dad dragged me back home in less than two weeks."

"How could he?"

She blew out a sigh and shook her head. "There isn't enough time or tequila for that messed-up story." She turned pleading eyes to him. "Can we just not, right now, Finn?"

He decided to give her that, went into the kitchen, and grabbed an ice pack from the freezer. His original plan had been shot to shit when she showed up looking like a prizefighter's practice partner. He'd wanted to take her to his room and remind her exactly how damned good they were together. Then he'd intended to find out why she'd pulled the shit with Heidi a few months back. Shit *he* had cleaned up, no less.

He sat down next to her again, gently putting the ice pack to her face. "You owe me, Tyndale."

While her one eye widened, she lifted a hand to wave the pack away, but he kept it in place. "How can I possibly owe you, Finn?"

"Your expensive prank had to be cleaned up by somebody. That somebody turned out to be me, and I'm still salty about that shit. You owe me."

She pushed against the ice pack. This time he let it drop between them. Remorse filled her eyes. "I'm sorry, Finn. Know that doesn't count for much now, but —"

He grabbed the pack and put it back on her face. "No need to apologize to me. I just don't fuckin' get it. Why did you do that shit? Were you hung up on —"

With a sigh, she sat back and pulled the ice from her face. "No. Not really, I just hated that Block was suddenly willing to help her when it was clear on the Fourth of July, she didn't give a single damn about him."

His lips quirked. "Sounds a little like you, if you ask me."

"What?"

He shook his head "Never mind. I still don't understand why you thought anyone would put it together that your prank meant for her to stay away from the Riot brothers."

She blew out an exasperated sigh, closed her eyes, and turned her head to the side. "Looking back, I don't either, Finn, but at the time it seemed like the right idea."

He twisted the top off her beer and handed it to her. "Rumor has it, you've learned your lesson."

She sipped her beer and shrugged a shoulder. "Yeah."

They fell into a lengthy silence while they sipped their beers. Even if she didn't want to talk about it, he had to ask. "Why doesn't Mensa know about this shit?"

That humorless smile reappeared. "The moment Dad heard Mensa was patched into the club, he told Auntie Celeste he no longer had a nephew."

He stared at her. "And you come to the clubhouse every chance you get... to poke the bear? Or what?"

Her eyes widened and he fought smiling. Working her up pleased him like nothing else. "I told you, Finn. It's the only place where I feel safe."

She polished off the dregs of her brew and tipped her head to the side in agreement. "And I wouldn't mind seeing Dad face down all the brothers. Most of y'all would lose your minds, and it would be epic... as long as nobody got arrested."

"Yeah, your daddy being a judge, we'd all find ourselves in lock-up at least for a night."

He wondered why Mensa never mentioned his uncle being a judge... but then Mensa had patched in four years before Finn began prospecting. Still seemed odd to him that nobody talked about that.

"You're thinking awful hard over there, Finn," she said, standing. "Do you recycle?"

He grabbed her bottle and went to the kitchen. After he downed the rest of his, he tossed both bottles in the recycle can. "Figure out what you want to eat tonight."

"I can't stay here, Finn."

His teeth sunk into his lower lip while he leaned into a hand on the counter. He didn't miss her eyes focusing on his soul patch. "Be a cold day in hell before I take you back to that abusive asshole."

"I have to be there in the morning," she said through clenched teeth.

"What time?"

They may have only spent one weekend together physically, but Finn had devoted quite a bit of time to studying Riley. From the way her body straightened, he knew she was lying before she spoke.

"One in the morning."

"Why? Is that curfew?"

"I won't sleep here."

He smirked. "Hard to sleep while we're fucking, babe."

She closed her eyes and hung her head. Then she glared at him. "I don't remember you being so damned cocky."

He straightened and smiled. "Things change in a year. Now, don't lie to me this time. What time do you have to be there for Jonah?"

She grimaced. "I was lying, but not by much. It would be good if I was there before Dad leaves for work, and really, it helps if I sleep in my own bed."

"Then I'm coming with you."

She threw her hands up for a split second. "Are you nuts? Dad will lose his mind if there's a biker in his house."

He leaned toward her. "I'll lose my mind if he hits you again, and something tells me he's itching to do that even if you follow his dictates."

Her chest heaved as she stared at him.

"What time do you need to be there, Riley?"

"Six-thirty would be good, six forty-five at the very latest. Jonah is up by seven and I have to... well, you don't need —"

"Don't hide things from me, woman. You have to what?"

"Help him get dressed if he needs it, get him some breakfast. Figure out his schedule and whether we need the in-home nurse or not... though normally I do that each night, so —"

"Can you do that from here?"

She nodded. "It depends on how Jonah's doing, but probably yeah."

"How old is Jonah?"

"Twenty-three."

His head reared back. "Really? What are you? Twenty-four?"

She gave him a fake smile. "Flattery, who'd have thunk it? You're close, I'm twenty-five."

Two years younger than him.

"Doesn't your dad have the bank for a caretaker?"

Her expression turned rueful. "More help means more chances of someone leaking his secrets or giving other politicians dirt on him."

He narrowed his eyes. "How is your brother having a medical condition 'dirt'?"

She barked out a laugh. "Ha! Dad *gave* Jonah his medical condition. Don't you have to get to Twisted Talons soon? The bar opens at four, doesn't it?"

His brow arched. "Club shut it down for tonight. I'm free for the next twenty-eight hours, since I don't go in until six tomorrow evening."

They spent over an hour watching the last part of *Ironman 3* and sharing a couple cigarettes. He hadn't shared smokes with another woman, and he really liked the intimacy it created. Once the movie ended, he made her dinner, more like breakfast for dinner. Nothing fancy.

Riley insisted on helping him by drying the dishes. "After this, I have to shower."

"Why?"

"We were smoking during the movie."

He frowned. "What's your point? The smell bothers you that much?"

She chuckled, though it held zero humor. "No, but it bothers Dad so much that he might shove me hard enough to either bloody my nose or bust open the drywall. Neither is good, but that last always ends up in a double beating for me because it isn't *his* fault there's a hole in the wall. It's *mine*."

His breath caught in his chest. Four hours ago, he didn't think anything could make him angrier than seeing her with a black eye from her father. Turned out hearing the asshole relished beating her twice for shit he caused made him so angry he saw red.

"Have at it, Riles. You can grab one of my t-shirts to sleep in if you want."

She doubled back and sidled up to him. "We aren't going to have sex?"

"Nope. Not tonight."

"Why?"

He ran the sponge over the non-stick skillet one last time and put it in the dish strainer. "I want to get to know you better."

"But why? You know me pretty well already."

He shook his head. "No, I don't. I have no idea why you consider a biker compound to be your safe haven." His head tilted for a moment. "That's interesting to me."

She looked offended. "So, you like that I've been abused."

"I did *not* say that," he said, his tone firm as steel.

"Sure sounds that way to me."

He dried his hands on a dish towel. "You aren't the first woman to be abused. Why not go to a library? The mall? The beach? Fact you chose the Riot clubhouse interests me."

Her lips twisted in contemplation. "Dad forced me out of the library — threatened the lady's job."

"No," he breathed.

"Yeah. He sent cops around to get me out of the mall... and the beach and parks worked until bad weather. Plus, when I got to be sixteen or so, he hired someone to tail me because I was getting drunk at the beach."

"Seriously?"

She shrugged as she met his gaze. "Seriously. Then again, by the time I was sixteen, he expected me to be Jonah's full-on caretaker."

Finn's head began to throb. "Surely the cops knew shit was wrong?"

She nodded. "Yeah. Except the Sheriff lost the election."

That had happened nine years ago. He'd been active duty with the Air Force, but he remembered the news coverage from when he came home on leave. "Wasn't that because of money problems?"

She shook her head while aiming a thin, hard smile at him. "Because dad paid off someone in election regulations."

"You're joking?"

"No. Dad knows it's about the little things and who you know, not what you know."

"Jesus," he muttered, running his hands through his hair.

"Not so interesting now, am I?"

He leaned toward her. "Don't fuck with me, Riles. All of that makes you more than interesting. Makes you a fighter."

"Ha! As if. I'm under his thumb. That's all there is to it."

Finn crossed his arms. "No, you're doing all you can to fight back. I love when people fight back."

She sighed. "If it weren't for Jonah, I'd have run... or I'd be dead — not sure which."

He hesitated. "Why doesn't Mensa know?"

She kept quiet.

"I thought he didn't know, Riley." His hands went to his hips. "How could he —"

"He *doesn't* know. Or, his parents may suspect, but I don't think he has any idea."

His eyes widened. "If he had even a clue and didn't do something, I'm kicking his ass."

She shook her head. "No, he doesn't know."

He narrowed an eye at her. "I thought y'all were close."

She grimaced. "Dad doesn't normally hit me where people can see. Mensa and Auntie Celeste think I have a bad back when I'm moving slow."

"Why do you still —" he cut himself off. "Your brother is the reason you're still there."

Her lips pressed together for a moment. "Yeah, I moved out at eighteen because Jonah had a great caretaker... but Dad found me."

"He found you?"

"More like he used Jonah to force me back home."

Between the growing pain in his head and the pained expression on her beautiful face, Finn struggled to get his thoughts together. "You're old enough, you should get... something like custody of your brother."

She scoffed and trudged to the sofa in the living room. "Sure, except that requires legal action."

He sat next to her. "He can't control everything, Riles."

"No, but he's been in the legal system here for decades, Finn. He'd find out and stop me." Her shoulders had risen as she spoke, and they sank with defeat. "Hell, he's up for re-election — most of the time people keep the incumbent, but he's got a woman who's hungry for his spot. So, he'd squash —"

"Riley, that makes this the perfect opportunity to fight back."

"I'm not supposed to fight back," she said, her eyes widening like she hadn't meant to say that.

"Explain."

"Forget it, Finn."

He stretched an arm along the back of the sofa and leaned toward her. "Not a fuckin' chance." He paused. Things clicked suddenly. "You haul ass the minute shit gets heated, and me and a couple other brothers always wondered why. Most club bunnies... their eyes light up when fights break out." He sighed in disbelief. "You were raised to take it."

"Christ turned the other cheek."

That drew him up short. "What... Are you're throwing religion at me?"

"We must all walk in the path of the Lord."

He stared at her. Could she be pranking him? Everything in her expression was serious.

"Mensa doesn't seem religious."

She nodded and gave a small smile. "Yeah, according to Dad, Uncle Dean came to our church and then convinced Auntie Celeste to convert to Catholicism."

"You really believe you're not supposed to fight back?"

She nodded. "Yeah, but the night he killed Mom and hurt Jonah so badly, I knew no loving God would stand by and let him get away with that."

Finn tilted his head. "But he did get away with it."

She stood. "Yeah. That's when I lost faith in the church, but I still had to go, since I was thirteen."

His eyes narrowed. "If you lost faith, then why don't you see that you need to fight back?"

Her head tilted. "Just because I lost my faith, doesn't mean I lost the habits that church ingrained in me. And seriously, Finn... Dad takes diabolical to a whole other level."

He gave a short head shake. "Take your shower. I need another cigarette."

She dipped her chin and pointed an inviting expression at him. "You sure you don't want to shower with me? Might be better than nicotine."

That tempted him, but he resisted. "I'm sure, woman. I was serious earlier. I want to get to know you better... and be certain you're in this with me not because I'm a brother, but because you're in it *with me*."

Chapter 3

Claims You

Finn

Finn cued up his favorite heavy metal playlist to distract himself while Riley showered. He'd imagined bringing her here over the past few months, but he hadn't expected to have her here so soon. Between songs, he noticed the water had shut off, so he turned down the music. Even though she only spouted off two lines, the religious quotes illustrated how little he knew about Riley.

Maybe heavy metal would offend her... he doubted it, given how loud and prevalent it was at every Riot MC bash, but at this point, anything was possible with Riley.

A knock sounded from the door just as he heard the bathroom door open down the hall. Few people dropped by his place after eight at night, and he needed to get rid of whoever it might be.

He opened the door three inches and saw Cynic standing on the stoop. "Nic, what brings you by?"

"Can I come in? Fuckin' mosquitoes are eating me alive."

Finn let Cynic inside and closed the door. "Something wrong?"

Cynic held his hand out, palm up. "Mensa said you got the extra set of keys to the bar. I need those since Two-Times is training to handle shit while I'm out of town."

Finn dug the keys out of his pocket with a headshake. "Still don't understand why you want a third person. Mensa and I got it covered."

Cynic's head tilted marginally. "Officers decided, man. They feel more comfortable with Two-Times in the loop." Cynic's eyes darted to the side, then his head turned sharply in that direction. "What the hell happened to her eye?"

Finn saw Riley standing frozen in the middle of the hallway.

He liked seeing her in his house, wearing his shirt. Part of him could get used to that.

Neither of them answered Cynic's question.

Cynic's eyes widened on Finn. "Did *you* do that to her?"

Finn's fists clenched. "Fuck, no!"

Somehow Cynic seemed to stand a little taller. "Why is she... is there more going on here?"

"No," Riley muttered.

At the same time, Finn said, "Yeah."

Cynic chuckled and stared at his boots for a second. "Right. Seen this play out once before. If she hasn't been to a doctor – call Silverman."

"It's just a shiner," Riley said.

Cynic's lips twisted and he nodded at her. "Yeah, but that still means you got hit in the head. She gets dizzy or some shit, take her in."

Riley's eyes narrowed on them. "You aren't a doctor, Cynic."

Cynic grinned. "Neither are you, Riley. And if that's your first black eye, they can be serious."

"Not my first black eye, and probably won't be my last."

The charged current in the air was palpable.

"It fuckin' will be if I got anything to do with it," Finn bit out.

Cynic glowered. "You've had more than one shiner – why?"

"Not your business," Riley said, her tone both snide and relishing.

Finn turned infuriated eyes to her. "Tone it down, Riles. He's trying to help."

She settled her hands on her hips. "And I told you, *not one of y'all* can help me."

Cynic stepped closer. "You may be a fixture in the clubhouse, but you don't know the half of what the Riot can do."

She scoffed. "Won't matter."

Cynic shook his head. "You lied to me."

"Excuse me?"

He glanced at Finn and seemed reluctant to speak. "Three years ago, the first time I noticed you —"

"Cynic," Finn started.

Cynic waved a hand at him. "Yeah, I know. None of us wants to revisit that," He looked back to Riley. "But, I *asked* you if someone hurt you. Those bruises on your ribs weren't just healing up after an accident. You lied about the whole thing."

Riley's posture stiffened and Finn wished he could get the chip off her shoulder. "So what if I did? It was years ago, and it doesn't matter. I'm just easy ass hanging around the clubhouse."

"Not any fucking more you're not," Finn said.

Her big brown eyes widened on him. "It isn't up to you, Finn."

Cynic leveled a serious look at her. "It is if he claims you. Fact you're here says it all to me."

"He can't 'claim' me. I'm not anyone's to claim."

"Why not?" Cynic asked. "Hell, why have you been spending time at the clubhouse, if not to land a brother?"

It struck Finn that she didn't always make herself available to the brothers. She hung around a lot, but not with the brothers. She'd shoot the shit with Sandy and other club bunnies more than she would vie for the attention of one of the brothers.

"He'll get hurt," Riley mumbled.

Cynic shrugged a shoulder. "He's a man, he can handle whatever you dish out."

"Not me —" She rolled her eyes at her words. "It's complicated, Cynic."

"Uncomplicate it."

Finn moved forward. "She's right, man. It's messed up."

Cynic's brows furrowed. "'Cause of her cousin? Mensa never cared who or what she did before."

"He cared, he just put on blinders," Riley muttered.

"It's her dad," Finn said, bracing for Riley's reaction.

Cynic shrugged. "So what if he's a biker-bigot? He'll get over it."

Riley charged into Finn's personal space. "Don't you say another word, Finneas," she hissed.

He tipped his chin down to meet her gaze. "It's gonna come out one damn way or another, Riley. And Cynic can help."

Her eyes widened. "Nobody can help – and I don't want Mensa to know."

"Tough shit, we don't keep secrets, woman," Cynic said.

Finn turned to Cynic. "Her dad beats her. He's a judge and pushes his clout around to protect himself."

Cynic frowned. "She's a grown-ass woman, she can get out."

"My brother needs a caretaker," she said in a small voice.

Cynic's expression morphed from sheer anger to careful calculation. "I'll talk to Fiona. She probably knows of some good services."

"Don't have the money," Riley sing-songed.

"Cross that bridge later," Finn sing-songed back at her.

Riley stared at him for a beat, then muttered, "You are annoying."

Cynic pointed a finger at her. "Doesn't matter if he's annoying. You aren't anybody's punching bag. Fiona will call you."

Riley's head cocked to the side. "She doesn't have my number."

Cynic grinned. "You just *think* she doesn't. Sandy will get it to her. Especially once I tell her why we need it."

Panic laced Riley's tone. "No! You can't tell Sandy."

"Girl, there's not a thing for you to be ashamed of. You keep goin' back —"

The panic seeped into Riley's eyes. "He'll hurt my brother."

"That's gonna change," Cynic said.

She shook her head. "That's a promise you can't keep."

Cynic's chin dipped. "Didn't make you a promise, but you work with us, this will get resolved."

"Why? Why would you all bother?"

"You know what happened to Fiona. That shit is not on in our world."

Riley's eyes narrowed just a touch. "But I'm just —"

"Mensa's cousin and apparently Finn's woman. You're one of us."

"Sandy isn't gonna judge," Finn said.

She let out frustrated, but still cute, growl. "Let me give you my number. Keep Sandy from pitying me for as long as possible."

Cynic handed her his phone. "I respect that, but Riley, there's a difference between pity and someone who cares about you showing empathy and trying to help you."

She tapped in her digits and met Cynic's eyes. "Can't say I have a ton of experience with people who care about me."

Cynic took his phone back. "That's all gonna change, lady."

Finn nodded. "Damn straight. I'll walk you out, man."

Riley reached out and patted Cynic's bicep. "Thanks, Cynic. I know I can be a pain in the ass, but I appreciate the help."

Cynic lifted his chin. "Not a problem, woman."

Finn followed Cynic to his candy-apple red chopper, putting a cigarette between his lips as they went.

"Don't light up around me. I'm almost six months cigarette-free, but it's still fucking hard." He pointed a finger at Finn. "You need to quit."

Finn jerked the lighter away from the cigarette. "This shit's got me stressed, man."

"You really taking an ol' lady at your age? You aren't even thirty."

Finn lowered his voice. "Not sure yet."

Cynic's head reared back. "You got her at your place. That shit sends a message."

Finn sighed. "Only because Mensa couldn't see her like that."

"Forgot about that," Cynic whispered, then asked, "Why aren't you sure?"

Finn's body shook with a silent chuckle. "Should be obvious, 'Nic. She's been with most of the club... I want to know that she gives a damn about me – not just settling for the only brother who'll take her."

Cynic nodded. "Makes sense. Didn't know you cared about her. It's not a savior complex?"

"Shut the fuck up, asshole."

He chuckled and held his hands up. "I'm just playing devil's advocate. Keep you both from getting hurt."

"Right."

"Gotta tell Har."

Finn's brows drew together. "Do you? I mean, it could wait since it doesn't involve the club."

Cynic's eyes widened. "Not yet, but with her Daddy's position, it's only a matter of time, Finn."

"Yeah. You're right."

Cynic blew out a breath. "You won't like this idea either, but Mensa needs to know tonight. In the morning, at the latest."

"She isn't —"

"Exactly. She'll be pissed and argumentative. Get that shit out of the way, she wants to hide it from him and that won't fly. Plus, he'll be pissed as fuck at you, and I wouldn't blame him."

"Right," Finn sighed. "You're wise beyond your years."

"Shut the fuck up, Finn. I'm not that much older than you."

Finn smiled. "Eleven years is a lot, man."

Cynic ignored the dig. "Another thing, Gower and Gower does family law – they might have ideas on what Riley can do about her brother."

Finn nodded slowly. "Yeah. Hadn't thought of that."

Cynic grinned. "Also why we need to tell Har."

"You're right. Ride safe."

Riley

"Aurora, you gotta come get me."

I leaned against the wall near the window in Finn's living room. Through the slightly-opened blinds, I could see him talking to Cynic. My call to Aurora served two purposes: I wanted her to come get me if possible, and it would keep me from trying to eavesdrop on Finn and Cynic – which wouldn't be cool.

"You started this call telling me that he drove your car there," my best friend said.

I wiped my free hand down my face. "Yeah... a car with both the oil and check engine lights on. Either Dad's stupid sabotage has gone awry or he doesn't care if he leaves me stranded." A small smile crept across my face. "Please, help me out. You'll get to meet a real, live biker."

She laughed. "Riles, I met more than one when you took me to Twisted Talons two months ago. That isn't the treat you think it is because the good ones are already taken."

"You shouldn't need a treat to help a sister out," I said, with more tone than I'd intended.

"Don't be like that. You know I'll help you, but honestly... I think this is *exactly* what the doctor ordered."

"What?" I nearly yelled, and moved to Finn's bedroom. "You're crazy! How is this even—"

"I remember how you talked about that weekend."

I scoffed. "I didn't 'talk about' it."

After a rueful chuckle, she said, "I'll let you hang on to that crazy idea. But I definitely heard how bitter you were *after* that weekend and he snubbed you. You care about him."

My argument died on my lips. Aurora could read me like nobody else. Worst of all, she was right on both counts. I'd talked about that weekend incessantly for days, and I'd definitely been bitter ever since.

But I didn't care about Finn. Not like that... did I?

Crap.

Another call came through my line. "Hang on Aurora." I saw Jonah's contact info. "I'll call you later. Jonah's on the other line."

"All right, but take care of yourself, sweetie."

I pressed the button to take Jonah's call. "Hey, Jay. You hitting the sack soon?"

"Dad's mad, sissy," Jonah said in a small, shaky voice.

I clenched my teeth. No matter that I should be used to it, I hated hearing Jonah talk like he was still a scared twelve-year-old. Part of it was the psychological fear of Dad's abuse, but other professionals said it was part of the brain damage Jonah endured. More than one caretaker had told Dad to get Jonah a private therapist. He'd do that for two or three weeks and claim an issue – money, insurance, the therapist not being a good fit – then he'd stop the service.

Just enough time for Jonah to feel like he was making progress, only for Dad to take it away.

"Remember, he isn't mad at you."

"Are you coming home?"

"I am, but you'll be sleeping, honey," I semi-lied.

"He's really mad, Ry-Ry."

Sounds of the phone jostling filled my ear.

"I'm more than mad, daughter. You aren't with your friend. Come home *now*."

"Dad, I —" My words died as Finn took the phone from me.

"Are you looking for your punching bag, sir?"

My eyes widened and I hissed, "You're gonna make it worse." Thank heavens I didn't use Finn's name in case Dad heard me.

Finn's eyes lit with a nasty grin. "I'm the good Samaritan who found her stranded on the side of the road. I'll get her home once I get some oil for her car. It's Sunday, and the auto stores are closed – so it'll be in the morning."

Seriously? Did he have any clue how much angrier Dad had to be hearing that?

My heart sank. Dad would take that anger out on Jonah.

Finn moved closer to me, locking eyes with me. "Oh, and if you touch her brother, there are some family services who are gonna be interested."

Oh no. Dad didn't do threats. I'd learned that the first time I'd reported child abuse to my junior high guidance counselor.

"She'll be there when she gets there... sir." Finn ended the call and I snatched my phone back. (If I had anything to say about it that would be the *last* time a brother took my phone!)

Finn stood in front of me with a brow arched and a satisfied look on his face like he'd saved the day.

I leaned toward him. "Do you know what you've done? My brother's scared to death and he's gonna get pummeled now!"

Finn crossed his arms and gave a single shake of his head. "Nope. Your dad can't wait to meet me. Said he'd store it up."

I tossed my arms up in frustration. "Finn! He'll still smack Jonah around. Please... just take me home."

He pulled out his phone and started tapping out a text. "Nope."

I inhaled deep to argue with him some more, but then I realized, I didn't need him to take me home. My car keys were still in my purse. I turned on my heel and grabbed my bag.

My progress to the front door stopped when Finn wrapped an arm around my belly.

I grabbed at his arm with my free hand. "What is your problem? I'm going —"

Finn whirled me around, his hands cupped my face, and he crouched so we were eye-to-eye. "You aren't even wearing pants, Riles. I know you're worried, but I just texted Cynic telling him to meet Mensa at your house."

"What?" I breathed.

"They aren't gonna let anything happen to Jonah," he said dropping his hands.

Defeat rolled over me and my body sagged. "You might as well hit him yourself, Finn. Dad doesn't care about the Riot MC brothers. He'll blame Mensa and Cynic for it just like he blamed Mom for what happened to Jonah. And seriously, Dad probably hit Jonah the moment you ended the call."

Finn blew out a breath. "Not going to happen that way, Riley. Cynic and Mensa know what they're doing."

My eyes widened when his words hit me. "Mensa can't know what Dad does!"

Gently, Finn took my purse from me and tossed it on the couch, then he curled a hand around my neck. "He's gonna find out, babe. It all has to come out, and I know you're scared, but you'll be better off once he knows."

Shame and embarrassment welled up inside me.

His thumb stroked a soft spot behind my ear. "I don't like when you're quiet, babe. You don't normally shy away from speaking your mind."

I fought an eye roll. "That isn't really true, Finn."

He dipped his chin to aim a dry look at me. "Back in September, you reamed out a hang-around for talking shit about the Riot when he thought none of the brothers would hear about it. You don't hold back, so don't start now."

My eyes narrowed a touch while I gave a head shake. "You weren't even there that night."

His chin dipped even further. "Yes, I was. Spent the whole fuckin' night watching you."

I struggled against a frown. "Why were you just watching me?"

"Told you earlier, I'm not down with sharing. Now, let's go to bed."

My gut told me Cynic and Mensa couldn't handle Dad, or worse, they'd arrive too late. "At least let me text Jonah."

He nodded. "Fine, but make it quick, babe."

I opened up my text thread with Jonah and hit the microphone icon to record a message. "Hey, Jonah. Can you let me know that you're okay? You're going to bed soon, so I hope you get this in time."

I sent it and waited. Then I prayed the weight in my chest would dissipate, but only Jonah's response would ease my worry.

Twenty minutes later, my phone chimed and I saw he'd sent me a voice message back.

"Hi, sissy. I'm okay. Dad went downstairs. He's still mad. Cousin Kenny came by and Dad yelled at him."

I exhaled with relief and the phone chirped again with another message. I played it.

"Don't be mad, sissy, but I'm glad you aren't here right now. Good night."

Hearing those words, I hung my head.

"It's gonna be all right, Riley," Finn said.

I wandered to the couch and put my phone in my tiny purse. "I sure as hell hope so, Finn. Jonah gets scared when Dad's this angry, and I wish I was there for him."

He wrapped his arms around me, and I lightly put my arms around his waist. As much as I wanted to enjoy his hug, I didn't trust it. The other shoe was always ready to drop in my world.

He squeezed me tighter. "I'm sorry, Riles. In the morning, shit's gonna change."

I tipped my head back to look up at him. "Please, Finn. Do me a favor, and don't make promises you can't keep."

A small smile played on his lips. "That wasn't a promise. That's a fuckin' guarantee. Your dad isn't gonna terrorize you or your brother any more."

Chapter 4

Paved the Way

Riley

The driveway to Dad's house seemed even curvier when experiencing it on the back of Finn's Harley. We were later than I'd have liked, but I suspected it took Jonah longer to fall asleep with the drama last night.

From the side yard, Mensa ambled up to us. His face had a hard set to it and anger blazed in his eyes. "What the fuck, Riley? Why didn't you come to us? God! You had to know you could come to our house."

My eyes widened with my mounting irritation. "No, I couldn't! Your mom wouldn't be able to stand up for me... Uncle Dean's the only reason she was able to get out of the church. She'd never go against Dad, even if she believed me. You have no idea how brutal he is."

His hands came up like he was exasperated. "Cynic mentioned cigarette burns... multiple ones, at that, tell a tale. Hell, I'd have gotten you out of there."

"You'd have gotten your ass kicked... until you joined the Riot, anyway."

"What cigarette burns?" Finn demanded in a steely tone.

I'd forgotten he was even there. For that matter, I hadn't realized Cynic had seen those scars, especially since he only mentioned the bruising earlier at Finn's place.

"I asked you a question, Riley," Finn bit out.

I closed my eyes. "That's how I know smoking bothers him. They're on my upper thigh. There's just four of them."

Mensa spluttered. "*Just* four of them. You're downplaying this shit. Stop it. *One* burn is too fuckin' many."

Finn stared at Mensa. "Where is the bastard? He inside?"

Mensa ran a hand through his wavy hair. "No, he left around five-thirty this morning. Cynic followed him."

"That's gonna go over well," I muttered.

My cousin glared at me. "He was in his new Bronco. Uncle Jack isn't going to spot him in that."

I trudged toward the front door.

"Are you packing your crap?" Mensa asked from behind me.

I turned around. "I can't leave Jonah behind."

Mensa's eyes widened. "No shit, Riley. Mom took the day off work, and we're moving him into our house."

My jaw shifted. "He's going to come to get Jonah back."

"So," Mensa said.

I sighed. "If Auntie Celeste fights him, he'll bring in the cops."

"Let him," Mensa said, his eyes lighting up at the prospect.

"Jonah doesn't need that kind of ugliness."

Finn came closer. "Neither of you will suffer another damned day. Let's get you and your brother out of this place."

"I texted my Fortnite handle to you," Finn said.

"Awesome," Jonah said.

I didn't realize Finn played video games. If someone would have told me Jonah would be exchanging Fortnite handles with a Riot MC brother, I'd have laughed my ass off. Yet, here we were. Jonah and Finn had struck up a conversation about online gaming and now it was like they'd known each other five years rather than for sixty-five minutes.

I heard the front door open and my spine straightened. Finn noticed if the set of his jaw was any indicator.

Mensa's nostrils flared. "Are you serious, Riley? The door opens and you go stiff. God, I wish you'd have told me."

Aunt Celeste bustled into the room, going straight to my brother and smoothing his unruly hair. "Hello, Jonah. How are you?"

"I'm good, Auntie Celeste."

She grinned, turned her grin to me, and it shifted to a regretful smile. Her familiar, spicy perfume hit me just before she hugged me tight. "Sweetheart, if I'd known —"

I pulled back. "There would have been nothing you could have done."

Her eyes filled with a stern resolve. "We'll agree to disagree on that, Riley Jean."

"Are you sure Jonah can stay with you?" I asked, stepping back a pace.

"As sure as the sky is blue today. And I don't care what Jack says or does when he finds out. I'm livid that we didn't see the signs, Riley. I *knew* that you were too young to have a bad back that made you hobble around like an old woman. I ignored my intuition and I'm so sorry that I did."

I squeezed Auntie Celeste's hand. "Don't beat yourself up —"

Her cheeks turned pink. "Don't beat myself up! You're family, honey. I should have seen it..." She trailed off, then her lip curled when she met my gaze. "Your poor mother... she was defending Jonah that night, wasn't she?"

I couldn't hold her steely, blue-eyed gaze.

She blew out a breath. "We're going to make this right."

She was wrong. There was no way to make any of this right.

I shook my head and turned back to her. "Let's get Jonah settled at your house."

Mensa sidled up to Aunt Celeste. "I loaded his suitcase." He looked at me. "We'll get him settled, but you and Finn need to deal with your car. He mentioned the oil light. Really wish you'd have told me Uncle Jack fucked with your car."

Aunt Celeste glared up at Mensa. "Kenneth, I don't care if you're a biker. You aren't going to use that language —"

"Ma, I had to take her car in to be serviced a few months back because of oil issues. It stands to reason that Uncle Jack did that to her car, and it'd have helped if I'd told the service guys exactly what had happened instead of guessing."

Aunt Celeste closed her eyes and shook her head in small shakes. "I can't believe Jack and I grew up together. Where did things go wrong?"

"That church might have somethin' to do with it," Finn muttered. "But Mensa's right, babe. Let them take care of Jonah for today, and we can get your car taken care of now."

My eyes slid to Jonah. He grinned. "Yeah, Ry-Ry. I'm cool."

"Seems I'm outnumbered, but since you're sure, J, I'll see you tonight."

Jonah's eyes slid toward Finn and his grin twisted into a smirk. "Or tomorrow works. You have a boyfriend now."

It was crazy to me how his injury kept him from being able to do certain things, but he could pick up on a budding relationship as though nothing had ever happened.

My lips tipped up. "We're not really —"

Finn stood. "Let them get moving, Riley. There's a storm comin' today, and riding in the rain sucks."

Aunt Celeste gave me another hug. "There's room for you, too, if you need somewhere to go, sweetie. You're *always* welcome. You understand me?"

I nodded. "I understand. Call me, if you need any help tonight."

The moment the door closed behind them, Finn moved in front of me. "I think you need understand something else, Riley."

I shook my head. "What's that?"

"Your aunt had to make sure you understood that you're welcome at her house. I'm pretty sure you need to understand that your brother's right."

My brow arched. "Not what you said yesterday afternoon, Finneas."

His hands settled on my shoulders. "I said I wanted to be sure you want me for me. Not because I can make you an ol' lady. No way for me to figure that out if we don't spend time together... alone, if possible. Your brother picked up on that, and he basically paved the way for us."

I nodded. My belly filled with butterflies which made no sense. I'd been with Finn. It had been a year ago, but spending time with him shouldn't make me nervous.

Hell if I wasn't, though.

My nerves gave way to dread as I thought about Dad finding out Jonah and I had flown the coop.

"I don't know what's goin' on in that head of yours, but I know I don't like that look on your face. Let's go. If you're worried about your father, don't be."

"Ha! As if it's that simple."

He pulled my forehead to his lips for a quick kiss. "It is that simple. If he's pissed, it doesn't matter. You won't be here, and he isn't getting to you."

Even though I tried to fight it, my head shook ever so slightly.

"What? Tell me why you're shaking your head."

"I want to believe that, but I just can't trust it."

"Yes, you can, babe."

My head tilted. "Why?"

"Because you can damn sure trust me."

I stared at him.

He gave me a small smile, that soul patch stealing my attention. "Trust me, Riley. Please?"

I bit my lip. Then I nodded. "I trust you, Finn."

Finn

He'd have never guessed the words, '*I trust you, Finn,*' could be such music to his ears.

Even though Riley fought him for no apparent reason, winning that battle made it that much more satisfying when she relented on anything – no matter how small.

Or in this case, how big because hearing she would trust him filled him with triumph.

Her warm brown eyes met his gaze. "But you have no idea what you're up against."

He laughed. "Baby, you heard Cynic. You have no idea the half of what the Riot can do, but I'll keep your warning in mind. You got any other bags? Need anything else while we're here. If I get my way, it'll be the last time you're here."

A faraway look entered her eyes for a moment. "Yeah. Give me a minute, it'd be good if I got something out of Dad's office."

He gave her some side eye. "What do you need from his office?"

"I don't have all Jonah's medical info – like the therapists he's seen in the past and stuff. Plus, I'm pretty sure there's a separate insurance card for him in there. It'll be good for Auntie Celeste to have that. If this works out, I'd like Jonah to see this one therapist who was making great headway with him, but Dad cut her off after two weeks."

He followed her to the back of the house. "Why'd he do that?"

Over her shoulder, she shot him a wry look. "Said she wasn't competent. I'm pretty sure she picked up on how abusive Dad could be. Once Jonah takes a shine to someone, he really comes out of his shell."

"Didn't seem to have a shell earlier."

She chuckled. "That's because he loves anyone who can talk Fortnite. I had no idea you were into online gaming."

He leaned against the doorway to the home office, while she pawed through a lower desk drawer. "It's something to pass the time and take my mind off life's bullshit."

She looked up at him. "You're so carefree. Life hasn't dealt you any bullshit."

He sighed. "I put up a good front, Riles. Life deals everyone bullshit."

His eyes darted around the room. He could deal with the deer head mounted on the wall, but the huge stuffed bison head staring down at him from behind the desk made his skin crawl. "You done in here? This room's creeping me out."

Her brows drew together as though she couldn't believe him, then she glanced over her shoulder. "Yeah, I've never liked what Dad did to Billy the bison either."

"He named it?" he choked out.

She grinned and shook her head. "No, I did. Helps me not be so weirded out, even if it makes me more than a little crazy."

"Whatever works, woman."

She folded a document and tucked it into her back pocket. "I take it you don't hunt."

His mouth opened, but he paused. "Once. Not really my gig. If it was just a deer on the wall, I could deal, but that bison... not even close."

Back at his house, Riley scrambled off his bike and he missed having her warmth at his back. He swung off and saw Riley's eyes glittering at him.

"Where's my car, Finn?"

He shoved his hands in his pockets. "Had a prospect take it to be serviced."

She squinted at him. "How could they possibly? I have my keys."

"Yeah, but yesterday I used the keys from the wheel-well and those were on the kitchen counter. Prospect used my spare house key to go inside and take care of your car for us."

Her chest heaved as she took a deep breath and nodded. "So, I *could* have gone with Jonah to —"

He closed the distance between them. "Letting you go – whether it's with your brother or on your own – defeats my purpose. Makes it impossible to get to know you better with the side benefit of spending quality time together... naked."

She laughed. "You can't be serious."

"Why not?"

"You just up and decided that since it's my last chance with the club, you're gonna make sure I don't waste it *and* you're possibly going to claim me along the way?"

"Sounds about right. Why are we rehashing this, woman?"

"Because you could have anybody. Why me?"

A car drove by, faster than usual, and Finn realized he didn't want to have this conversation with her outside. He took her hand, unlocked the door, and led her inside the house, but crowded her so she backed up against the closed door.

"Why the fuck *not* you? But to answer your question... how about this." He lowered his lips to hers and kissed her with everything he had.

She whimpered, then pressed forward and drove her fingers into his hair. His hands slid down to her waist, pulling her to him. He'd forgotten how Riley went from zero to one hundred in the bedroom – there was no 'slow' with her. That turned him on even more. He wanted her naked, but they had time for that. With effort, he pulled away from her.

"You're such a great kisser, Finn," she whispered.

"So are you, Riles, but I'm serious. We need to get to know each other."

A questioning look crossed her face. "What is there to know? I'm pretty sure you've got my life story after the last twenty-four hours. I'm at the mercy of a power-drunk, over-zealous father, and just trying to take care of my younger brother. In my free time, I love going to the clubhouse because it's the safest place I know and the brothers have excellent taste in beer."

With a chuckle, he grabbed her hand. "You're right. We do have great taste in beer. Come on, we'll hang in my room until lunch."

"Naked?" she asked, peeking up at him.

"After a while, maybe. Action flick or comedy?"

"Umm..." she hesitated.

He stopped outside his bedroom door. "Hell, don't tell me you don't watch movies."

She shrugged and smiled. "I prefer music when given the choice."

His brow jumped at that. "That's doable. Rock, metal, alternative, or country."

"Are those my only options?"

"What else is there?"

"Pop, but I'm picky about that. Punk, electronic, techno, jazz, reggae, opera – but I'm not in that kind of mood, Christian, hip-hop, seriously, there's lots of other options, Finn."

He wandered into his bedroom, sat on the bed, and tugged off his boots. "You're right. But since we're here, your options are limited to those four."

She paused and tucked a lock of her straight brown hair behind her ear. Her hair was parted down the middle, and on any other woman it wouldn't be half as appealing. With Riley though, she had a natural glamour that reminded him of a movie star. Her lips seemed larger and fuller because of her small chin, and those brown eyes were always so bright and expressive.

The way she stood in his room, watching him, he had the urge to give her what she wanted and get naked. Yet, hearing her go on about music encouraged him to stick to his guns. He shrugged out of his cut and draped it over the arm of a nearby chair.

"Take your shoes off, woman. I'll play some music for you."

He pulled out his phone and opened his Pandora app. While he toggled through his stations, he heard more rustling than just her toeing off her shoes. He glanced up in time to see her pull her bra out from the bottom of her shirt. "Riley."

"What? If we're hanging out here until lunchtime, then I'm not wearing a bra."

On the one hand, he didn't blame her for wanting to be comfortable, but on the other hand knowing she wasn't wearing her bra had him itching to feel her up.

Alternative rock music filled the room and he settled himself under the covers in his bed.

She stood on the other side of the bed with a brow cocked. "Really? We should skip the hassle and just get into bed naked."

"Patience, Riles. Besides, wouldn't you like to get to know *me* better?"

She folded the sheets back and climbed onto the bed, laying down on her belly. "You can tell me your life story while I suck your cock and stare up into your eyes."

"I should spank you for that." His words hit him and he felt like a supreme jerk. "Sorry, babe, I shouldn't have said —"

She put her finger to his lips. "That weekend we spent together, you spanked me, and I *loved* it. So, don't feel like you can't say things to me, Finn."

He pulled her finger from his lips and intertwined their fingers. "Okay. Why are you so forward?"

Her eyes slid to the side and back. "Isn't that what you want? I mean, most bikers aren't after a timid woman. Not from what I've seen."

He chuckled. "I don't think what a biker wants on a random Saturday night and what he wants in his bed permanently is the same thing, woman. Forward was the wrong word. Kenzie and Trinity aren't aggressive like you are."

"What do they have to do with anything?" she asked.

"I tell you we're going to hang in my bedroom, and you immediately want to get naked. What's with that?"

She shrugged a shoulder and scooted closer to him. "We're going to end up there anyway, I'm just saving time."

"Taking my time to get to my destination is half the fun, Riley," he said, snaking his hand around her waist and under her shirt.

He had his hand on the small of her back. She squirmed in an effort to get him to move it further up. He shook his head. "Slow can be fun, woman."

She slid her hand up his chest. "And *more* fun can be had by going fast, Finn."

God, she was tempting. That was one of the things he really liked about her. She reveled in tempting him, almost to the point of teasing, but not quite. His dick was on board with her, but he fought against it — again.

"What do you want for lunch?" he asked.

Her eyes widened and she glanced at his alarm clock. "I don't know. That's like three hours away."

"So? What do you want to eat? If it's fast food, we have less time since we'll have to leave the house."

Her gorgeous brown eyes filled with mischief. "I want your cock for lunch. If you're good, I'll let you have my pussy at the same time."

On a growl, he rolled on top of her. She grinned and wrapped her legs around his thighs.

"Don't you know... your pussy is dessert. Now, what do you want for lunch... no, what's your favorite thing for lunch?"

She swiveled her hips, rubbing against his erection. "I don't have a favorite."

"Bullshit," he bit out, fighting against the urge to rock into her.

Her eyes softened and she slid a hand up the back of his neck, into his hair. "I'm serious, Finneas. I'm not fussy about food. As long as it isn't Vienna sausages, it's all good."

Those fingers wove their own brand of magic and he lost his battle. He lowered his lips to hers and kissed her. She opened her mouth. He took his time, sweeping his tongue against her lips, then just touching the tip of her tongue.

"Mmm," she hummed.

She tried to push her tongue into his mouth, but he kept control of the kiss. With one hand, he pulled her leg free of him. Her hands came to the fly of his jeans, and he stopped her progress.

"No, babe. Not yet."

"Finn... I want you," she whispered.

"Want you, too, but it's not time yet."

He dropped his lips to hers again, but this time he lost his control. He took her mouth with a vengeance. If he wasn't mistaken, he felt her lips widen into a smile, and she returned the kiss with her own form of vengeance. His hand slid up under her shirt, and he squeezed her breast. Kneading the soft, warm mound, his hips bucked of their own accord.

He rolled to his back, taking her with him. She broke the kiss and sat up on his lap. He watched her hands grab the hem of her shirt.

He grabbed her hands. "No, Riley. Slow it down."

"Why?" she demanded.

"Makes shit better."

"Finn, I'm ready to burst, I'm so fucking hot for you."

He brought her hand to his crotch. "Pretty sure *I'm* ready to burst, woman."

Her mischievous grin lit her face. "Then let's go, baby."

He shook his head. Loving the frustration filling her face. "Make out with me some more."

"I want you now, Finn."

"Nope," he said.

"What are you... what is this? A game to you?"

His jaw shifted. It would seem that way to her, but it wasn't. "You can have me... when you actually *need* me."

Their hands still rested at his crotch. She pulled his hand to the waistband of her shorts. Next thing he knew, she'd shoved his fingers inside her panties and had guided his index and middle finger into her hot, slick pussy. "If that isn't *need*, Finn, I don't know what is."

He loved feeling her liquid heat. That had to be why he gave in to fingering her for another thirty seconds. It wasn't until he noticed her riding his fingers that he stopped.

"Finn!"

He yanked his hand free and licked his fingers.

Oh, yeah. She tasted even sweeter than the last time.

Whether she knew it or not, she'd pushed him over an edge he didn't know he was riding. He wrapped a hand around her neck and pulled her down to him. Once her chest met his, he grabbed her hands, pulled them behind her back and wrapped his hand around her wrists. Then he cupped the back of her head and brought her lips to his.

He kissed her, nipped at her lip, and sucked on her tongue. She let out a cross between a whimper and a moan which restored some of his sanity.

He broke their kiss just long enough to ask, "You okay?"

"Yes," she whispered.

"Prove it," he whispered.

Her eyes met his. "What?"

"Prove to me you're okay with this," he said, giving her wrists a squeeze.

Her arms wiggled and he held tighter. Understanding filled her eyes and her lips tipped up just before she took his mouth with an aggression and hunger he'd never experienced before.

He felt her arms struggle against his hold, but he wouldn't tighten his grip. He didn't want to mark her. Not for a while, anyway.

Her tongue twirled around his and he nipped at it. She moaned and her hips bucked against him.

He dragged his lips along her jaw. "You want something, baby?"

"No, Finn. I fucking *need* you. Now."

His plan had been to do this closer to lunch, but that was shot to shit. He let go of her hands. She brought them up to cup his cheeks and she kissed him again.

He shoved her shirt up.

She broke away from him so he could pull the shirt over her head. Her dark eyes flared with lust. "It's about time."

Her perky tits with rosy, budded nipples were right there for the taking. He sat up and sucked one nipple into his mouth while he plucked at the other with his fingers.

She bounced in his lap, even as her hands went to his jeans. "Dammit, Finn. I need you inside me."

Pre-cum leaked from his incredibly stiff cock. He wanted... no, he *needed* to watch her get off before he fucked her. For once, he had her right where he wanted her.

He lowered his hand to her shorts. "You're gonna get my fingers, baby. Make you come in my lap. Then I'm gonna fuck you so hard, you're not ever gonna look at another brother."

The fire shining from her eyes should have blistered his skin. "Finn... God, I *need* you and your thick cock."

He sucked her other nipple. "I'll give you what you need Riley, but I'm calling the shots. Get your shorts off, baby."

Riley lifted one leg off him and shucked her shorts in a flash. He had his shirt half-way up his torso when she yanked it over his head. She leaned forward and kissed a trail along his chest, nipping his pecs near his nipple. He wrapped an arm tight around her waist. Holding her on his lap, he got back to working her up with his hand, and his mouth sucking on her luscious tits.

Her head tipped back with her moans. "Finn. Oh, God, don't stop."

She writhed against his fingers. He wished his cock were inside her, but he'd fantasized about this very moment for months. Watching her unravel before him, listening to her beg for his dick, tasting her anyway he could have her. In short, making her his, whether she knew it or not.

"Look at me," he demanded when he sensed she was close.

Her head tipped forward, warm, brown eyes meeting his gaze.

"What do you need baby?"

"You."

He shook his head. "No, baby. That's not what I asked. What do you need? How do you want it? Harder, faster, rougher?"

She bit her lower lip. "Yes, Finn. All of that."

He reached around and pulled on her hair, hard. "Like this?"

Her head tilted backward and she moaned.

"Look at me," he demanded.

Her eyes found his and he rubbed at her clit as hard and fast as he could with the calloused edge of his thumb.

"Yes! Shit! I'm gonna —"

"Come, Riley. I got you, and I love to watch you come undone."

Once her pussy spasmed and clenched around his fingers, his control slipped again. He sucked at her shoulder and planted her on her back. As fast as he could, he shoved his jeans and boxer briefs off, lined himself up with her, and thrust inside. The sensation of her pulsating pussy overwhelmed him. He'd never get enough of her.

Same thing he thought last year.

It was good to know some things didn't change. Except this time, he'd make sure she stuck around.

Chapter 5

Anyway I Can Get It

Riley

The brain did crazy stuff in an effort to survive, like blocking out certain types of pain. It was the only explanation for why my mind had blocked out how insanely fantastic Finn and I were together.

Effortless and perfect.

An elegant explosion of lust.

Yes, he could work me up like nobody else.

I felt the familiar sensation – the inkling that Finn and I could be something special. Something I'd dreamed of for so long it seemed more an elusive mirage than an attainable dream.

I couldn't go there. Dad had a way of ruining all the goodness in my life. As much as I wanted to be optimistic, I also didn't want another dream to be crushed.

The bed jostled as Finn climbed in behind me. He wrapped an arm around me. "You're on the pill, right?"

"No, an IUD because periods freaking suck."

The air seemed almost tense. I looked over my shoulder. "It's okay, Finn. An IUD prevents pregnancy, and I got a clean bill of health at my check-up last month."

"Yeah," he sighed. "How soon can you get it taken out?"

My breath left me in a whoosh. "What? You... want me to have it removed?"

He used his hand at my belly to shift me to my back. Once he settled on his side, he gently tugged at my waist and I mirrored his posture. His eyes raked up and down my naked body before he aimed a serious gaze at me. "Yeah, I do. I make you mine, I want kids with you. The more the better, the faster the better."

"What happened to going slow?"

He grinned. "What happened to going fast means more time for fun?"

"Smart ass," I muttered.

The serious look on his face didn't fade.

"You're for real?"

He nodded once. "I'm getting hard just thinking about you carrying our baby."

"You're my age."

He shook his head. "Couple years older. I'll be twenty-eight soon. I've been ready, Riley. Just needed the right woman. If you hadn't... that doesn't matter now, but that's what I want and I can't stop thinking that you're the right woman."

The conviction lacing his words, that determined look in his eyes – I was getting wet all over again.

I wanted that – but in two years, maybe three.

"I didn't know you were so driven," I said.

He dipped his chin. "I am. Probably why I get along with Cynic. He was that way until his ex-wife screwed him over. He's lucky he found Fiona."

He was right about that. Before he found Fiona, Cynic had a lousy outlook on relationships. It was probably why I gravitated to him early in my time hanging around the club. He'd said at the time, he was always down to fuck, but never going to commit. I'd thought I could change that, but I quickly gave up that idea.

I shook off thoughts of Cynic and focused on Finn. "You're full of surprises, Finn."

He tucked a lock of my hair behind my ear. "I'm really not, babe."

My finger traced the lines of a tattoo on his arm. "But with me? I don't even know how you take your coffee!"

He grinned. "That's what we were supposed to do before you jumped on my cock."

My eyes widened. "I did not."

"You pretty much did, begging to get naked. Well, here we are babe. And so you know, I take my java anyway I can get it. Hot, iced, black, creamy, it's all good. Or as you said earlier, 'I'm not fussy.'"

I chuckled. "All right. And so you know, I don't drink coffee."

His eyes rounded with alarm. "What? Jesus. Where do you get your energy? Don't say Red Bull!"

I laughed. "No. Sometimes I drink tea, but mainly I have Pepsi One."

He clutched his chest. "Oh, God. We're doomed."

"Why? Are you a Coke guy?"

He pushed me to my back and hovered over me. "Coke is the *only* right answer."

I slid a hand through his close-cropped hair, smiling. "Agree to disagree."

His eyes twinkled and he dragged his very hard cock through my wetness. "I agree to fuck some sense into you."

I laughed. "Not happening, but I'll always agree to you fucking me."

The tip of his cock pressed inside ever so slowly. "Why not try to fuck some sense into me, baby? Am I always gonna have to do the work?"

I spread my legs and shoved him to his back, loving this playful side of him. "Oh, it's on, Finn. I'm gonna make you see sense just before you see stars."

He smacked my ass and smiled. "You fucking better."

"Get dressed," Finn said when I came out of the bathroom.

The clock indicated it was a quarter to noon. "Why? I thought we had until after lunch to get my car."

He grinned. "I said we'd be hanging here until lunch. It's lunchtime, and I'm hungry."

I pulled on my shorts and crossed the room to pick up my bra. "Okay. Don't you have food in the house?"

He pulled his Nirvana t-shirt over his head. "I got a sudden hankering for barbeque and whiskey. There's a place down the street. We'll walk."

"You said there was a storm coming in today. What do you mean we'll walk?" I asked, pulling on my shirt.

"Sun's shining right now, and we won't melt even if we get caught in the rain."

He put on his boots and his cut. After I put on my shoes, he grabbed my hand and guided us out the door.

I tried to pull my hand away when we were on the sidewalk, but he held firm. "This is weird," I mumbled.

"What? Me holding your hand? Deal with it, Tyndale."

I peeked up at him. "So you're a barbeque guy?"

"Good barbeque, absolutely. Really, I'm a mood eater. Something about being with you puts me in the mood for good smoked meat and sweet and tangy baked beans."

"And the whiskey?" I asked.

He grinned. "It's always a great chaser to good food. Noticed you don't normally hit the hard stuff at the clubhouse, why?"

I shrugged a shoulder. "Not anybody's old lady. I never knew when I'd get kicked out of a brother's room, and I needed to be able to drive home. Can't even imagine the beat-down I'd get if I ever got pulled over on a DUI since that would be sure to make the news."

He stopped us on the edge of the restaurant's parking lot. "Your religious upbringing doesn't play a role at all?"

My laughter was all kinds of rueful. "If anything it should have turned me into a complete lush, as controlling and restrictive as it was, but no. The religion has nothing to do with it."

He stared at me for a moment. "I'd love to get you good and sloshed on some Jack... and *Coke* just to see what you're like. But something tells me we need to be on our toes for a while."

I nodded. "Yeah. That's for sure."

Over an hour later, I feared Finn would have to roll me back to his house, I was so full. Finn held me tight to his side as we walked back in a comfortable silence.

I broke it to ask, "Are there people in your driveway?"

He gave a short grunt. "Looks that way. Pretty sure Cynic's there with Fiona, but I don't know who those other two are."

As we came closer, I saw Gamble and Victoria chatting with Fiona and Cynic.

Gamble aimed an incredulous look at us. "You went for barbeque and didn't invite anyone? What the hell, Finn?"

"What are y'all doing here? Besides freaking my girl out," Finn said.

I wasn't freaked out until Finn said that because nobody had ever been so in tune with my reactions.

Cynic draped an arm around Fiona's shoulders. "Fi wanted to find out more about Jonah. Victoria's working family law with Gower and Gower, so chatting with both of them at the same time should get shit moving."

Overwhelming humiliation flooded my body. Again, Finn sensed my reaction and moved in front of me. "It's cool, Riley. Don't get embarrassed."

That was easier said than done, but I managed to nod my head.

Fiona came closer. "Let's go inside and you can tell me about your brother."

While Finn unlocked the door, Victoria said, "Cynic says your dad's a judge."

I nodded. "Judge Tyndale."

"I've never had him preside over any of my cases. He's mainly civil suits these days, right?"

"I think so, I try not to talk to him about work."

She nodded. "I can see that. My coworkers say he's a real hard-ass."

We followed Finn inside. "That's one way to put it."

I couldn't tamp down my awkwardness around these people. It was always bizarre being around old ladies when I'd been with their men, but now they were all getting into my dirty laundry.

Finn put six bottles of beer on the coffee table. Cynic grabbed two and handed one to Fiona, who had settled on the couch.

She patted the cushion next to her. "I won't bite. Tell me about your brother."

I sat down and took a deep breath. Finn twisted the cap off a bottle and gave it to me.

Fiona leaned toward me. "I also don't judge, Riley. What's in the past is past. Cynic told me about the bruises and cigarette burns he saw on you. If your dad did all that to you, I can't imagine what he did to your brother."

Even after a shot of whiskey at lunch, I needed the extra liquid courage and I sipped the beer.

"He never beat Jonah," I started and felt everyone's eyes on me.

Finn sat next to me, slinging his arm over my shoulders and pulling me to his solid frame.

I kept my eyes locked with Fiona's. "The night Dad hit Jonah, it was because Mom had stepped in to keep me from being beaten. Dad lost his mind on her. Then Jonah —" I swallowed back my tears of guilt and frustration as visions of that awful night assaulted me.

Finn gave my shoulder a reassuring squeeze, and I pushed past the memories.

"He was twelve and wanted to protect me and Mom. Dad clocked him, though. Said it was me and Mom's fault he'd knocked his son out. But that hit was more than just a knock-out – it was so much worse. I called 911." Tears were streaming down my cheeks. "I should have kept him from killing Mom instead of calling for help."

Fiona grabbed my hands and pulled me away from Finn to give me a hug. "Oh, my God. I can't imagine... how old were *you* during this?"

"Thirteen – almost fourteen, really – my birthday was the next week," I whispered.

She pulled back. "My God, that's so fucking young!"

"What an awful time to lose your mom," Victoria said, then added, "Not that there's ever a good time, but God, that's horrendous."

My lips pressed together and I gave a single nod.

"Your dad never... went to jail or any of that shit?" Gamble asked.

I swallowed the lump in my throat. "He blamed it on Mom, said he found her beating us and he acted in self-defense of his children."

Cynic perched a hip on the arm rest of the couch near Fiona. "Any investigator should have seen right through that."

My head tilted a touch. "Hard to see through the money he threw at it."

Gamble's brows furrowed. "He paid off everybody?"

I glanced at him. "It didn't hurt that he had the church elders on his side."

"What do they have to do with it?" Cynic asked.

My chest tightened just thinking about it. "Mom had sought counseling at church about her marriage; that's the process at our – no, *his* church. If a woman wants to separate or take action against her husband, she's supposed to talk it out with trusted elders first."

Victoria sat across from us in a recliner. She squinted at me. "You're my age, roughly. So, this would have been what? Twelve to fifteen years ago?"

I nodded. "Roughly. Anyway, all I knew was that Mom was 'disciplined' for wanting to get out of the marriage."

"Disciplined?" Cynic asked, his tone edgy.

I glanced at him. "That's what they call it. Basically, she was publicly shamed and called out for seeking advice. They didn't quite accuse her of making up the problems she had with Dad, but she was expected to bend to the will of her husband."

I took a deep breath. "Dad used that to his advantage in the investigation. Told them about the scene at church. Claimed she was abusing me when it was always him, and Jonah got in the way, which was how he got hurt. That's the only shred of truth in his story. But the church elders came forward and made him look like a God-fearing man and served as great character witnesses, not that it got that far."

"God," Fiona breathed. "Not to change the subject, but tell me what happened with Jonah's head injury. From what Cynic's told me, he's still suffering, so it was more than a concussion."

Gamble was perched on the arm rest of the recliner and he rubbed his hands down his denim-clad thighs. "And Mensa doesn't know about any of this shit?"

"Not until last night," Finn muttered.

My head wobbled. "He knew Mom died and it was a violent death. Uncle Dean had convinced Auntie Celeste to join the Catholic church about five years prior — so they didn't know about the discipline."

Gamble shook his head. "But didn't *you* tell the cops what happened?"

Victoria looked up at him. "Even if she did, the words of a fourteen-year-old girl wouldn't have been taken as seriously as those of a man like Tyndale. A judge with a reputation and church leaders on his side. No way." She frowned. "I don't know who the district attorney would have been back then, but I'm sure they wouldn't have pressed too hard to make a case either."

"Whole damned world is fucked up," Gamble grumbled.

Victoria shook her head. "Not the whole world, honey. Just corrupt officials."

Cynic pointed at her. "I'd say you should report this to the Bar, but I'm sure he's got connections there too."

Victoria shrugged. "It would go to the Commission on Judicial Performance. I'll ask around about the Bar anyway, though. Does your brother get disability of any kind? Is he working? Or has Judge Tyndale had him declared incompetent and established a guardianship?"

I shook my head. "Jonah had a part time job months ago... and Dad made him quit."

"Jesus. This is enough to make me want to smoke," Cynic muttered.

"I told you," Finn said.

"No smoking! You just quit," Fiona said.

Victoria's lips pressed into a line. "Would Jonah know if he's getting disability payments or anything like that?"

"He might. Most of the time, it's like nothing happened, and then there are moments when it's like a twelve-year-old boy is in front of you."

Fiona rubbed my bicep. "Does he need to be in a home?"

I looked at her. "I'm not an expert, but any time Jonah makes gains with a service or therapist, Dad cuts it off."

Cynic stood. "I want to punch this asshole. Who does that to their kid?"

"An abuser," Fiona said.

I looked to Victoria. "I'll have to search Dad's office about the incompetency —"

Victoria waved a hand at me. "Don't bother. I can check the legal databases. Keep you out of his space."

Finn rested a hand on my thigh, but looked at Victoria. "If her dad had Jonah declared incompetent, what can Riley do?"

Victoria turned her hands up. "That'll depend. I need to research it. The easiest thing would be to ask him to give up the guardianship to her — if you want that — but it's also the *least* likely to happen. It's why I asked about disability. Judge Tyndale is probably cashing that in and my hunch is that he's not going to give up that gravy train."

"Right," I whispered.

"Another avenue would be to have him re-evaluated to be declared competent. It would require a doctor or medical examinations, I'm sure."

Fiona looked at Gamble and Cynic. "Doc Silverman won't work, by the way."

Victoria nodded. "Yeah. Judge Tyndale is gonna come out with guns blazing – figuratively speaking."

"Too bad it isn't literal," Gamble said.

"Shooting that asshole would be too kind," Finn said.

Victoria's head tipped to the side. "It would save her a ton of legal fees, though."

I chuckled silently.

Finn

Finn felt her body shaking with silent laughter, and he admired her even more. Not everyone could unload to four people and find a way to chuckle about 'guns blazing'.

He recalled her saying she wasn't a fighter, but he intended to shine a light on her strength for her to see.

"What kind of job did your brother have?" Gamble asked.

"He was working data entry remotely – part time. We both were. Boy, did Dad let me have it after that one."

Cynic stopped pacing and sat on the arm of the couch near Fiona. "Let's back up. Why were you always the one getting hit?"

The sound of her sigh made him brace.

"Dad *loved* that he had a son. Jonah could do no wrong. He would tell Jonah that I deserved to be hit because it was punishment for my sins. Then he'd spout off the corresponding Scripture."

Finn gave her a sideways glance. "Why do I suspect you're not telling us something, babe?"

She turned to him. From the pain in her eyes, he wished he hadn't asked.

"I feel awful just thinking this, but part of me feels sure that if Dad hadn't hurt Jonah, he'd have groomed him to be the same way."

"You're right," Fiona said.

"What?" Riley asked, turning to Fiona.

"You heard me. That shitty behavior is taught. Though, even if I haven't met him yet, I think your brother would have fought against it anyway."

Riley scrubbed a hand down her face. "Yeah, I just feel horrible thinking that night kept Jonah from becoming like Dad."

"Don't waste your energy worrying about that," Cynic said.

"I'll try," Riley said. She looked at all of them. "Should we go meet Jonah? I feel like that would make things easier. Especially since I have a shift tomorrow."

Finn fought his irritation. "Thought you didn't work with a black eye?"

She aimed a dry look at him. "My makeup skills will hide it by tomorrow."

"Not very well, they won't," he said without thinking.

"Finn —" Riley started, her tone laced with attitude.

"Where do you work?" Gamble asked.

"The Easy Fix hardware store."

"The one near the clubhouse?" Cynic asked.

She nodded.

"Does your Dad ever go there?" Gamble asked.

She scoffed. "No. He's all about the larger chains."

Finn couldn't stop himself from asking, "Are the owners members of the church?"

She shook her head. "No. Back to my question, do we want to go meet Jonah? He seemed to be having a good day today."

Fiona shifted on the couch. "Maybe later in the week. I'd like to talk to Dr. Verla. And that should give Vickie time to research things on her end."

Riley locked eyes with Victoria. "What's your rate? I'm not sure if I can —"

A cunning look crossed Victoria's face. "If your dad's corrupt, my boss may do it pro-bono."

"But —"

Cynic cleared his throat. "Woman — you don't worry about it. You're Riot, whether Finn claims you or not."

She glared at Cynic. "That isn't true and even *I* know it."

Cynic grinned. "You're not Mensa's cousin? You're his family. Either way, I'm an officer, so I'll talk to Har, Brute, and Block. You aren't footing this fuckin' bill."

Fiona glanced at her watch. "I hate to say this, but I have to get back to the practice."

Victoria checked her phone and grimaced. "Yeah, my lunch hour's almost over, too."

Gamble rose and pointed a finger at Finn. "Your ass should have invited us out for barbeque. I love that fuckin' place."

Finn stood. "Then get a to-go order, Gamble. Not my job to feed you, since I'm not a prospect any more."

Victoria stood and wrapped an arm around Gamble's waist. "Someone's getting hangry. I'll get back to you when I've heard anything, Riley."

"Okay. It's no rush."

Finn aimed wide eyes at Riley. "It certainly can't wait too long, either, Riles. I'm not gonna be responsible for my actions if he lays a finger on you again."

Fiona gave Riley another hug. "I'll be in touch tonight after I talk to Dr. Verla."

Once all four of them left, Finn closed and locked the door. He turned around and found Riley sprawled out on the couch with her forearm draped over her eyes.

"Seeing as all we did was talk, it makes no sense, but that was exhausting."

The sight of her curvy, petite body on his couch lit something inside him.

He lowered his body on top of hers and she moved her arm. Her eyes opened, giving him full view of her exhaustion.

"You ever tell anyone all of that shit?"

"Aurora."

His eyes slid to the side as he recalled the one night she brought a friend to Twisted Talons. "That the woman you brought to the bar?"

"Yeah."

"Did she grill you for an hour like they just did?"

She shook her head once. "She just listened."

"Right. Questions from Fiona alone are a lot. Add Vickie to the mix, that shit's draining as fuck."

He felt her chest rise beneath him with her deep breath. "Yeah, that's true."

"I'd offer you some caffeine as a pick me up, but Pepsi products haven't come through these doors since Gram died ten years ago."

"Your grandparents drank Pepsi?"

He dipped his chin. "My grandma did. Gramps only drank Coke. They bickered about it all the damned time."

Her eyes skated around the room before locking with his. "So, I remind you of your grandma?"

He shook his head. "Nope, but I like the idea of bickering with you about the superior soda for another forty or fifty years. It'll be fun."

She laughed. "It doesn't sound like much fun to me."

His hand slid down her thigh and then back up and under the leg of her shorts. "Since you're drained... I've got something that could fill you up."

She smiled and shifted her legs. "Is that so?"

"Yep," he said, lowering his lips to hers.

Her hand slid into the hair along the side of his head and she gave the kiss back to him. It almost surprised him since other women might have said they weren't in the mood after such a heavy conversation. But not Riley. She had a sexuality unlike other women, and he especially liked that.

Her hips swiveled as he snuck his finger under her panties. He found her already wet.

"Love that you're always ready for me, baby."

"I love what you do to me, Finn."

He nipped at her lower lip. "Good."

Three sharp knocks sounded from the front door.

He lowered his mouth to her neck and hissed, "Goddammit."

"Who could that be? Can we ignore them?" she whispered.

He raised his head and withdrew his hand from her shorts. "Nope. That should be the prospect with your car."

She grinned. "Oh, good. Then I'll be able to go to work tomorrow."

He stood. "We're chatting about *that* later. Gamble kept me from pushing it with you, but..."

"I need money, Finn. Whatever was wrong with my car probably wasn't a cheap fix."

He went to the door to avoid arguing with her.

Dylan, a nineteen-year-old prospect, stood on the porch looking around as though he was concerned about something.

"There a problem?" Finn asked, stepping onto the porch.

Dylan shook his head. "I don't think so, but I felt like I was being followed."

Finn looked up and down the street. "I don't see anything, but how the hell are you getting back to the clubhouse?"

A Honda Civic pulled up to the curb and Dylan grinned. "This bitch I've been banging is picking me up. Later, man."

Finn slugged Dylan in the bicep. "You aren't gonna ask a brother if he needs anything else?"

Dylan's eyes widened. "Do you need anything else, Finn?"

"Yeah, since you didn't tell me what was wrong with her car."

"Oh yeah, sorry about that." Dylan dug into his back pocket and pulled out a folded invoice. "It's all detailed on there, but she's lucky it didn't blow a gasket was the main thing I got from them."

Finn unfolded the paper with a frown. "That really doesn't help me here, man."

Dylan grimaced. "Sorry, man. I'm not good with cars. They said it's drivable and those lights aren't on any more. Didn't know I needed to know all that shit."

He glared at the prospect. "Who the hell is sponsoring your ass?"

"Gamble. Is that everything you need? Or do you need to bust my balls some more?"

Finn rolled his eyes. "No, but think about that shit the next time before you plan on getting laid after doing what a brother asks."

He stood in the doorway and watched Dylan leave. Behind him, Riley tugged the door open wider. "You went easy on him."

He raked a hand through his hair. "Don't remind me."

"What did Dad do to my car now?"

He turned around and narrowed his eyes. She backed up and he followed her inside. "Now? What do you mean? And why are you so sure it was your dad?"

"He used to disconnect my battery. One school morning he forgot to reconnect it. I told him the car wouldn't start, and I watched from the house as he 'fixed' it."

"Why?"

"To keep me home over the weekend."

He shook his head. "No offense, but I really think I hate your father."

She smiled. "Join the club."

That made him even angrier.

"What?" she asked.

He tamped down his anger, willing himself not to fume. "He's fucking robbed you, Riley."

"True," she said in a cavalier tone. "But why do you seem angry?"

His chin dipped. "Have you seen Vickie with her dad? He's been hanging around the clubhouse every so often."

"Not that I recall."

He nodded. "Yeah. The way they are together... I can see he'd do anything for her. *Anything*. She loves him, and their bond is practically visible." He tossed his hand out toward her. "You don't have that from your dad and it makes me sad, which in turn angers the fuck out of me."

"Oh," she said, nodding once.

He squinted one eye. "What's that mean?"

"I thought when you said he robbed me, you were talking about him killing Mom."

He tossed both hands in the air. "That too! Jesus, this shit is so fucked up." His hands cupped her shoulders. "There shouldn't be a club to join where your dad's concerned."

If she had any response to that, he'd never know. Her phone rang. She looked at it, a worried frown pulling at her lips. "Why is Sandy calling me?"

He could guess. "Answer it. She's persistent as fuck."

"Hi, Sandy. What's—"

He heard the high pitch of Sandy's questions from two feet away. It was all he could do not to yank the phone away from Riley.

"I'm sorry, Sandy."

"You got nothin' to be sorry for," he bit out.

Riley grinned. "Yeah, that was Finn."

Pause.

"I didn't want anyone to see me differently, and I didn't want you to pity me."

"Wouldn't be pity," he muttered and sank onto the couch.

She sighed. "Believe me, Finn educated me about pity and empathy. I mean, he just groused about it again."

He couldn't hear what Sandy said to that, but the bizarre look on Riley's face piqued his curiosity. For a fleeting moment, her gorgeous eyes filled with fear mingled with wonder. Then she turned and paced away from him.

She stopped mid-stride and shouted. "Holy crap on a cracker!"

Finn shot up and moved to her.

"Finn has a cat!"

Gramps had a cat. Technically, Gramps inherited Grandma's cat, since she'd adopted the Balinese cat a year before she passed away. She'd called him Beau of the Ball, because of his breed, but Finn had immediately called him Baller, which Gramps had liked much better than Beau.

Now, Baller seemed to know his owner was gone and he bowed to no human. He only deigned to pay attention to Finn when he doled out the food. The rest of his hours were spent... probably sleeping, but Finn was pretty he was planning an evil coup of the house.

The feline snaked between Riley's ankles and Finn froze. Riley's smile made his heart pound and his breath catch.

It hit him that she'd probably never had a pet.

Dammit. He'd have to keep her from bonding with Baller. He didn't want her to get hurt.

"What kind of cat is this?" she asked, her excited tone twisting him up.

"An old one. And grouchy."

Her eyes widened at him. "Cats are supposed to be grouchy."

"Says who?" he demanded.

"Says Jonah."

That brought him up short.

Into the phone she said, "Yes, Sandy. I'll bring Jonah to meet you. He'll love meeting Joules... that is if we can get him away from Finn."

His phone rang and he pulled it from his back pocket. Har's name lit up the screen.

"Hey, Prez."

"Rumor has it you're claiming Riley."

"Probably."

Har paused. "You aren't sure?"

He sauntered toward the kitchen, away from Riley. "Let's say, I'll be sure soon."

"Is he fuckin' with her?" Finn heard Mensa ask in the background.

"What's Mensa doing there? He's supposed to cover for me at Twisted Talons."

Har's tone almost sounded teasing. "I'm at Twisted Talons talking to Cynic."

"I see."

"Her dad know you're in the club?"

Finn's lips tipped up. "Not yet, but he's dying to meet me. I expect he'll be more pissed when he finds out we moved Jonah."

"Mensa says his mom covered that."

Finn hesitated. "Are you telling me to hide that I'm with the Riot?"

Har sighed. "No, but I'm saying don't poke the bear too much. From everything Cynic and Mensa shared, I want to have our shit tight before he knows about us."

"Got it, Prez."

"Why her?" Finn heard Mensa ask.

"That's none of his fucking business," Finn muttered.

"You're right. That's why I didn't repeat it," Har said.

"Is that everything, Har?"

"Yeah. Later."

He put his phone away. Ten minutes later, Riley said goodbye to Sandy, and someone knocked on the door.

"Who the hell is that?" Finn grumbled to himself.

Baller darted to the back of the house.

Finn opened the door to a uniformed Biloxi police officer.

"Are you the homeowner?"

"Yes, sir."

"Do you own that white Toyota?"

Unease skated up his spine. "My girlfriend does."

Riley slid her arm around his waist, nudging the door open a little wider. "Is there a problem with my car, officer?"

The cop looked between them both, then focused on Riley. "I need you to come downtown with me."

"How come?" she asked in an innocent tone.

"Orders were to be on the lookout for a white Toyota Corolla with your plate, then bring you downtown."

Finn straightened. "She isn't going anywhere without talking to her lawyer."

"She isn't under arrest."

Riley let out a growly sigh. "Do you even know why you had to look for my car?"

"Ma'am—"

"It's because my father doesn't like me not being at home under his thumb."

Finn crossed his arms. "Last time I checked, her hanging out with her man isn't breaking a law, officer. It isn't even breaking a neighborhood ordinance."

The cop shook his head, and speared Riley with his eyes. "You need to make your way downtown. And if your father's concerned about you…" His eyes darted to Finn. "Maybe there's a reason for that."

Luckily, the officer went back to his car and didn't hear Riley whisper, "Oh. My. God. I cannot believe he just said that."

Finn shut the door. "Let it go, Riles."

Her eyes widened at him. "Oh, I need to let it go, huh? Well, next time don't tempt fate with the ordinance stuff."

"Why?" he asked, fighting laughter.

Her lips quirked skeptically. "This is the South. For all we know, there's a law that says you can't put your arm around someone's waist on Mondays."

He chuckled. "You're funny, babe. The upside to this is that your dad tipped his hand a little."

"How do you figure?" she asked, wandering back to the couch.

"Your car was on a BOLO, *or* that officer was specifically told to look for your vehicle. I'm guessing your dad cashed in a favor to make that happen."

She leaned her head back on the couch cushion. "Yeah, so..."

"So, we might as well go to him."

Her head shot forward. "With Mensa?"

He shook his head. "I was thinking a cop would be better."

Her jaw dropped open. "Are you crazy?"

"Maybe, but your dad can't have everyone on his payroll."

A faraway look hit her eyes. "Sure seems like he does seeing as what happened to Mom."

He sat next to her, pulling her close. "I get that. What time does he get home?"

"Six most days, six-thirty on bad days."

The rumble of a motorcycle cut through the air. "Jesus! Who's here now?"

"I don't know, but I'm kind of glad they are."

He looked over his shoulder at her while moving to the door. "You're tougher than that, Riles."

"Where is Riley?" Mensa demanded when Finn opened the door.

"I'm right here."

Mensa turned to Finn. "Don't go to her house."

His body tensed.

How did Mensa know that was the plan?

"Why not?" Riley asked.

Mensa stared at her so long, Finn wondered if he'd heard her. Finally he said, "Because it's not safe – not that I should have to tell you that."

She cocked her head to the side. "What are you hiding?"

"Not hiding anything. Jack was just at Mom's. He's more pissed than she's ever seen him," Mensa said.

"If he's come and gone, then I'm going to Auntie Celeste's and spending—"

"No, you're not," Finn said.

Her big brown eyes landed on him like heated stones. "You have to work tonight. You said so last night."

"Cynic gave him the week off," Mensa muttered.

That was news to him, but earlier Cynic *had* texted to tell him he had the next three days off.

She put her hands on her hips. "Well, I still want—"

"Jonah is twenty-three years old and most days as adult as I am. He's good, Ry," Mensa said.

She sighed. "Fine, but I still don't —"

Mensa stalked toward her. "Keeping you two separated forces Uncle Jack to choose who he's gonna go after. And as Mom pointed out, she doesn't want Jonah trying to protect you again."

Riley closed her eyes, but the pain still slashed across her face. Finn wanted to punch Mensa for putting that there, but he knew that was misguided.

"Why do you look so angry?" Riley asked, but her eyes were pointed at Mensa.

"Because I'm pissed that my cousins have been abused all their lives and I had no fuckin' clue."

"None of it's her fault," Finn bit out.

Mensa's eyes cut to him. "Didn't say it was, and I'm not pissed at her." He ran a hand through his unruly, wavy hair. "Hell, I'm pissed at myself and the whole fuckin' world."

Riley walked over and wrapped her arms around Mensa. "Don't be mad at yourself."

Mensa buried his nose in her hair. "Christ. How could he do this shit to you two?" His head came up and his eyes blazed at Riley. "Hell, how can you still be so sweet after everything he's fucking done? Taken from you?"

She leaned back and shrugged a shoulder. "I can't fall apart around Jonah. Then where would we be?"

Chapter 6

Power Over You

Riley

Mensa's words had hit me hard. I didn't want Jonah trying to protect me again, either. For years I had blamed myself for all of it. Only recently Whitney had shifted my perspective.

One afternoon back in the spring, Sandy caught me hanging around the bar in the common room. She insisted I go with her to pick up the cuts for prospects that had earned their patches. We walked into the shop and I discovered how much the smell of leather comforted me. Who knew?

Nadia, the owner of the leather shop, introduced us to her niece, Whitney. She was a year or two older than me, and we got to chatting and exchanged numbers. A few days later, I hung out with her and told her about my brother – though not my father's role in all of it.

She tipped her margarita at me. "You know, life deals us all shit at different times. Sounds like you got yours really early. No matter what though, you can't blame yourself for your brother's injury. He did a brave thing and sadly has to pay the price for it. You didn't ask him to do it and you had no idea he would step up like that. It isn't your fault. Stop giving that idea power over you."

No matter how much I tried to heed her words, I struggled. It might have been Dad who dealt all the blows, but if I hadn't set him off it might not have gone so far. Mom wouldn't be dead and Jonah would be living a better life.

Mensa gave me an extra squeeze and I backed away.

"Give us a minute, Riles. I need to talk to Mensa for a moment," Finn said. The set of his jaw surprised me. He looked as angry as Mensa.

My brows furrowed as confusion settled inside me like a lead weight. I struggled with trusting men outside the bedroom, and Finn's anger at Mensa didn't add up. Why would he get mad at Mensa? I'd be mad if Uncle Dean had done something bad to him.

Finn stepped closer to me and squeezed my hand. "You got that look on your face that says you want to run. Both of us are pissed, but not at you, and not really at each other. Does that make sense?"

Any time men were arguing, I ducked out. If I was going to make a fresh start, I needed to grow a spine. I chuckled nervously. "Not really, but I'm not going anywhere, Finn. Whatever you have to say to Mensa, it has to do with me, so I'm staying put."

The anger in Finn's expression softened for a second as what appeared to be pride flitted across his face. "Glad you feel safe enough to take a stand, honey. But —"

I put my hands on my hips. "No buts. You want to get to know me, well, here we are, Finneas. I'm tired of running away to avoid conflict. No matter how uncomfortable it makes me, I'll listen to you two argue."

"There's nothing to argue about," Mensa grumbled. "I care about you. Seems Finn cares about you, but —"

Finn glowered at Mensa. "Like she said, 'no buts.' I care about her, that's all that fuckin' matters, Mensa. We both care about her.

"But her dad fucked up. Cop came by half an hour ago. Told her to go downtown because there's a BOLO on her car. I want to take a cop with us and let them see how he treats his daughter."

Mensa shook his head. "But Har doesn't want him to know who you are."

Finn shrugged. "Somebody like Dennizen would keep it quiet about who I am."

I scoffed. "Dad won't fall for that, Finn. He's great at being one of the boys with cops and anyone in charge."

My cousin nodded. "She's right about that. Though your plan has potential. It's gonna take some planning. Not sure *Dennizen* is the right cop to take with you. Uncle Jack's probably going to know Dennizen works homicide."

Finn's eyes darted to me and back to Mensa. "Vickie said he mainly hears civil suits these days. Maybe he won't know who Dennizen is."

Mensa shrugged. "Maybe, but you still gotta get Dennizen on board, and that's gonna take some planning."

Finn fell silent. Relief built inside me for a split second, then he said, "I'm gonna talk to Roman. See if Trinity and her friend Olivia can help."

Oh, no.

Roman wasn't my biggest fan. No doubt he'd told Trinity to steer clear of me, so I didn't know if she despised me or if she just avoided me because her ol' man said so. Then again, it could be a little bit of both. Either way, I hoped I wouldn't have to be around for that conversation.

"We could all do dinner," Finn said, his tone firm.

"Great," I muttered.

"What's that mean?" Finn asked.

Mensa laughed. "Means her first strike was because of what she did to Roman."

"Mensa," I said, fighting an urge to mouth off at him.

He shot me a short, but incredulous glare. "You know the brothers talk." He tipped his head at Finn. "You're going to be with him, he should know. It happened two years ago; I'm surprised he didn't know already."

Finn shook his head. "Hadn't earned my patch yet, and prospects don't get much time to chat."

Mensa pulled his keys from his pocket. "I have to run, but still say it's a bad idea taking her around Jack."

Finn wobbled his head and kept his eyes on Mensa. "Yeah, but that cop had to have reported in and her Dad's gonna know she's here."

I stepped closer to them. "Then I'll go to Aurora's."

"No," Finn said.

At the same time, Mensa said, "No way."

My cousin's words and firm tone concerned me. "Why would you care if I go to Aurora's?"

Mensa's dark eyes gleamed in the setting sun. "Her sister has a thing for Jonah."

My head reared back. "What? Denver? No, they just...," I trailed off, recalling how Jonah and Denver would talk while playing games on their Nintendo Switch. "How did I miss that?"

A satisfied smile curled Mensa's lips. "Aurora didn't want to point it out to you."

My eyes widened. "She told *you* but not me?"

His smile twisted into is smirk. "She had that extra shot of tequila. Patrón always makes women chatty."

I narrowed my eyes. "Really?"

He nodded. "Told me Denver wasn't the only one who had it for a Tyndale."

"She likes men," I said.

Mensa chuckled. "Yeah, she assumed I'm a Tyndale, too."

Oh, crap.

"Thought you had to go, man," Finn said.

Mensa gave him a chin lift. "I do. Don't miss church."

"As if. Later."

We walked Mensa out to the drive and watched him roar away on his bike.

I kept my eyes pinned on the road. "I can't stay here."

"Why?" Finn asked.

He infused that single word with so much tone, I couldn't help but look at him. "He'll come for me, Finn. I *am* his punching bag."

Finn's nostrils flared with his inhale. "Not any more, you're not. Let's go inside."

"We should go to the clubhouse."

He gave me a dry look. "That's a Band-Aid on a bullet wound, Riles. Let's see what he does."

I bit my lip. "Finn —"

He sighed. "The sooner we get him out of your life, the sooner you can get back to normal."

"Normal? Finn, there's not much normal in my life. Jonah —"

He shook his head. "Un-uh. He's capable, Riley. May not have seen much, but it's clear he could be semi-self-sufficient. I want to get you to where your only care and concern is how we're gonna fuck and where. The less you have to think about, the sooner you can focus on being yourself."

"I'm already myself."

His brow arched. "My guess is you're a shell of yourself. I can't wait to watch you come alive."

I left that comment alone and headed straight to the kitchen. Earlier, I'd spied a carton of strawberries in the refrigerator, and I needed to satisfy my sweet tooth.

"What's the story with Roman?" Finn asked, locking the front door.

"Don't worry about it," I said, grabbing the strawberries from the fridge.

I was a foot from the counter, when Finn grabbed the strawberries out of my hand.

"Hey! What are you doing?"

He crowded me from behind, guiding us forward. He put the container on the counter. "What did you do to Roman?"

I tipped my head back, but ran into his strong shoulder. "I don't want to talk about it, Finn. Just let me eat some strawberries."

His body retreated an inch. Then he snatched the pint and ran toward the living room. "You want 'em, you gotta come get 'em, baby."

I whirled around. "Are you serious?"

He grinned and winked. "Bet your ass, I am. They're an aphrodisiac. You aren't eating these without me."

"Finn, I am not —"

"Come get 'em. Or are you scared?" he asked, then ran down the hall out of sight.

"Oh, it's on, Finneas!" I shouted.

I zipped around the corner and realized I wasn't entirely familiar with the layout of the house. Finn hadn't given me a tour yesterday. But, this wasn't a mansion, so I knew I'd find him sooner or later. I also knew his bedroom was on the opposite end of the house. The first room I peeked into was an office, and he wasn't there.

"Finn, I'm not joking. I'm craving sweets and I'm not in the mood for this."

"What's the story on Roman?" he asked, from the room adjacent to the office.

I barged into the room and tagged the light switch. The bedroom appeared to be a guest room with a full-size bed made up with a sky-blue quilt. Surprisingly, Finn stood leaning a shoulder against the wall, the pint container open in one hand, and a strawberry in his other hand. The shield tattoo running from his wrist to his knuckles contrasted against the red berry.

He looked at the fruit and then at me. "Tell me, or I'll eat all the juicy ones."

I gasped. "You can't eat those. They aren't washed yet."

His bearded lips twisted with a sly smirk. "Can't say that scares me. What did you do to Roman?"

My lips pressed into a hard line and I debated telling him, but it wasn't a good memory. "This started out fun, Finn, but I'm serious. I don't want to talk about it."

He put the strawberry back into the container and snapped the lid closed. With a shrug, he straightened from the wall. "That's too bad because I'm not giving you *any* strawberries until you do."

"You said I had to catch you."

His brows arched. "Yeah, and you haven't done that yet, either."

He darted past me and out the door.

"Gah!" I cried and ran after him. For some reason he slowed down when he entered the living room and I hopped up on his back. "Take that!"

He laughed and wrapped his free hand around my thigh holding me in a piggy-back position. We leaned forward as he guided us into his bedroom. Next thing I knew, we turned around, then my back was on the bed and some of his weight was on me. Fear surged through me for a split second before he let go of my leg and twisted so he was on top of me.

"Did I scare you?" he asked, concern filling his eyes.

"For *maybe* a second, but — how did you know?"

His head bobbed with a short nod. "I'm in tune with you, Riley. Felt you get stiff. You weren't sexually assaulted, too, were you?"

I shook my head. "Thankfully, no."

"Good. Now what did you do to Roman?"

I tipped my head back as much as I could on the bed. "Oh my God, you're a dog with a bone."

"Yeah, so tell me."

Righting my head, I met his resolute gaze. "I didn't really do anything to *Roman*. I thought I was doing something for myself."

He twirled a finger in the air. "Keep going."

"At the holiday party two years ago, I noticed Roman wasn't around. Somebody had brought a bunch of new women in, so the brothers would have variety, I guess."

Impatience filled his eyes. "Yeah... get to the part about Roman."

I sighed. "I had a feeling he'd show up but was just running late. Most of those other women hadn't been to the clubhouse before, and I told them Roman was off-limits."

Finn scoffed. "That doesn't stop most sweet-butts from making a play."

I twisted my lips, hesitant to admit anything more. "Yeah, but I also told them he was a serious player and that he had a woman. I may have also said that he'd deny it if they called him on it, and sweet-butts or not, most women don't like it when men lie."

Finn's full lips pressed together as realization washed over him. "I remember being behind the bar as a prospect for that party. You were the one who cock-blocked him."

I shook my head. "I wanted him for myself, Finn. It was never my intention to cock-block him."

He aimed some side-eye at me. "There's more to this if it's what led to your first strike like Mensa mentioned."

I closed my eyes to keep from rolling them. "I gave you the gist." I opened my eyes. "Can I have the strawberries now?"

He shifted, grinding his hips against me in a tease. "I don't want the gist, woman. I want all of it. Not gonna judge you, but I gotta know what I'm dealing with here before I go asking Roman to do me a solid."

"If y'all are brothers, it shouldn't matter, should it? Thought you had each other's backs, no matter what."

He exhaled hard through his nose. "We do, but I don't like having egg on my face. Especially when I can prevent that shit."

That made sense, and I didn't want to embarrass him. I'd never had a man care so much about what I'd done in the past or how I was feeling now.

"You're right. Roman came in through the back door and I happened to be right there when he did, which I thought was a sign. I came on to him, and he brushed me off."

Finn gave me a chin dip. "Yeah."

I took a deep breath. "I stuck around in the kitchen, helping Sandy make punch and shooting the shit - as well as some tequila. It didn't take long for Roman to make his rounds and get rejected. He found me and dragged me down the hall toward his room. I thought he'd come to his senses. Problem was I didn't know he'd figured out what I'd done."

"Cut to the chase, Riles."

"Yeah, well, he said really mean things and I didn't react well."

His teeth grazed his lower lip. "What's that mean?"

My eyes slid to the side. "I may have tried to spit on him."

His torso jerked. "What? Are you shitting me?"

I grimaced and shook my head, shame filling me. "I'd blame the tequila, but —"

"No, you can't do that. It may not happen often, but I've seen you shoot tequila. Unlike other bitches, you can handle your liquor."

"I know, but he insulted me and —"

"And that's an excuse. Did you ever apologize?"

"Not really. I mean, he got married and... it's more like I just avoid him," I said, but the last part sounded like a question.

Finn hung his head. "Dammit." He raised his eyes to me. "You're lucky as hell you weren't tossed out permanently that night."

"Yeah," I said on a sigh.

"Something tells me we need all the help we can get, and he and Trinity are our best shot at talking to Dennizen. You're gonna have to apologize to Roman, babe."

Guilt and dread washed through me. "Fine. Can I have my strawberries now?"

His eyes warmed and he kissed me, a lingering kiss I felt down to my toes. He broke it and smiled at me. "Yeah, but a gorgeous woman tells me we have to wash 'em first."

Finn

Finn took the pint container into the bathroom.

"What are you doing? We need to hull the berries," Riley said from the bed.

He looked over his shoulder at her. "Babe, don't tell me you cut all your strawberries? Live a little."

She padded to the bathroom doorway. "That's fine, but I'm not eating them in bed. I meant it when I said I wasn't in the mood. This has been a very long day."

He rinsed a strawberry, shook the excess water from it, and held it up to Riley's lips. "Lucky for you, it's almost dinner time, and we'll hit the sack early tonight."

She bit into the strawberry and chewed. He twisted and tossed the stem into a small garbage can.

After they ate four of the berries, she asked, "Can we skip dinner with Roman?"

He stared at her for a beat. "Part of me wants to give you that, but the thing is, we can't avoid any of my brothers for very long. Especially not for something that, frankly, you should apologize for anyway."

Her face fell and she took a deep breath.

He spoke before her. "I'm not trying to make you feel bad, Riley. I just want to clear the air between you and the others."

"Fine," she muttered. "What are we eating for dinner?"

"What do you feel like? I got steaks, chicken, or ground beef in the freezer – pork chops, too, but we had pulled pork at lunch."

She gave him a strange smile. "Yeah, I'm porked out."

He shook his head, not making the obvious joke.

"Decide, and I'll cook."

"I'm surprised you don't want to order in."

"I'm a decent cook, Riley. Too much restaurant food grates on me."

She grabbed the strawberries. "I'll put these away."

He wrapped an around her waist and gave her a peck. "I lied. We'll have steaks. I'm guessing your dad didn't feed you steak very often."

Her head tilted. "Only if we were having company, so no."

He followed her into the kitchen. "Grab a beer when you put the fruit away. Gonna let the steaks marinate in beer."

She shot him a look. "That sounds like a waste of good beer."

With a freezer bag in hand, he grinned at her. "Don't knock it until you try it."

A few minutes later, he put the bag with the marinading meat in the fridge. He was headed back toward the bedroom when his cell rang with his mom's ring tone.

"Hey, Mom. What's up?"

"My blood pressure most likely. Is this a good time to talk?"

His mom's tone concerned him. He turned back to the living room and sat on the sofa. "I guess. What's wrong?"

"Nothing's wrong exactly, though you won't see it that way. Your aunt and uncle are meeting with a realtor about the house."

He clenched a fist. "It isn't out of probate yet."

She sighed. "No, but it should be any day now… according to the lawyer, anyway."

"They know I want to buy it."

"Yes, but the market's been crazy in other towns in the South. They want to see if selling it —"

"Gramps would shit a brick if he knew they sold this place to some big ass investment firm. That's the only reason the prices are so damned high, Mom."

"I know that, honey, but your uncle just found out he's losing his job at the end of the year."

He laughed bitterly. "So, selling this house is going to help him? Hell, me paying rent to them is better than putting it on the market."

Mom's voice became stern. "You don't know how hard it is to raise kids, Finneas."

"Not yet."

"What does that mean?" she asked in a sharp tone.

Fuck.

"Nothing, Mom."

"Don't give me that. You may be twenty-seven, but I know when you're hiding something. If you're serious about this house business, you need to come clean with me. Your Aunt Laurie and Uncle Steve are already convinced you have anger issues and that you probably have untreated PTSD from being in the military."

He leaned his head back. "That's news to me, seeing as Uncle Steve says the men who serve in the Air Force are wimps who couldn't even hack it as Army reservists."

"Let that go, Finneas. They also don't think you being in that biker group —"

"It's a club, Mom."

"I know that. I said 'group' not 'gang', but they question your decisions over the past year or two."

"What the hell? I served this country for four years to protect everyone's right to freedom, Mom. Which means I'm *free* to join a motorcycle club if that's what I want. Whether or not I have PTSD has no bearing on me buying the house. I got money saved for this, but not if they go pricing it based on inflated prices from the investment groups."

"I know that, dear, but do you hear how angry you sound?"

"Of course I'm angry. I'm trying to keep the house in the family for fuck's sake."

"Yes, but money does crazy things to people. Calm down. As it stands, they haven't heard back with a possible price range from the realtor because I haven't agreed. Seeing as none of us have been in Biloxi since the funeral last year, I'm not certain that they've chosen the right person for the job."

"Good."

"I can't stick with that argument very long, Finn. In fact, Aunt Laurie suggested you find a good realtor."

"Oh, fuck no."

"That attitude won't help either of us, here. Now, you managed to change the subject on me. What did you mean by 'not yet'? My knee-jerk reaction was that you've knocked up a woman, but we raised you better than that."

"I'm seeing a woman that I'm pretty serious about."

"Oh, how long has this been going on?"

"That's not the point, Mom."

She chuckled. "It most certainly is. You don't want to give them any more reasons to keep you from buying the house, do you?"

He paused to get his thoughts together. "She and I were together the night before Gramps passed. I didn't tell her about Gramps dying because... well, that was a crazy time for all of us."

"Yeah," his mom whispered.

"Anyway, things cooled off for a while because of life issues, but now we're together and I'm thinking it might be serious."

"Might be?"

He heard that question in stereo and glanced over his shoulder at Riley. With his free hand, he gestured for her to sit next to him on the sofa. She arched a brow at him and planted herself in the recliner with her feet tucked under her ass, keeping eye contact the entire time. His lips quirked into a small smile. "Yeah, Mom. It's a little too soon to tell, but she definitely does it for me, and I'm —"

"Eager to start a family like your grandfather did," she finished.

That drew him up short. "What do you mean?"

"About what? Gramps and Grandma were married in their early twenties. Uncle Steve was born before Grandma was twenty-five and I came along just after Grandma turned thirty – which, to them, was pushing it."

"Yeah, so?"

"So... from a young age, you said you wanted to have a family just like Gramps and Grandma. Then that one girl broke your heart before you got out of the Air Force."

"I don't need a reminder, Mom."

He could hear the smile in her voice. "Yes, but from the way you talked about it, I knew what bothered you was that you weren't any closer to having the family you wanted." She paused. "Then you went and joined the Riot brothers. I really thought that was a phase."

His jaw clenched, but Riley shifted in the recliner and he forced himself to relax. "It isn't a phase, Mom. They're my brothers."

"Yes, I know. You made that very clear. At least Westley didn't hear you say that."

He bit his lower lip and looked toward the window. "Biological brothers are different, Mom."

"So, what's her name?"

His eyes skated back to Riley who alternated between watching him and examining her fingernails. "Her name's Riley."

"That's a pretty name. When are you bringing her to meet us?"

"Not sure, Mom. She's got work and so do I," he said, not wanting to mention Riley's situation.

She hesitated. "That almost sounds like a fib, but I'll let it go for now."

"Thanks, Mom. And thanks for the update, even if I don't like it. Tell Wes and Dad I said hey and I love them."

He ended the call and Riley tilted her head. "You told your mom we're serious? And how many biological brothers do you have?"

"Come over here, please."

She stared at him for a moment and he wondered if he'd have to ask twice, but then she slid her legs out from under her and came to the sofa. He quickly rearranged them so they were laying down on their sides facing each other.

"I have a brother named Westley who's eleven years younger than me."

Her eyes widened. "That's a swing."

He grinned. "He was a surprise. Also part of why I went into the military. The delivery was complicated. Mom and Dad had to tap into my college savings to pay hospital bills."

"Wow," she breathed.

"Yeah, but it's cool. Wes being born changed a lot of things, but it made me see the value of family, and I'll always wish Mom and Dad had had a kid between me and Wes. No matter how much people complain about their siblings, big families are the shit, Riles."

"Didn't sound that way if your aunt and uncle want to sell the house out from under you."

He tucked a lock of her hair behind her ear. "How much were you eavesdropping?"

She shrugged a shoulder. "Your rant about serving in the military was hard to miss, Finn. Most people think you're laid-back, but you get loud when you really care about something."

"Can't argue that."

Her eyes slid to the side. "She wants to meet me?"

He chuckled. "She likes to meet everyone in my life. I may have a younger brother, but she still treats me like her only son sometimes."

She nodded. "I noticed you didn't tell her about my... problems."

His chin dipped. "Yeah. There's time for that, and I don't want her to worry. Nothing she can do for us, since she's in Atlanta."

"Did you grow up there?"

He shook his head. "Not really. We lived here until I was ten. Then dad got a promotion and we moved to Atlanta. Probably how Wes came along, but I try not to think about that shit."

"Yeah, I get that."

He heard her stomach rumble and he smiled. "Let's hit the kitchen. We got broccoli to cut up and I don't know if you want a baked potato with your steak or something else."

Chapter 7

Mom's Here

Riley

The scent of steak, french fries, and broccoli hung in the air while Finn and I did the dishes. He had 'grilled' the steaks in a fancy Ninja Foodi contraption because he was out of propane for his outdoor grill. When we finished eating, he insisted on washing the dishes and me drying.

It struck me that I hadn't ever worked alongside a man in the kitchen. Dad always ate frozen dinners for some weird reason. I made sure to clean up after Jonah if he did anything in the kitchen – though that was rare. At the clubhouse, Sandy kept tight reins on the communal kitchen. Being with Finn like this was comforting and strange all at once.

"You're way up in your head there, Tyndale," Finn said.

I finished drying a sheet pan and put it on the counter. "Sorry."

He tilted his head toward a cabinet. "You can put that pan in there. I don't care if you're quiet and caught up in your thoughts, as long as you're not plotting how to get to work tomorrow."

I put the dishtowel on the counter. "I'm trying to obliterate that convo from my mind."

He grabbed the towel to dry his hands. "Riley, your dad's got no outlet right now. It would not surprise me for him to do something to you at work."

My eyes widened. "He wouldn't make a public spectacle, Finn. Really, I don't think you understand how important his image is to him – especially with the re-election coming up."

He shook his head and stepped closer to me. "That's not what I'm talking about, babe. He might show up when you're leaving to 'take you home,' and then what?"

I shook my head. "He doesn't know I've got a job."

Finn closed his eyes and sighed. "I just want to know you're somewhere safe. Right now, the safest place for you to be is with me."

"I have to keep a job, Finn. It's bad enough how erratic my employment history is. Makes it impossible to get a credit card and build my credit rating, the whole shebang."

His expression shifted like he had an idea but didn't want to share it. "You said you did data entry, right?"

"Yeah," I drawled.

Finn shoved his hands in his pockets. "Last I heard, Har's had some issues with his assistant."

"You mean Julie?" I asked.

He nodded. "I didn't realize you know her."

I tilted my head. "Not that well. She, um, looks down her nose at sweet-butts."

"Thought you weren't one – isn't that what you said yesterday?"

I nodded. "Yeah, but she knew I'm around the clubhouse regularly and she just seemed very judgy."

Finn nodded. "I think if Har could replace her easily, he would."

I shook my head. "I don't want to take her job out from under her."

He pulled his hands from his pockets and crossed his arms. "It wouldn't be taking it from her. She fucked with Cynic a while back. She's smart enough to not flirt with Gamble, but she's been over-friendly with some of the customers. Men with wedding rings on their fingers, no less. Har told her to knock that shit off, but she hasn't."

Even though Dad didn't know about my job at the hardware store, he would find out eventually. I hated having to change jobs so much. The idea of having a job where two or more brothers would be around to keep him in his place definitely appealed to me. Being an assistant at a body shop wasn't my dream career, but then again, I didn't have a dream job, since my only goal was to make certain Jonah and I both survived each day.

"I'll think about it."

"You do that. Tomorrow you're taking the day off."

"Again?"

"Yep. Hell, if I knew Cynic was giving me the rest of the week off, I'd have taken us to Atlanta to see my family, but that's a long-ass ride. Plus we need to get this shit sorted, the sooner the better."

"Right. Can I see Jonah tomorrow?"

"Only if I go with you, but really I'd prefer it if you lay low."

I sent a quick text to Aurora while Finn took a shower.

> Finn won't let me leave. That's a serious red flag right?

For good measure, I added in a couple red flag emojis.

In no time, she texted me back.

> I say this with love, but honey, you are the red flag. He isn't keeping you captive. He's keeping you safe. There's a difference and I want to smack your dad for this.

I shook my head while my thumbs whirled over the screen.

> Smack him for what?

She sent me an eye-roll emoji.

> For preventing you from seeing a healthy…maybe even loving… relationship when it happens.

My brows drew together. Neither of us had said word one about love.

I jumped a foot in the air when Finn said, "I think your friend Aurora is a smart woman."

He stood right behind me.

"It's not cool to spy like that, Finn."

His blasé shrug rubbed me the wrong way, but his words caught me off-guard. "It wasn't intentional. I'd apologize, but that little exchange gives me a heck of a glimpse of who you are. She's right, Riley. She mentioned a loving relationship. We're not at a point to talk about love, but I'm keeping you safe because I care about you. A lot."

My phone vibrated with another text, but I held it near my leg so Finn couldn't read anything else.

I smiled up at him. "Aurora's right about a lot of things. I care about you, too, Finn, but this day… no, the past three days, have been whoppers so far. I don't want to rely on you too much, which is why I'd like to go to work."

"What do your bills look like? That hunk of metal in the driveway has to be paid off and you don't have rent to pay, right?"

I gave him a weak glower. "Yes, but that's hardly the point."

He nodded once. "Tell your boss the truth. They don't understand, it's a sign."

A laugh erupted from me. "A sign? I don't think any of the other brothers believe in signs."

Finn shot me a closed-lip smile. "Tiny does. He totally believes in auras and juju and shit."

"Fine. I'm taking a shower so this day can finally be over."

He wrapped an arm around my waist, pulled me close and kissed me short but sweet. "Have at it, babe."

Part of me didn't know what to do with Finn being so sweet. Another part of me waited for him to be like my dad and follow the sweetness with something mean. I shoved that thought aside. It wasn't right to think he would treat me like dad. Aurora told me repeatedly that *nobody* would treat me as badly as Dad did.

Thinking about Aurora made me check my phone to see the message she'd sent me earlier.

> I haven't met him yet, so I can't say if he's loving toward you.

That message was followed by another one.

> Maybe we should do lunch, and I'll assess in person.

Finn and Aurora... I wondered what she'd make of him.

Mid-morning the next day, we rode to the compound on Finn's Harley. After we dismounted, he grabbed my hand and we walked toward the clubhouse.

"You know Roman works late hours. We could hang in your room," I said.

Finn chuckled. "It's the middle of the week, and he hasn't had any pyrotechnic shows all month."

I sighed. "Did you call him or something?"

"Or something," Finn muttered.

The back door opened and Roman sauntered out to one of the picnic tables where he sat down.

We drew even with him and his brows rose with what seemed like impatience, adding to his disinterested and impervious vibe.

After a beat, he said, "I won't make this easy on you."

On the one hand, a tiny part of me understood that, but on the other hand I couldn't help but resent him a little for being so aloof and hard-assed.

As usual, Finn seemed to read my thoughts. "Can't blame him, babe. Somebody pulled that shit with me, they'd be done."

I summoned up my courage. "I'm sorry for what I did at the holiday party two years ago. I never should have tried to spit on you. I apologize."

Roman's chin lowered ever-so-slightly. "And the meddling with the other women?"

I knew better than to repeat what I'd said to Finn – about wanting Roman for myself. Finn didn't want to share me and I didn't want to remind him of my promiscuity. "I'm sorry that I lied to the other women about you."

Roman's head turned and his eyes narrowed. "I'm not trying to bust your balls on this, but that doesn't sound very sincere."

I tilted my head. "Seeing as how you were married pretty soon after that, I suspect Trinity might be happy I kept you from those other women."

A hint of a grin tugged at his lips. "You're probably right. It's still bullshit, though, but it's a moot point. And I'm pretty sure Finn will keep you in line."

Finn wrapped an arm around my shoulders. "That's the plan."

Roman's jaw shifted. "Is it true? Your dad beats you… even at your age now?"

I pressed my lips together to keep from frowning. "If it weren't for Jonah, I'd have left a long time ago."

"Doesn't matter," Roman said in a blistering tone. "He's blessed with two children, and he abused them both. But beating a daughter… that deserves serious retribution."

My body froze with surprise, but heat bloomed in the middle of my chest, filling me to my belly. Mensa, Finn, Cynic, Gamble, and now Roman – were all pissed and itching to dish it back to Dad. The idea that anyone would do that for me was so foreign, I had an overwhelming urge to cry.

"I'm glad we're on the same page," Finn said. "I want to ask you a favor – though I might have to run it by Har first, also."

Roman aimed a dry look at Finn. "Then maybe you should wait until you've done that."

Finn shook his head. "I'm thinking Detective Dennizen will feel as adamant as I – we – do about Judge Tyndale paying for his crimes."

"He's homicide," Roman said.

Finn nodded. "He might still be able to hook us up with the right people. And by right people, I mean officers who won't be swayed by Tyndale's position or money."

Roman's lips pursed. "Tall order on both counts, man. Cops don't earn what they should most of the time." Roman looked from Finn to me. "What do I have to do with this?"

I held my hands up in surrender. "This is all Finn's idea."

Finn squeezed my shoulders. "I was thinking we could have dinner: you, Trinity, Olivia, Dennizen, me, and Riley."

Like a cat uncurling, a sly grin crept across Roman's face. "You cooking?"

Finn nodded.

"You better not let me down. Gonna have to break out those crawfish beignets, your Cajun corn maque choux, and depending on what Dennizen likes, that jambalaya you made during Bike Week last spring wouldn't be a bad idea either."

I couldn't keep my mouth closed. "Wait. Beignets are sweet... adding crawfish sounds like a crime."

Roman laughed. "I said almost the same thing, but... think crab-cake, only much better."

Finn held me a little closer. "Besides, this dinner isn't about you, Riles. I mean, it is, but it's about getting on Dennizen's good side."

With a deep breath, I said, "For all we know, he won't want to go through the trouble. I'd say Dad is a whole lot of trouble."

Roman's head tipped in contemplation. "I've only been around Olivia and Travis together once so far, and from a couple conversations we've had, I don't think he'll shy away from taking your father down. The problem is that he doesn't handle domestic violence."

"Her mom's murder wasn't self-defense like he claimed. Not sure if there's a way of re-opening that case or if that's a district attorney issue, but if it's reopened, that would have a much harsher punishment than assault and battery," Finn said.

Anger suffused Roman's features. "Nobody mentioned her mom being murdered."

I told Roman about that night, and everyone's role in it.

His jaw clenched. "I'll get Trinity to —"

The back door opened and Trinity strolled out wearing designer skinny jeans with a shimmery silk blouse. She grinned at Roman as she closed the distance between them. "You'll get me to what, hubby?"

From the way Roman's teeth sunk into his lower lip and he stared up at her, I suspected he wanted to roll his eyes at her calling him 'hubby.' He snaked an arm low around her hips and pulled her closer. "Call Olivia, *cher*. Finn and Riley want to have dinner with her, Travis, and us. They have a pressing issue and they're hoping Travis can help."

Trinity's chestnut brown eyes darted from Roman to Finn and finally to me. I didn't miss her taking in my black eye, since Finn hadn't given me any time to cover it up with concealer before we left. She looked at Roman. "I take it this has something to do with her eye."

"Yes," Roman said after a moment.

Trinity tilted her head a touch. "Liv tells me her detective is quite the foodie."

Roman chuckled. "I know. Lucky for them, Finn's something of a foodie, too. He has a knack for Cajun food and I think it'll be right up Dennizen's alley."

She gave Roman a pointed look. "He has a first name, you know."

Roman grinned at her. "I know, but for this, we need him in a more official capacity."

Finn

One thing had become clear to Finn in the past two days: if Riley asked for anything, his immediate reaction was to give it to her. He wasn't whipped, rather he admired her perseverance so much he believed she deserved anything and everything her father had kept from her. Which meant that when she suggested hanging at the clubhouse all day and even into the night, he wanted to give into that, but he didn't trust leaving her car at his house. Somehow, he figured, Judge Tyndale would pull something tricky and Finn wanted to be at the house to confront anything head-on.

Listening to Trinity speak to Olivia, he thought of all the ingredients he needed from the store. It was still a few days before November and the start of crawfish season. With any luck the seafood counter would have some crawfish on hand. He hoped they were good ones because he couldn't wait to rock Riley's world with those savory beignets.

His thoughts were cut short when he heard Trinity's tone become stern. "Liv, do not ambush your boyfriend with this. That won't be cool and they need his help. I don't have all the details, but Finn's... woman," she trailed off, her eyes met Finn's and he nodded. "Yes, he has a woman named Riley and her father's been beating her. There's more to it than that, but he's also a judge, which is the biggest reason Travis needs to be forewarned before dinner tonight."

"Tonight?" Riley whispered.

"You don't have time to waste," Roman muttered, taking the words out of Finn's mouth.

Trinity ended the call and locked eyes with Finn. "She's got to call me back. To be honest though, you or Roman might have been better off contacting Travis directly. She's pretty determined for him to hear more about Riley, come hell or high water."

"Oh, boy," Riley muttered.

Trinity smiled at Riley. "She can be pushy, but only when she really cares about something... so, it's a good thing."

Finn nodded. "That's cool. Have Roman text me if they're in or not, and what time. Six-thirty or seven is cool with us. In the meantime, we've got to hit the grocery store."

Riley aimed wide eyes at Finn. "We can't do it here? There's more room, that's for sure."

Roman said, "Dennizen doesn't like being here. Not unless there's police business."

Finn grabbed her hand and gave it a reassuring squeeze. "He's right. Besides, it would be best to tell him about your sitch at the house – that way there aren't as many people eavesdropping or butting in."

Prior to tonight's dinner, Finn had never used the huge round table in the formal dining room. For once he was grateful that Gramps and Grandma hadn't bought a rectangular table. He might be wrong, but he could swear the circular seating arrangement put everyone more at ease. Or as much more at ease as possible, given the heaviness of Riley's situation.

Travis Dennizen sat with an elbow on the table and his sharp brown eyes locked on Riley. "You haven't mentioned it, yet, but I would imagine you want your mother's case reopened."

Riley's head canted to the side while her lips twisted. "Not really. I don't see anything changing with that."

Finn shook his head. "You don't know that, Riley. But getting him charged with murder, hell, even manslaughter, would carry a harsher punishment than having him arrested for assault and battery."

Dennizen lowered his chin in a slight nod. "I'd have to approach my lieutenant to get the case reopened. Your dad being a judge, he'd hear about the request. There's another detective closing in on retirement, but he's very tight with bailiffs and a couple female clerks. I'd have to be able to keep it quiet from him."

"Would it be better if he acted out in front of an officer?" Trinity asked.

Riley frowned. "We'd have a hard time getting him to do that."

Dennizen sipped his beer. "That's true. It's my understanding there's an election coming up. As much as I hate politics, that's probably your best option. His opponent, Shirley Calhoun, is hungry for that spot. Her public relations people would have a field day with this."

"It can't come from Riley, though," Finn insisted.

Dennizen nodded once. "You're right, but it makes no sense for Calhoun to get that info from anyone else, though."

"Mensa would do it," Finn said.

Roman chuckled. "You sure about that?"

"He was pissed as fuck last night."

Olivia picked up her wine glass. "Pissed doesn't mean he wants to ruin family ties."

"The moment Mensa joined the Riot, Dad said he didn't have a nephew. There isn't a bond to break."

"If I'm the opponent, I don't know if I'd take this one," Olivia said, sipping her red wine. "It'll be secret sources and stuff that's easily disputed or worse, discredited."

Dennizen sat back in his chair. "That's Calhoun's call to make, Livie."

Olivia shot Dennizen a sassy smile. "You're right. The real question is: will the added press help to reopen the case without getting you into hot water?"

Roman threw his napkin on top of his plate. "Probably won't hurt, and bad publicity would keep him from having to ask about the case out of the blue."

Riley sat next to Finn. She held her fork over her plate, but he noticed her other hand was in her lap, twisting with nervousness.

He rubbed her bicep. "What do you think, Riley? Do you want to open this up to public scrutiny?"

She turned questioning eyes to him. "I figured it wasn't up to me. It's only because of you and Roman that we're having dinner with Detective Dennizen."

Finn took a deep breath. "Yeah, but your father's taken enough from you. This will likely get messy and public, so the choice should be yours. But, you'd also get justice for your mom if it goes right."

Riley's rueful laughter filled the dining room. "Very little in my life ever goes 'right,' Finn. Of that you can be certain."

"That's going to change, and not just because of Finn," Roman said.

She aimed a pointed look at Finn. "All jokes aside, I want to talk to Jonah first. He'll be mentioned in these stories too, and... he should be prepared, if possible."

Dennizen opened his mouth to say something, but someone knocked on the door and Finn stood. He kept eye-contact with Riley. "Crazy as it makes me, I hope like hell that's your dad."

"You couldn't be that lucky," Roman muttered from across the table.

Finn took one look in the peephole and cursed.

"What?" Riley asked.

He glanced back at her. "Mom's here. Don't freak out."

Riley paled while Trinity and Olivia laughed. Loud.

"Now, *that* makes you crazy. Any woman is gonna freak about this. I'm feeling anxious and I just met you," Olivia said.

Trinity, who sat next to Riley, reached over and gave her hand a squeeze. "It'll be fine."

"Right," Riley mumbled.

He opened the door, unsure if Dad and Wes had come with Mom. All three of them might send his woman over the edge.

"Hey, sweetie," Mom said. "I didn't know you'd have guests."

He did his best to use a gentle tone. "Yeah, Mom. Are Dad and Wes with you?"

"No. Your dad couldn't get off work and Wes has testing."

He stepped aside. "Come inside and meet everybody. I'll get your bag in a minute."

She wrapped him in a warm hug. "That's all right, Finneas. I'm staying at the Hampton Inn." She took four steps inside and locked eyes on Riley. "You must be Riley."

He'd have wondered how Mom knew that, but everyone had stood from the table. Roman had an arm around Trinity's waist, keeping her tucked tight to his side. Dennizen's posture wasn't much different except he had his bulky arm draped along Olivia's slim shoulders.

"Yes, ma'am," Riley said, in a meek voice Finn had never heard from her.

Finn had no doubt her dad did that to her. Made her feel weak and small in any unexpected situation. In an effort to tamp down his anger, Finn introduced his Mom to everyone.

Roman shot a gleaming smile at Mom. "It's nice to meet you, but we were just leaving. Trinity hits the office early every morning."

Before Mom could say anything, Olivia said, "And my man never knows when he's going to catch a case since crime never stops around here, so we're going to get going, too."

Once the other couples had left, Mom gave Finn a remorseful look. "I didn't mean to break things up."

"You didn't know, Mom."

She tucked a chair under the dining table. "I also should have called."

That was true.

"So why didn't you?" Finn asked. "Not that I'm unhappy to see you, but it's a six-hour drive to get here – assuming no traffic and there's always traffic in Peachtree. Is something happening with the house?"

Mom wandered closer to Finn. "No, and yes. After talking to you, I was thinking your aunt and uncle should see how you're taking care of the place. It might, possibly, open their eyes."

Finn's mouth slipped. "Nothing's gonna make them see past the club."

"Why would they have a problem with the club?" Riley asked.

Silence invaded the room.

Finally, Mom said, "They don't have a problem with the club."

"Just me being in it. Like that has a damn thing to do with my ability to handle homeownership." He narrowed his eyes on Mom. "If they're money-hungry, you won't change their mind."

"It's worth a try," Mom said, her gaze averted.

"You just had to meet Riley," he guessed.

"Finn," Riley murmured.

Mom smiled at them. "It's okay, Riley. He's got my number. To be fair, I knew he was hiding something. I just didn't expect it to be about you, though."

Finn's voice sliced through the room. "Mom."

Riley tentatively stepped closer to him. "It's okay, honey." She looked at Mom. "What happened to me is a long story."

Mom tipped her head to the side a touch. "It appears that someone hit you. And I know it wasn't Finn."

Riley scoffed. "Of course not. The Riot brothers are the best men in town. I don't know why Finn's aunt and uncle don't see that."

Mom swung her smile from Riley to him. "She's loyal. And good at changing the subject."

Finn's eyes widened. "She's also standing right here, Mom."

"I didn't mean to be rude."

"You weren't, Mrs. O'Halloran."

Finn glanced at Riley. "She was, and I don't like you being pressured into sharing if you're not feeling it."

"He's right, Riley. I'm sorry. I hope whoever did that pays a price."

Riley's expression shifted to defeated.

Mom whipped her eyes to Finn. "She can't be serious."

"It's complicated, Mom."

She crossed her arms. "I could swear your club uncomplicates things like this."

Finn sighed. "We're working on it. Do you want a crawfish beignet?"

"You have some left over?"

Finn grinned. "No, but I made extra batter, so..."

"If you're willing, but —"

"It's no problem, Mom. You want a beer? Or, Trinity brought some white wine."

Mom grinned. "Only if Riley has a glass, too."

Chapter 8

Missed This

Riley

While Finn walked his Mom to her car, I poured another glass of white wine. I liked Finn's mom, but I sensed she wanted someone better for him. Probably someone who didn't come from such a dysfunctional home.

"Don't get too loose, woman," Finn said from the other side of the kitchen.

I turned around. "Why not?"

He sauntered to me. "Because I want you to remember tonight." His gaze wandered to the side and back to me. "And even though I don't want you thinking about him, your dad's been too quiet so far."

I ignored the bit about Dad. 'Out of sight, out of mind' was a great mantra for this week. Though I knew that could lead to problems.

"I'm not trying to upset you, but dealing with Dad's always better when I'm loose. Not to mention, I'm still feeling a little edgy after that dinner and then meeting your mom."

Finn's hand slid up my back and he maneuvered himself so his hips pinned me against the edge of the counter. "One more glass, but that's it, because trust me, sweetheart, I got a better way of taking that edge off."

Heat swirled through my body. I didn't want Finn to do that - I *needed* him to take the edge off as only he could.

I lifted up on my toes, grazing his well-groomed beard with my nose and brushing his lips with mine. "Yes, please."

He pulled his head back, grinning. "Glad you're on board, but after we finish our drinks."

I shook my head. "You don't have a drink."

His grin twisted into a smirk. "Not yet, I don't. You're standing in the way of the cabinet where I keep the whiskey."

I stepped to the side. "If I didn't know any better, Finn, I'd say that you like teasing me."

He reached up to grab the whiskey and I admired his long, lean frame. His blue-gray eyes twinkled when he caught me staring. "I'm far from being a tease, Riles."

I deliberated that. "You've definitely put effort into withholding sex from me."

He barked out a laugh. "Not even close, woman. Held off until we both couldn't take it, yes. But that's not withholding."

"Fine. But make your drink a shot, and I'll polish this —"

He turned to me. "No, babe. We got chemistry, but it's always zero-to-one-hundred with you. I'm trying to show you things can be different."

I sipped my wine. "Maybe I don't want different."

With a small head shake, Finn poured a finger of whiskey into a high ball glass. He added a splash of ginger ale and put the two-liter back in the fridge. "I misspoke. Variety, babe. There's more than one way to get to our goal."

"Okay," I drawled, too chicken to ask why he wanted to show me that.

He stared at me for a moment while he sipped his drink. "Not to overanalyze it, but you stayed away from home to avoid your dad, and because you were hanging in certain places, you started drinking, right?"

I tilted my head back and spoke to the ceiling. "Yes, can we stop talking about my freaking dad?"

He chuckled and I looked back at him.

"Sure, sweetheart. But I'm just saying, you got the drinking under control, but my guess is that you use sex to avoid thinking about your problems."

"I have sex to feel good, Finn. It has nothing to do with my problems."

With a tip of his drink at me, he asked, "You don't use it to forget? Not ever?"

I swallowed some wine. "Maybe once or twice."

He nodded. "Right."

His mouth wasn't fully closed, so he might have had more to say, but I couldn't keep quiet. "I don't need to be fixed, Finn."

He downed the rest of his drink. "Never said that."

I finished my wine. "Actions have a way of speaking, too."

With a slow nod, he set his glass aside and stalked to me. He took my glass from me and put it on the counter. "You're right. Your actions ever since I've known you have said that something's wrong. I just hadn't put it together until three days ago. Now, I plan to rectify shit. You're great in bed, Riley, but I want you slow and sweet, not just hard, hot, and fast. You get me?"

I inhaled deep and exhaled slow and steady. "That makes sense, Finn. I just really don't like to think about all the ways Dad fucked me up."

"I don't either, woman. Let's stop talking about him and go to my room."

I turned to lead the way, but Finn grabbed my hand and turned me back around, yanking me to his hard body. He held my hand down by my side, lowered his lips to mine and kissed me hard. Harder than anyone had ever kissed me. Next thing I knew, his hands were at my ass, hauling my legs up. My little black dress bunched up when I locked my ankles behind his waist. I wrapped my arms around him and held on while he took his time trudging to his bedroom.

The moment his shins hit the bed, he lowered us down. His head tilted which allowed him to take my mouth with even more aggression. This should have freaked me out, but instead I loved it.

A grin pulled at my lips and Finn broke the kiss. "For someone who says *I* go from zero to one hundred, I'd say *you're* the one who doesn't know how to go slow, Finn."

His brows shot up. "What can I say, having your legs wrapped around me does shit to me. Don't worry, though, I'm gonna make love to you nice and slow, Riley."

I worked my hands between our bodies and undid the top button of his jeans. His mouth trailed a path from my lips down my neck and along my collarbone while his hands tugged my dress up.

"Love your tiny black dress, Riles, but it's got to go."

I arched my back to help him pull it off me.

His eyes widened when he caught sight of my lacy, transparent, black bra. "That bra doesn't do shit to hide your nipples, woman."

My head tilted. "Not when I'm around you it doesn't."

"Get it off while I deal with my jeans," he ordered, his voice rough and urgent.

I smirked. "Are you going to lose control, Finn?"

He stood naked at the side of the bed, and his eyes blazed at me. "You're gonna lose a bra if you don't do what I said."

That idea made me wetter. Still, I didn't have money to burn on a replacement bra, so I quickly unclasped it and tossed it aside.

I loved seeing Finn like this. No, I loved knowing I made him like this — barely hanging onto his control and hungry for me. That heady rush never got old, and I hoped it never did.

He planted his knees on the bed and lowered his body onto mine. "What's running through your mind now? You look like a bus is about to run you over."

I smiled and shoved thoughts of a future with Finn out of my mind. "Nothing, everything's cool."

He hovered over me, resting his weight on his forearms. His thumb came up and traced my lower lip. "You're lying, but I'm gonna let it go. Whatever has you freaked, I'm gonna make you forget it."

I raised my hips to guide his cock where I wanted it. "If ever there's a man who can do that, it's you, baby."

His eyes warmed. "Now you turn on the sweet." He kissed me, slow and methodical. "I'll take it."

I woke up in the morning uneasy about the day ahead. Unless I was sick, I didn't get days to myself. Every day had me tending to Jonah in the morning and work immediately afterward. My mind went into overdrive thinking about how I should be helping Auntie Celeste with Jonah. I spied the time on Finn's bedside clock. If I skipped breakfast and hurried in the shower, I could help her get Jonah started for the day.

The moment I shifted my body, I realized Finn had his arm locked around me.

How had I missed that?

It wasn't any wonder, really. Him spooning me felt as natural as peas in a pod.

"You goin' to the bathroom?" he asked, his voice rough with sleep. It was downright cute to hear him like that, though I could never share that with him.

"Yeah," I croaked, because mother nature wasn't very kind to me.

He let me go and I took care of business in the bathroom.

It took me a while to wake up in the mornings. While I washed my hands at the sink, I didn't react as fast to Finn coming into the bathroom. He crowded me from behind, reached past me and grabbed a small container of Listerine breath strips. I watched absently as he put one on his tongue, then held one out to me. On autopilot, I took it from him.

His hands roved my arms, down to my hips and my thighs. "Don't know why you didn't sleep naked last night, but at least you're just wearing this tank and panties."

Suddenly, his fingers wrapped around the hem of my tank and he whipped it off me – the momentum taking my arms up and getting my attention in the process.

"What are you —" I trailed off when his lips landed on my neck. He nipped and sucked at me. My breath caught and I leaned my head to the side. Our eyes locked in the mirror. He let out a growl of approval. Then he straightened and shoved my panties down my legs.

"Missed this," he said, one hand sliding around my hips, then down between my legs to my pussy while the other hand glided up to knead and massage my breast. That was when I noticed he was naked.

"You missed what?" I whispered.

His index finger dipped inside me. "You, all drowsy and cute in the morning. But damn if you don't wake up ready to take my cock."

"Finn," I moaned, grinding against his finger.

"Yeah," he breathed, then craned his neck and kissed me.

Now I understood why he gave me the breath strip. I tried to twist toward him, but he held me in place.

"No, babe. I want you to watch."

He lined himself up and pushed in just an inch.

I growled and shifted to get more of him. He thrust a little further, but it still wasn't enough.

He groaned. "Look at you, Riley. Grinding on my dick, your tits bouncing."

My head tipped back with my laughter. "You're holding one, so more like one tit bouncing."

He chuckled and massaged at my breast until his fingers worked their way to my nipple and he pinched and rolled it.

A shot of sensation ripped through me from my nipples to my clit. "Yes," I moaned.

"Oh, yeah, baby. Gonna make you come harder than last night. Want your juicy, hot pussy to milk me dry."

My hips jerked to keep up with his pace. He lowered his mouth to my neck, but this time he didn't nip at me. He sucked with intention.

"Finn... you're going to mark me."

His fingers rubbed my clit in fast, furious circles. "Damn right. You're mine, woman."

Any retort I had died on my lips when pleasure flooded through my body.

Just when I thought I would start coming down, Finn pushed forward, slightly bending us over the counter and his hips bucked.

"Open those eyes, Riley. Watch me fuck you. See what you do to me. Watch us both come."

My eyes opened and it hit me what Finn meant when he said, "Missed this." I had an instant memory of that weekend at the clubhouse. Both mornings, he'd woken me up with sex. Only now, I realized our last morning together it had bordered on more than just sex. *How could I have missed that?*

"Riley," he called.

My eyes caught his in the mirror. "Harder, Finn," I breathed.

A contrary look seeped into his eyes and he slowed his pace. "Slower, baby. Make sure you see it and feel it."

I didn't complain because watching him take me from behind was an erotic and beautiful vision. Not to mention, he was close and there was no way he would finish without picking up speed.

He maintained a slower, steady speed for all of six thrusts before he lost control and pounded into me harder and faster. I braced myself against the vanity and met his thrusts. With my eyes riveted on our reflection, I felt my second orgasm building, not just because of Finn's fingers and cock working me up, but because of the way he stared at me.

At us.

Nobody had ever looked at me that way.

Finn lowered his body closer to mine. "I'm close, Riley. Need you to get there."

I swiveled my hips and put my hand over his, showing him what I needed.

He kept pounding into me, his fingers continued to work my clit, and my release hit me a second before he stilled and shouted with his orgasm.

After a moment, our eyes met and he gave me a cocky grin. His lips kissed along my shoulder and he went back to the spot on my neck.

"Finn, you're going to leave a mark."

"Yeah."

"Your mom isn't going think much of me if you do."

He lifted his head, his eyes were weighty. "That's wrong, baby. She'll see how serious I am about you."

I fidgeted and he gently withdrew from me. His hands went to my hips and he guided me around to face him. To my surprise, he lifted me up and put me on the vanity.

"Finn, you are crazy!"

"Nope. Can see that look in your eyes, you don't think I should be serious about you."

I shook my head. "It's that you could have anyone, Finn."

His lips tipped up. "Yeah, but they aren't you."

"Right. They won't have as many problems."

He grabbed a wash cloth from a wire basket behind me, turned on the tap and after a moment he slid it under the faucet. "Everyone has problems, Riles. Yours just happen to be more serious than most. Now, I'm gonna clean you up —"

My eyes widened. "I can handle that, Finn."

His eyes widened in return. "Know that, but I want to and then we're gonna make breakfast."

A faint sound hit my ears and then I heard another sound added to the mix. "Who would call me or you this early in the morning?" I asked.

He handed me the washcloth and opened the door. "Shit."

I set the cloth aside and scurried to my cell, but as soon as I grabbed it, the ringing stopped. Anyone who knew me knew better than to leave a voice mail, so I took my cell back to the bathroom and cleaned up. By the time I finished washing my hands, my cell dinged with a notification.

There was a text message from an unfamiliar number.

> Hey, it's Victoria. Sorry if I woke you, but I'm swinging by Finn's place right after I get through this drive-through line at Starbuck's. Do you want anything? I'm grabbing a Chai latte because I'm not feeling coffee today.

Crazy as it made me sound, I always assumed the old ladies who were my age hated me because I'd been with their men. Though, Gamble had never shown any interest in me, so maybe he'd shared that with Victoria.

Before I could tap out a reply, the phone vibrated on the counter.

"Hi, Victoria," I answered.

"Good morning. I'm sorry to be pushy, but I've got news and I'm coming to see you. I assume you're still at Finn's. Gamble's calling him right now for me to make sure."

I fought a chuckle. "Yeah, I'm still at Finn's. As fast as you're talking, are you sure you need any kind of latte?"

"Hardy-har. I'd almost think you spoke to Gamble, but no. I'm just eager to share this news and I'm not doing it over the phone."

"Okay," I drawled. "Part of me wants to be excited, but I know better than to get excited about things that concern Dad."

I could hear the smile in her voice. "I always tell people to trust their gut. Now, I'm getting a soy chai latte, are you in?"

This felt weird, but I ignored that. "I've never had one, but I guess I'll try it."

"Excellent. See you in a few."

I came out of the bathroom and found my burnt orange blouse laid out on the bed, but Finn was nowhere around. It stood to reason that he wanted me to wear this, but I had no idea why. The flowy cotton top routinely fell off my shoulder, which meant I had to wear a strapless bra, but since most were so uncomfortable I tended to opt for no bra.

And that had to be why he wanted me to wear the blouse.

Finn's arms snaked around me from behind. "That shirt is fuckin' hot, Riley."

"Yeah, but I'm gonna wear something else."

He shifted back. "Why?"

I faced him. "Because Victoria's on her way over, and I'm guessing your mom will be swinging by this morning too. Neither one of them need to be around me wearing a shirt without a bra."

He cocked a brow. "You wore that at the clubhouse. Vickie won't care. And if Mom judges you for that, well, I'd rather get that shit out of the way now. It's not up to her or anyone what you wear."

A grin overtook me. "If it's not up to anyone... that would include you, too, wouldn't it?"

He gave me a dry look. "Leave it to a judge's daughter to use logic on me. You're right, but I'm just saying, I like you in that and I especially like the idea of easy access."

Since when did a man saying something like that to me turn me on?

He chuckled. "Seems you like that idea, too."

I shook my head. "Doesn't matter, Finn."

He smiled. "Sure, it does. But, you don't want to wear that, I'm damn sure not going to push you. It was a suggestion."

The doorbell rang and my eyes widened. "Shit."

He laughed. "If that's Vickie, I owe her huge."

I shook my head and changed into the blouse and tugged on a pair of jeans. Before I went out to the living room, I checked myself in the mirror. The blouse slid down my shoulder, and luckily it wasn't blatantly obvious that I was braless.

Finn's eyes roamed my body while his lips curved into a huge smile. "So fuckin' sexy."

His compliment filled me with pride, but I still shook my head. "Thanks."

The doorbell rang again, Finn answered, and Victoria swept inside carrying her legal brief case on her shoulder and a drink carrier in her hand.

"Chai latte for you, I forgot to ask if you wanted hot or iced, so I made the executive decision for iced. And a venti mocha latte for Finn."

Her upbeat attitude was contagious, but I resisted because good news was a rare thing for me.

I moved toward the dining room, until Finn and Victoria sat down in the living room. Finn patted a spot next to him and I planted myself on the couch.

Victoria took a deep breath. "If your father wasn't pissed before, my hunch is he's going to be pissed now."

That flew in the face of her upbeat attitude.

"Why?" Finn asked.

Victoria ignored his question and shot me a questioning look. "Your mother's maiden name was Daniels, right?"

With a slow nod, I said, "Yeah."

Victoria grinned. "I didn't find much about your brother. My paralegal is digging deeper on that, but I *did* find your mother's parents changed their will after her death."

I nodded. "Sure, if they were leaving something to her, they'd have to change it, right?"

Now Victoria nodded slowly. "Yes, that's true. Did you get to see them very often?"

I shook my head. "The last time we saw them, I was probably seven or so. In fact," I shot Finn a furtive glance, then focused on Victoria again. "This house reminds me of their home because of the smell."

She swallowed a sip of her tea. "Right, then you probably don't know that they had money."

I shrugged. "Not really. I mean, Dad never spoke about them to me or Jonah."

A sly look crossed Victoria's face. "Yeah, I bet he didn't. My paralegal is also working on getting her hands on the case file for your mom's murder. My guess is that they tried to get the investigators to take a harder look at your dad, but it didn't work."

I dipped my chin because that made sense.

Finn put his coffee on the end table. "Why's Tyndale going to be pissed now, Vickie?"

"What I've found so far is that Mrs. Daniels, her grandmother, left Riley a large sum of money. She also left funds to Jonah, but the bulk of the money went to Riley. I'm no financial adviser, but it's in a trust to you and Jonah. Since your dad kept it from you, most likely, it's sitting in an account gaining interest, though I'm guessing not much interest."

My shoulders rose in a small shrug. "Well, that's nice, but it doesn't really help much. Jonah needs care and insurance—"

Victoria shook her head. "It's over three million dollars, Riley."

My mouth went dry and my mind tripped over itself. "Say what?"

She chuckled. "You heard me. I mean, medical bills will eat up money fast, but I would think you can take care of your brother with that kind of —"

"No fuckin' wonder he beats her," Finn muttered.

I turned wide eyes to Finn. "What?"

Finn turned his hands up. "He's got to be pissed that money went into a trust just for you. I'm not saying he premeditated your mom's murder, but a man who beats women and children... the idea of you getting that kind of cash would eat him up."

Victoria's head wobbled as she thought about it. "That's the thing though. I'm not sure he's aware of how much money was bequeathed."

"Why wouldn't he know?" I asked.

"Your grandmother's lawyer is Smith Wharton, and while that doesn't mean anything to you, he's incredibly savvy. And sly as a fox, from what my colleagues say. Anyway, the language of that will stipulated only your legal representative would be informed of the amount."

Finn picked up his coffee. "I'm guessing Tyndale pulled some favors or some shit to find out how much money was involved."

Victoria tossed a hand out. "You could be right, but if he had, I'd think he'd have pushed harder to gain control of the trust, and that would be on record, but isn't." She gave me an assessing look. "You don't look excited by this. Most people would be thrilled to have so much money coming to them."

I gave her closed-lip smile. "Most people don't have a dad like mine to deal with, and really, I'm guessing it'll take a while to get the money."

Victoria shook her head. "Not with this type of trust. This doesn't have to go through probate, Riley. I'll text you Mr. Wharton's number and he can advise you on how to get access to the cash." She pulled out her phone and her eyes rounded. "Shoot. I didn't realize it was so late. I gotta run, but look for that text."

I stood when Victoria did. "Thank you so much for looking into this, Victoria. I'm... kind of surprised you were willing."

Her head cocked in question.

I shrugged. "I mean, after what I did to Heidi and all."

She pulled her bag higher on her shoulder. "You apologized for that, right?"

I nodded.

"There you go, then. People make mistakes. Yours was a little... bizarre, but as long as you apologized, meant it, and aren't going to do anything crazy like that again, then I'm good with that."

I smiled. "Well, thanks. Not everyone is that gracious."

We walked her to the doorway and watched her drive off.

Finn closed the door and wrapped his arms around me. "That's some pretty great news, woman."

"Might be," I said.

He shook his head and slid a hand under the back of my shirt. "Gotta be more positive, Riley. Shit's turnin' around for you and it's only gonna get better from here on out."

Before I could respond, he lowered his lips to mine and kissed me. The kiss turned into a make-out session and Finn took full advantage of the 'easy access' of my blouse. My hand had just slid under his shirt when someone knocked on the door.

"Damn," Finn whispered against my lips.

"Yeah," I breathed.

He righted my shirt and I stepped aside so he could answer the door.

"Hey, sweetie," his mom said.

"Hey, Mom. Come on in."

With a smile, I moved next to Finn. "Hi, Mrs. O'Halloran."

If she found it odd that I was right next to the door, she didn't let it show. Instead, she returned my smile. "Call me Nina, please."

"Nina," I murmured.

Her gaze darted to Finn and her expression changed. "What's going on? You look pleased as punch."

Finn draped his arm around my shoulders and pulled me close. "My woman got some epic fuckin' news, that's all."

Her eyes closed as shook her head, then she opened them. "You and that mouth, Finneas." She glanced at me. "You don't seem half as thrilled."

"I am. It's just a little unreal to me right now, that's all."

She arched a brow and Finn chuckled.

"She lies, Mom. She's waiting for the other shoe to drop, but I'm convincing her it doesn't have to be that way."

Chapter 9

The Idea

Finn

Finn wanted Riley and his mom to get along, but deep down he knew that didn't matter. As infrequently as Finn saw his folks, the two women just needed to be civil to each other... though if they could be more than that, he'd love it.

Riley's nervousness around his mom and other people bothered him. No, the fact he knew it all stemmed from her abusive dick of a father bothered him. Add in the fact he couldn't do much about it, and it didn't *bother* him, it angered the hell out of him.

Mom strolled to the couch and set her purse on the floor between the end table and the couch. She turned around to face them. "Well, are either of you going to share this great news?"

He glanced at Riley and shrugged a shoulder. "It isn't really mine to share, Mom."

Riley sat in the recliner. "I just found out my grandparents left me some money, that's all."

He could see Mom's wheels turning, but he didn't want her getting nosier. "What brings you by, Mom? Are you here through the weekend?"

She sighed. "I have to leave tomorrow. Don't freak out, but I thought we could fight fire with fire where Laurie and Steve are concerned. Maybe we should meet with a realtor to see what the house would really go for. And I didn't know how much money you have for a down payment or if you have financing lined up."

Finn ran a hand through his hair. Years of being in the military and he couldn't break the habit of keeping it short. In fact, just sliding his hand through it, he knew it needed to be cut soon. "Mom, I have money saved, but I had hoped to have a little more time to save more."

Mom shook her head. "Why?"

He widened his eyes. "The more I can put down, the lower my mortgage payment will be. I plan to start my own business. I didn't finish trade school for nothing. It'll be better if I'm carrying less debt when I'm ready to open an AC repair company. With my Air Force record and the house as collateral, I should qualify for a decent small business loan."

Mom nodded. "I understand that, Finneas, but Steve is convinced that the house will go for over two-hundred seventy-five thousand."

He threw his head back with laughter. "Mom, has he taken a look at Zillow or any real estate site that shows comps in a one-mile radius? Seriously. You'll be lucky if the house gets a hundred and fifty grand."

Mom sighed. "You don't have to tell me that, dear. But it is what he keeps yammering on about, comps at three hundred K and all that."

"Those are probably new houses," Riley muttered, then looked surprised she'd even spoken.

He grinned at her. "You got that right, babe."

Mom turned her hands up. "Which is exactly why I want you and I – and Riley if she wants – to go to a local realtor and get the lay of the land."

His eyes slid to Riley. "What do you say, Riley? Want to go talk real estate?"

Her reluctant smile said it all. "Could we divide and conquer? I'd really like to go see Jonah today."

He shook his head. "You're stickin' to my side for the next few days, woman. I think Mensa and your aunt are right. You go hang with your brother and it's the perfect opportunity for your dad to strike."

Her jaw clenched, but she didn't say anything.

He realized he'd said too much in front of Mom if Riley didn't want her knowing about the problem with Tyndale. "But, we can go separate from Mom and swing by to check on Jonah after, if that works for you."

Riley shook her head. "No. I don't want to cause problems. I'll just call Jonah while you meet with the realtor."

Part of him wanted to argue against that, but her suggestion made sense. Plus, Mom seemed relieved at the notion of Riley not being with them while they spoke to a realtor. Not that it mattered one way or the other – they weren't going to list the house, since it was still in probate.

He nodded. "Sounds like a plan."

"She reminds me so much of Allison," Mom said while they waited in the lobby at the realtor's office.

"No, Mom. She's nothing like Allison."

Mom dipped her chin. "Brown hair, brown eyes, petite, and her father is abusive."

He did his damnedest to suppress his growl, but failed. "Why would you say that, Mom?"

She gave him a mock smile. "You said something about giving her dad the chance to strike. Most fathers don't wait for their chance, they have an open, honest relationship with their kids."

He shook his head twice. "Those four things are where the similarities end, Mom."

"Really?"

He looked her in the eyes. "Riley hasn't decided if she's on-board with having kids. Allison was nothing more than a yes-woman. Said anything she thought I wanted to hear, but never told me how bad things really were."

Mom's eyes widened. "And Riley has?"

He nodded. "Yeah. I let her take her time, but she opened up like a book, Mom. Then she did it again when friends of ours came by to try and help."

"Okay, but do you really want a woman who needs saving?"

He gave a humorless chuckle. "I'm gonna ignore how offensive that is, to her *and* to me, but I'll tell you right now, she doesn't need saving. She's only stuck around this long because of her brother. And like I said yesterday, that's her story to tell, not mine. She's one helluva fighter, Mom, and I admire the fuck out of her for it."

Mom shifted in her seat. "Well, I just wish I knew the whole story here."

"It's still a little early, Mom. But the better thing for you to do is try to get to know her. She warms up to you, she might tell you on her own."

One of the administrative assistants stood from her desk. "Mrs. O'Halloran? Ms. Greer is ready for you."

Half an hour later, Finn followed his mom out of the office and muttered, "That was a waste of time."

"No, it wasn't. By the end of the day, we'll have real comps, not whatever hot air Steve is giving me. Plus, his friend was all speculation. This woman knows we can't move forward without the house being out of probate."

"Pretty sure Uncle Steve knew that, Mom."

She hitched her purse up higher on her shoulder when they stepped onto the sidewalk. "It didn't sound that way, Finneas."

"Any word on the will?"

"Not yet."

"Good."

Mom stopped. "I have a conference call at four. In the meantime, can I take you and Riley to lunch?"

Finn looked down at his Mom. "Sure, but don't be too nosy."

Riley had her arm slung low around his waist while they stood waiting for a table at a small Italian restaurant. Mom had hurried to the restroom.

He kissed the top of Riley's head. "Everything good with your brother?"

She made a humming sound. "I guess. Nobody's telling me anything, but I get the feeling Dad's made things hard on Auntie Celeste."

"How the hell could he?" Finn asked.

She tilted her head up, skepticism shining from her brown eyes. "You'd be surprised, Finn."

"Not sure anything your dad does would surprise me, but lay it on me, woman. I'm serious."

She took a deep breath. "Jonah sounded preoccupied, and that's unusual for him. He claimed he didn't sleep well, which happens, but I'm guessing Dad dropped by late and tried to terrorize Auntie Celeste."

"But you're just speculating?"

She nodded. "Yes, because they're not telling me anything."

He pulled his cell from his back pocket. "Let me see if Mensa knows anything."

"I doubt he'll share with you."

He grinned at her. "You'd be surprised."

"Did you say there's a surprise?" Mom asked, joining them from behind.

"No, Mom."

A hostess led them to a table in the center of the restaurant.

Riley put her napkin in her lap, looked across the room, ducked her head for a moment, then cast a furtive look at his Mom. "Nina, would you mind changing seats with me?"

"Is something wrong, dear?"

"Not exactly, I just —"

Finn glanced across the room to where Riley had been looking. Two women stared in their direction. They both wore what appeared to be silk, button-up blouses with dress pants. One wore her steel gray hair in a bob, while the other kept hers much shorter in an almost pixie-style cut. Both ladies had a grandmotherly air about them, but from Riley's reaction, that might have been being too kind. The women caught Finn's eyes and turned away.

"Great," Riley whispered.

"Do you know them?" Finn asked.

Riley hesitated. "I used to."

From the corner of his eye, Finn saw the one with the bobbed hair walking toward them. The woman with the shorter hair had her phone to her ear.

Riley looked Mom dead in the eyes. "I'm sorry."

"For what?" Mom asked, as the woman stopped at the edge of the table.

This woman had shrewd brown eyes that bordered on being beady. She looked down her nose at them. "Riley Tyndale, you haven't been to church in ages."

"Mrs. Demps, it's good to see you."

Finn didn't know someone could look down their nose even further, but this bitch managed it. "You shouldn't lie, dear. If that were true you'd have come by our table or waved at the very least. Instead you're hiding." She paused and a small grin crossed her face. "Almost as though you're ashamed of something."

Mom leaned forward. "I'm sorry, but you're out of line."

Finn didn't disagree, but he knew how much Riley hated confrontations. "Mom, let it go."

Mom turned stunned eyes to him. "Not a chance, Finn. She can't waltz over here out of the blue and guilt Riley about not going to church. Especially when it's obvious she was attacked."

Mrs. Demps tilted her head at Finn. "By him, I'm sure."

Mom threw her napkin on the table.

Finn grabbed her hand. "Mom, don't give her what she wants."

Mom glowered at him, but kept quiet.

Riley crossed her arms and glared at Mrs. Demps. "Happy now? You've insulted me and... my man in front of his mother. Go back to Mrs. Lancaster and have a nice lunch."

His breath arrested in his lungs at her calling him her man. Mrs. Demps tried to stare Riley down, but Riley withstood the woman's glare.

As soon as Mrs. Demps left, their server came to the table. "Can I get you started with some drinks and an appetizer?"

"No appetizer, but we'll take a bottle of red wine – Syrah if you have it, three glasses, and three waters," Finn said.

Once the server left, Mom leaned over the table and hissed, "Finneas, I'm driving."

Finn lowered his voice. "It's okay, Mom. I can drive if you have one too many."

She narrowed her eyes at him and he grinned. Her brow arched and she looked at Riley. "Learn fast: my son might seem like a teddy bear, but he can be a bit of a steamroller when he wants to be."

He'd have argued with Mom about that, but hearing Riley's throaty laugh set him at ease.

Riley

I had to hand it to Nina. She defused the situation with her candid remark about Finn and suddenly I didn't feel half as mortified.

She aimed a patient smile at me. "I can see you just relaxed, but I'm hoping you'll tell me at least a little about what's going on because I *really* don't like that woman and what she had to say."

Our waitress came back with three wine glasses and the bottle of Syrah. She uncorked the bottle and asked Finn if he wanted to sample it first. I had been slightly surprised that Finn would order wine, but it didn't surprise me that he declined the sample.

Nina lifted her glass once the waitress left. "This isn't a very good toast, but it's all I've got. Here's to new beginnings and no more bad vibes."

I grinned and tapped my glass to hers and Finn's. The first sip of wine went down much smoother than I'd expected. "Are you sure you want to hear what's going on with me? It isn't fun and it might make you more angry."

She nodded. "I have a hard time believing that, but yes. I want to hear it."

Twenty minutes later, Nina stared at Finn with huge eyes. "Tell me you're doing something about this."

Finn sat back in his chair. "Told you that yesterday, Mom."

She shook her head. "I guess now I see why it's taking time."

We ate our lunch in peace and Nina lost her fight with Finn to pay our bill. I almost slipped up and said I should pay since I'd soon be a millionaire, but I couldn't count on that money. All of it needed to go to my brother.

We stood in the parking lot thawing out from the chilly restaurant.

Nina handed Finn her keys. "You drive. I'm feeling too buzzed." She looked at me. "And you sit up front."

I shook my head. "No, ma'am. I'm good in the back seat."

Nina looked like she would argue with me some more, but she relented.

When Finn pulled the car into his driveway, my sigh escaped me. His eyes caught mine in the rearview mirror, then he focused on the two older gentlemen standing in front of his house.

I hadn't seen either of these men in months. Mr. Demps had put on some weight and his gut hung over the top of his pants. He wore a blue-and-black plaid, short-sleeved, button-up shirt and looked ready to attend Bible study.

Mr. Coleman prided himself on staying fit, but he still showed his age. His gray hair had receded to the point it made a horseshoe shape around his large head. His square-frame glasses magnified his brown eyes. He wore khaki pants with a hunter-green polo shirt and brown leather boat shoes.

"I'm gonna guess those two men are married to Mrs. Demps and her crony," Finn said.

I lowered my chin in slight agreement. "One is. The other is Mr. Coleman, but they're both respected church elders."

Nina looked over her shoulder at me. "What denomination did you say the church is?"

"It doesn't matter, Mom," Finn said, turning off the car and opening his door.

I whispered, "They say non-denominational, but they're very evangelical."

"Okay," she whispered back.

On the walk leading up to the front stoop, Finn stood with his legs wide and his arms folded. Part of me thought it was a power posture, but it also prevented me or Nina from moving past him.

"You don't need to protect us from them," I muttered to Finn's back.

He turned his head just a touch. "Quiet."

"Hello, sir. We'd like to talk to Riley, if you don't mind," Mr. Demps said.

It had to be my imagination, but I swore Finn stood even taller. "I do mind, and you two need to leave. Now."

Mr. Coleman stepped onto the walk with a friendly smile. "Please hear us out. Riley's in a world of trouble, but nothing a little discipline won't fix."

I leaned to the side. "Discipline like you gave my mother?"

Mr. Coleman's smile faltered before he strengthened it, but it was fake. "You are very much like your mother, Riley. Jack only wants to be sure you aren't headed down the same path of sinning."

"The sinner here is her father," Nina said.

The way Finn's head tilted up, I knew he was calling up patience with me and Nina.

"You don't know what you're talking about," Mr. Coleman said.

"Leave. Both of you," Finn stated.

Mr. Demps had joined Mr. Coleman. "You know, you're worse than your mother. At least she was married. You're out here in skimpy clothes instead of at home taking care of your brother like a good daughter."

Finn pulled his phone from his pocket. "You've been asked to leave twice. I'm calling the cops now."

"There's no need for threats," Mr. Demps said.

Finn had the phone to his ear and I saw Mr. Coleman's eyes widen. "We're leaving." He glared at me. "You need to be in church on Sunday. We'll be praying for you in the meantime."

I clenched my jaw. Those men wouldn't be praying for me, they'd be reporting back to my father, just like Mrs. Demps reported back to her husband.

Finn tucked his phone back in his pocket once the two men were inside Mr. Coleman's Cadillac.

"Were you really going to call 911?" I asked.

"Was gonna call Mensa, but they didn't have to know that. He's at the bar which is just a few minutes from here. Either way, they left."

Inside the house, Nina sat on the couch. "How did they even know to find you here, I wonder."

"In some way, this is Dad making a flex. Having a church elder come here makes it clear that he knows where I am."

"He gets others to do his dirty work," Nina surmised.

"Sometimes," I said, planting myself in the recliner.

"I still don't understand why you can't report the abuse to the police," Nina said.

I pressed my lips together. "It becomes my word against his, and the real problem is that I can't move out because someone needs to take care of Jonah."

"Right, I keep forgetting that part. Probably because I can't believe a father wouldn't do everything he can to help his son – especially when it's his fault his son was injured." She shook her head. "I better head back to the hotel and get ready for my conference call." She walked over to Finn. "Give me a hug, honey."

"I'll walk you out, Mom."

She let go of Finn. "Not before I give Riley a hug, too."

That shocked me because before lunch I hadn't felt like Nina approved of me so much as she was tolerating me. I stood up and she wrapped me in a warm embrace. It struck me that she gave great hugs, like Finn.

After Nina left, I heard the door open and close. Finn settled on the couch facing me. "I hate to say this, but, we get you out of this mess, you're never talking to your dad again."

"Done and done, Finn. The only possible hang-up with that is if *Jonah* still wants to keep in touch."

He leaned forward and put his elbows on his knees, shaking his head. "Nope. You let him do that by phone only."

I nodded. "Sounds like a plan."

"Why do I think you don't mean that?"

I chuckled. "Because I think that it's up to *Jonah* more than you or me, so... we'll have to wait and see."

Finn crossed the small living room, came to me, and grabbed my hands to pull me out of the recliner. Fire burned in his eyes. "No. You get free of this asshole, you are done, Riles."

"Okay. Calm down."

His arms slid around my waist. "I know how you can calm me down."

I grinned. "A blowjob?"

"To start."

My fingers snagged on the loops of his jeans and he kissed me. He tasted like marinara sauce and hints of red wine. We both groaned when the doorbell rang.

I leaned my forehead on his chest. "Your place gets more visitors than the clubhouse."

"No shit, babe."

Finn draped his arm on my shoulders, guided us to the door, and he looked in the peephole. "I'll be damned."

"What?" I whispered.

He shook his head. With a grin, he opened the front door. "You could have texted, motherfucker."

Mensa came inside. "I did."

"Riley!" Aurora called from the drive.

I opened the door wider and saw her rounding the front of her lime green Kia Soul. "What are you doing here?" I called.

She opened the back passenger door to her car and Jonah got out. "Your cousin asked me to help get Jonah out of the house."

My eyes widened with my smile. "You are the best girlfriend, ever, Aurora! Jonah, you're gonna love Finn's house!"

Jonah ambled up the walk, and if I wasn't mistaken, his gait had improved.

"Did you have physical therapy this week?"

Jonah smiled. "No, Uncle Dean works out in the morning. He had me start exercising too."

"That's great, Jay."

After I gave them hugs, I led Aurora and Jonah into the living room.

Sitting on the couch, Mensa shot me a pointed look. "I'm guessing you made Finn text me."

I scoffed. "Like I could make Finn do anything. I talked to Jonah on the phone, but something tells me nobody's giving me the whole story."

Mensa twisted his lips to the side while he weighed his words. "Things have been ugly at the house each night, but I think Uncle Jack's run out of steam."

"Or he's going to focus on her now since his church buddies were just here," Finn muttered.

Aurora leaned against the arm of the couch, opposite Mensa. "Which ones?"

"Coleman and Demps," I muttered.

"Good times, then," she said.

"Not even close," Finn said. He looked at Jonah. "Want a tour? My gaming chair isn't as fancy as the one you have, but it's pretty cool."

Jonah's eyes lit up. "Yeah!"

"Why are you so gung-ho to see your brother?" Aurora asked after Finn led Jonah out of the room.

I recapped last night's dinner with Detective Dennizen and the idea of approaching Shirley Calhoun.

"That sounds like a decent strategy," Aurora said.

"I hope it will be," I said.

Finn and Jonah came back into the living room.

"You hope what will be?" Finn asked.

Jonah sat next to Mensa and I took the seat on my brother's other side. "I'm hoping Jonah is cool with the idea we came up with last night."

"What idea?" Jonah asked.

Finn sat in the recliner, but locked eyes with Jonah. "Some friends of ours suggested telling your story to the woman running against your father."

"My story?" Jonah asked.

Finn turned his hands up for a second. "Yeah, about the night your dad hit you."

Jonah wrung his fingers in his lap. "And Mom. Don't forget Mom."

I explained to my brother that if things worked out, police detectives might ask him questions, and that there might be reporters who wanted to talk to him, too.

After a long moment, he turned his big brown eyes to me. "Do it, sissy."

I squeezed his hand. "They're going to focus on you, honey. A lot. And... political ads get nasty."

Aurora paced the room, shaking her head. "Neither one of them has reason to drag Jonah through the mud." She stopped and stared at me. "It's you they might do wrong."

"I don't think so," Mensa said. "She was a minor at the time, and if he wants to refute the claims, Uncle Jack would be calling his daughter a liar, which still makes him look bad."

Aurora frowned. "Call me crazy, but there should be a higher authority she can go to and have this fully investigated."

"An investigation is one thing, making him pay is another, and I don't care how vindictive it makes me, he needs to pay," Mensa said.

Chapter 10

Exclusive Interview

Finn

Aurora's cell rang and she turned away from the group to take the call. From the corner of his eyes, Finn saw her shoulders rise. "Are you serious?" she asked.

She kept her back to them, but her head shook. "You know this is messed up, Dad."

Riley stood from the couch. Finn intercepted her before she reached Aurora, who had turned around. "Oh, yeah. His precious faith. It's all he hides behind to justify beating his wife and kids."

As much as Finn dug Aurora's spunk, he saw how tense it made Riley, and with a glance at Jonah, it was impacting him, too.

Mensa crossed the room and put his hands on Aurora's shoulders. "Did Jack call your dad?"

She nodded. "He knows I brought Jonah here."

Mensa shook his head. "No, you didn't. I'm the one who arranged this. I'll get Jonah back to my Mom's."

"He can't ride on your bike," Riley said.

Mensa shot Riley a look. "I'm saying, I'm the person responsible for this." He turned back to Aurora. "Make sure your dad understands that."

Finn grabbed Riley's hand and tugged her to the side. "Get a bag together. We're spending the night at the clubhouse."

She tipped her face up at him, her mouth opened and he could practically see the argument on her lips. Then the fight drained out of her and she sighed. "Fine. That's probably a good idea."

"I vote we stay here for a while. Dad doesn't know where I am," Jonah said.

The gentle, sweet smile on Riley's face hit Finn hard. He knew she'd aim the same kind of tender smile on a child, and he wanted to be the man who gave her that child.

"Unfortunately, Jonah, he *does* know where you are, because he knows where I am."

"Really?" Jonah asked.

Riley nodded. "Yeah. A police officer stopped by here because he saw my car."

"So. Fucked. Up," Mensa bit out.

Finn caught Aurora's eyes. "Take Jonah back to his Aunt's house. We'll follow you, make sure nothing happens."

Aurora's face set with determination. "Oh, I want something to happen, all right."

His eyes slid to Riley and Jonah pointedly, then back to hers. "No, you don't."

She followed his gaze and nodded. "I think I might like you for her."

"I'm right here," Riley muttered.

Mensa ran his hands through his hair. "Yeah, and we all need to go. Might seem like overkill, but I think Uncle Jack has some dirty tricks up his sleeve."

Riley gave Jonah a hug. "I love you, Jonah."

"Love you, too, Sissy."

He and Riley followed Aurora like they said they would. It was a quiet ride, and as they pulled onto the street for the clubhouse, it hit Finn how much he'd enjoyed having Riley at his back.

Riley dismounted and put her helmet on the seat, glancing around the lot. "Looks like everybody's here."

Finn nodded. "Got church in a couple hours. We have enough time to eat beforehand. Or we can wait until afterward. Not much going on these days, so the meet won't take long."

Riley shook her head. "No way. Those are famous last words, and I'm a girl who needs her food."

Two hours later, Finn sat next to Mensa in the meeting room for church.

Har cleared his throat. "Gonna keep this short, brothers. Not much has happened since we came back from Daytona. Block go ahead and run down our finances."

After they heard about money issues, there was a lull.

Cynic looked at Har. "There is something to bring to everyone's attention. Riley's got a situation, and we need to help her."

"What's the situation?" Brute asked.

Cynic summarized Riley's issues and her status with Finn.

Brute shook his head. "This really isn't a club matter, Prez. Hell —"

Finn didn't care if they fined him. "How isn't it a club issue? She's been with all but four men in this room. A threat to her absolutely is a threat to the Riot."

"It isn't. We aren't a battered women's home," Tiny said.

"Not saying we are, but what about Fiona? All the brothers rolled out for her."

"She's a president's daughter," Brute said.

Finn threw out a hand. "Riley's Mensa's cousin."

"It's different," Tiny said.

"So, we only protect women related to the gavel? That's bullshit," Finn muttered.

"No, it isn't," Tiny bit out.

Finn's eyes widened. "Sierra, Vickie, even Heidi had people gunning for them and nobody said shit when we stepped up for them."

Har said, "You're right, Finn. Riley deserves our help, but this *is* different. Tyndale's used his influence and that could hit the club businesses as well as individual brothers."

Finn looked down the table. "All due respect, Har, that's nothing new."

"The threat to our businesses is a new threat," Block said.

Finn shook his head. "Are you saying the drugs weren't ever in jeopardy if a cop busted us? It's always been risky, Block."

"He's got you there," Joules piped up.

"Did she decide if she's going to talk to Calhoun?" Roman asked.

"Who's that? And why does that name sound familiar?" Joules asked.

"Pretty sure she is. Jonah gave his okay on it," Finn said. He looked to Joules. "That's Tyndale's opponent in the election."

Brute's eyes widened at Finn. "Provin' my point, man. Politics isn't club business."

Har frowned at Brute. "It could be. Always better to know than not-know about shit."

Finn looked down the table at Brute and Har. "One thing that Riley said is that this is the one place she's always felt safe. I doubt Tyndale knows that, but he'd likely figure it out fast. There's been an attack on the clubhouse before, there's nothing to say he wouldn't do something similar."

Cynic nodded. "Yeah, we should limit cages comin' in. Put a prospect on the gate again."

Brute sighed, but kept quiet.

Har nodded. "Done. Anything else?"

Finn shook his head.

Har adjourned the meeting.

Finn followed Gamble to the common room. Victoria sat next to Riley at the bar. Sandy stood behind it with one of the prospects.

Cynic and Mensa dragged one of the round high-top tables behind Victoria and Riley.

"What are you doing?" Gamble asked.

Cynic aimed a dry look at Gamble and Finn. "I want to talk to her without yelling down the damn bar. I do enough of that at Twisted Talons."

Riley swiveled around on her stool. "Why do you need to talk to me?"

Mensa sat on a stool. "Because I want to know if you ever fought back. And 'Nic can help you learn to use a knife. Figure a gun isn't good for you if Jonah's around."

Heidi bustled through the front door. "Hey, Vickie!"

Block stood from one of the couches. "What am I? Chopped liver?"

She grinned. "You knew I was coming inside. I didn't expect Vickie to be here."

Block and Heidi took stools on the other side of the table from Mensa and Cynic. Riley tensed, but after a deep breath, she relaxed. Finn admired how she powered through her awkwardness.

Block arched a brow at Riley. "Why didn't you fight back?"

"Because most of the time Dad held back. When I was younger, I fought, and he showed me how hard he could really hit me in the stomach. I'd never been so winded before that night. Something I forgot around sixteen or seventeen. That's the only time he lashed out at Jonah, because he knew how much I love him. After that, I just took it."

Finn's teeth ground together while he pulled a pack of cigarettes from his vest pocket. "That is some goddamn bullshit."

Riley aimed a reluctant smile at him. "Yeah, I didn't want to tell you about that."

He widened his eyes at her. "Don't keep something from me because of my reaction, babe. It's not directed at you and I'd never take that shit out on you. Ever."

Heidi shook her head. "You take your Dad's shit to keep him from beating your brother."

Riley shrugged. "Jonah's the only family I have. What else am I gonna do? Pretty sure Mom would haunt me if I didn't make sure he's okay."

Heidi's lips twisted to the side. "Do you think your dad will hurt your brother without you around?"

"Neglect is its own kind of abuse," Riley muttered.

Sandy set a beer in front of Finn. "If there is a threat to her brother, you should have brought him here, too."

He gave her a dry look. "There's more to it than that."

Sandy narrowed her eyes. "I keep hearing that. Funny thing is, it sounds like an excuse, and a lousy one at that."

Riley patted Sandy's hand. "We'll bring him by. I promise. It may have to wait until this shit dies down, that's all."

"Probably easier to take her to him at this point," Finn said without thinking.

"I knew there was a reason I liked you," Sandy said, smiling at him.

Mensa groaned. "Why'd you have to go and say that shit?"

He looked at Mensa from the corner of his eye. "It slipped." He focused on Sandy. "It's going to wait, for now."

Sandy stared at him for a beat. "If it keeps him safe, then I'll wait. Drives me crazy that parents beat on their children." She looked at Riley. "And you stay away from him. You don't need to take that crap anymore."

"Yes, ma'am. Finn's made that pretty clear."

"Good," Sandy said, and wandered to the kitchen.

Mensa swallowed some beer. "How do you feel about Krav Maga?"

Riley shook her head. "When am I gonna have time for a martial arts class? I need to get back to work —"

Vickie shot her a pointed look. "Do you?"

Riley shut her mouth for a second. "I still need to earn my own money and take care of myself. What you found is for Jonah."

Block nodded. "Mensa's right. You need to take some kind of class to learn defensive moves at a minimum. If you're laying low, this would be the perfect time to try Krav Maga."

Gamble set his beer bottle on the bar. "She'll need to have an instructor come to her. If she's going to her dad's opponent with her story, the press is going to be breathing down her neck very soon."

Finn slid his arm around her waist. "Do you have a way of reaching out to Shirley Calhoun, Riley? It came up in church earlier, and I wasn't sure if you got the ball rolling or not."

"I don't, but I'll look into it. Worst case scenario, I might be able to play dumb and ask Dad's publicist who's handling her publicity. It's such a small world in that industry, they're all up in each other's business."

"Think that's true of a lot of industries, babe," Finn said.

"Have you considered reaching out to just one TV station? You could offer an exclusive interview. Then you wouldn't have all the reporters coming after you – at least not immediately," Victoria said.

Heidi nodded. "That could probably work. People believe news interviews much more than political ads."

Sandy brought a bowl of Chex Mix to the bar. "A bonus to using the news reporters is that would keep you from having to play dumb and possibly tipping your daddy off."

Finn looked at Block. "Doesn't Two-Times have a sister who's a producer at one of the local stations?"

Block hesitated. "I know she works at a station, not sure if they have news or not."

"Text him and find out," Sandy suggested.

"Oh, boy," Riley whispered.

Victoria smiled at her. "Look at it this way, the sooner it's done, the sooner you can move on."

Riley

For so many years, I'd wanted to tell people what Dad did to me. Since going to trusted people at school had never helped, the idea of calling a TV reporter never occurred to me. Now, everything was happening at what felt like warp speed. I felt so many things — excitement at the prospect of escaping Dad's wrath, fear at how Dad would retaliate — and I had no doubt he would. Then there was the sheer overwhelming thought of rehashing my story with a stranger and possibly having to go on television.

I glanced at Finn. "You think they can blur out my face?"

Sandy reached past Finn to grab my hand. "Honey, they'll do whatever it takes to get your story, I'm sure of it. Exposing a long-time judge of a crime *and* possibly re-opening a murder case? They will bend over backwards." The earnestness in her brown eyes made me believe her. She smiled and squeezed my hand. "Believe it, Riley."

I nodded.

A light knock came from the front door before Nadia and Whitney came inside.

"Hey, Sandy, what's shakin'?" Nadia asked.

"Not much, sweetie. Did you bring the karaoke machine?"

"We did," Whitney said, putting it down near the stereo system.

"What the hell, Sandy? I deal with open mic night once a week at Twisted Talons, now you got Nadia bringing karaoke here?" Cynic grumbled.

Sandy's eyes darted between me and Cynic. My brow rose as it hit me that Sandy was up to something.

"It'll be fun, 'Nic. Besides, nobody here sounds *that* bad, and some of us might even be pretty good."

"What are you smoking today, Sandy? That might be the craziest thing I've ever heard," Block said.

My phone rang with Aurora's ring tone. I slipped out of Finn's hold and wandered toward the stereo system where Whitney was messing with wires.

"Hey, Aurora."

"Hey, yourself. I'm parked outside the clubhouse. Do I need to use a special knock or something to get inside?"

I tipped my head back. This confirmed my suspicions that Sandy was up to no good. "No, you can just come inside. If you're parked in the back, don't bother with the front door. There's a door by the picnic tables." I paused because Sandy didn't have Aurora's cell number as far as I knew. "Who invited you out here, anyway?"

Aurora scoffed. "Your cousin. My guess is he thinks I still have a thing for him, but I don't. He's not actually interested in me, is he?"

I chuckled. "Hell if I know, but I suspect another woman told him to call you."

"Why?"

"Come inside and you'll find out."

I tucked my phone in my back pocket and went to the back door. Mensa followed me. I tossed him a look over my shoulder. "Are you in on whatever Sandy's got planned?"

His lips hinted at a grin. "A little. Is Aurora here?"

"Yes. You gonna sing karaoke too?"

"Fuck, no. I only did what Sandy asked because she's doing this for you."

"Why?" I asked, opening the door, and watching Aurora make her way to the patio.

Mensa side-stepped toward the kitchen. "Why not? Just another reason for people to drink and party, really. But you better keep the pop music to a minimum. Too much of that shit is revolting."

I grinned. "So judgy."

His eyes widened. "I'm right, and you know it."

Aurora stepped inside the clubhouse. "What does he think he's right about?"

"Musical tastes," I said.

At the same time Mensa said, "Pop music being the work of the devil."

Aurora tipped her head to the side, and her dark hair fell over her shoulder. "He might *not* be wrong. But why does it matter?" She looked down the hallway to our right. "What's down there?"

"Brothers' rooms. And the pop music matters because apparently we're doing karaoke tonight."

Mensa handed a bottle of Coors to Aurora. "No, Sandy's arranged for you to sing tonight because it's a great way for you to relax."

I cocked a brow at Aurora. "Wait a minute. Where's Denver? You normally hang with her in the afternoons."

I could read my best friend like a book, and not just because I'd known her for so long. Aurora couldn't lie to anyone because she wore all of her thoughts on her face.

Mensa shook his head. "You blew it, woman." He looked at me. "Denver is with Jonah."

Mensa mentioned Denver having a crush on my brother, but I was in denial. Not to mention, he was twenty-three and Denver was seventeen, though she would soon turn eighteen. It was close to six years between them, but I wondered if Denver's crush was a fleeting teenage-girl phase.

Aurora said, "Don't worry. They're gaming... in person rather than online for once."

I nodded. "Yeah. I don't want either of them to get hurt."

"She'd never hurt him," Aurora said.

"Maybe he's going to hurt her," I said.

Aurora didn't quite roll her eyes. "No way."

Mensa wrapped his hand around my neck. "You're borrowing trouble, Riley. Stop it because you damn sure got enough of it right now."

"Okay," I murmured.

"You must be Aurora," Whitney said from behind us.

Mensa's hand fell away from my neck and his eyes darted to Whitney. "Why are you still here?"

I scoffed. "Rude, much? What kind of question is that? She came with Nadia. They're related."

Whitney aimed a smirk my way for a split second. It dropped away in an instant when she refocused on Mensa. "Aunt Nadia doesn't know how to run the karaoke machine, but really, Sandy invited both of us. That's why I'm still here, Tyndale."

I opened my mouth to correct her, but Mensa leaned toward her. "My last name isn't Tyndale, Whitney. And I'm not a man you can wrap around your little finger like you do the men at the bar. Show a prospect how to run the damned machine. You need to clear out. ASAP."

My mouth dropped open and I stepped between them. "You need to apologize, Mensa. She hasn't done a damned thing to you."

Mensa lowered his chin and his dark eyes caught mine. "No, I don't. Something about her is off, and I don't like it. She's up to something and it isn't anything innocent like karaoke. A woman like her has no business being inside the clubhouse."

I shifted to look at Whitney. To my surprise, she had a demure smile on her face.

"You sound scared, Mensa. I thought it would take something more than a woman like me to scare a tough biker like you."

Mensa rolled his eyes. "Jesus. Listen to this shit. I don't have time for this." He shook his head and looked past me. "Make sure she's out of here before ten."

"You got it, brother," Finn said.

Mensa stormed off.

"Are you serious?" I breathed.

Whitney nudged my shoulder with hers. "If you think I'm letting Mensa determine when I leave, think again."

Finn crossed his arms. "You should think again, Whitney. Things are different here than they are at the bar."

She nodded. "I got that, but it's time to get this show on the road."

Aurora grinned. "It's about time. My girl can crush 'This Little Light,' but you really need to hear her sing Evanescence's 'Bring Me to Life.' It is," she lifted her fingers to her lips. "Absolutely chef's kiss."

My face was on fire even while her words filled me with pride.

"What's with the tomato impersonation?" Aurora asked.

"I just never knew you thought that."

Her eyes widened. "And I thought you had let it go – that dream of yours."

I shook my head. "It isn't a dream. We're just singing karaoke."

Whitney laughed and waved her finger around the group. "*We're* all doing karaoke. From what I've heard you sing a cappella, *you're* doing something else entirely."

"Stop it," I muttered.

"What are y'all doin' back there?" Sandy asked, standing in the middle of the common room. "It's time to get this started."

Fifty-three seconds into my karaoke song, Mensa sang the male vocals to 'Bring Me to Life.' It surprised me and thrilled me at the same time. I hadn't sang with him since we were kids and he visited our church a couple times. I'd forgotten how great his voice happened to be.

When we finished, Sandy let out a piercing scream like she was at a rock concert.

"I had no idea you could sing like that," Joules said as I made my way to the bar.

I glanced over my shoulder at Mensa, but he'd headed to a pool table. "Well, it's not like there are too many opportunities for singing around here."

"I didn't know Mensa could fuckin' sing," Cynic said. "That settles it, he's got 'Open Mic' duty from here on out." Cynic glanced at his phone. "Shit. I didn't realize the time. I gotta get over to Twisted Talons."

He aimed a look at me. "Finn said you're staying the night here. Late tomorrow morning, I'm showing you how to wield a knife."

I nodded, hoping I wouldn't have to ever use a knife. The idea of cutting someone didn't sit well with me, but I wanted to protect myself.

The distinct opening notes of Elle King's 'Where the Devil Don't Go' filled the room and I whipped my head around to see Whitney holding the microphone. For all her talk earlier, she was wrong. Her voice wasn't as raspy as Elle King's, but Whitney could still belt out the lyrics.

From the corner of my eye, I caught Mensa staring at her. The look in his eyes confused me. As much as he wanted her out of the clubhouse, I almost thought he watched her with lust in his eyes... but it also looked like anger.

"Stop staring at your cousin," Finn murmured in my ear.

I turned and our noses were almost touching. "I can't help it. She's really good, and the way he's looking at her. I'm not sure if he wants to wring her neck or kiss her."

Finn's eyes heated. "Some people like to do both."

My jaw dropped. "I am not thinking about my cousin that way, Finn!"

He laughed. "I love pushing your buttons."

I pointed a finger at him. "That's great, honey, but leave my cousin out of it."

Roman sidled up to us. "Have you considered singing, professionally?"

With a smile, I shook my head. "I'm not good enough for that —"

"Stop it," Finn said.

Roman nodded. "Listen to Finn. You *are* good enough to consider professional gigs."

I opened my mouth to protest, but Finn gave my neck a gentle squeeze.

He stared at me for a beat. "I already hate the bastard for hitting you and shit, but my guess is he took this dream from you, too. Wish I'd have recorded you just now because, babe, you and Mensa could practically be an Evanescence tribute group — but I think you're too good for that."

I kept quiet and looked away from Finn.

Roman said, "He's right. You should be singing at local events, the National Anthem, America the Beautiful, songs like that. If you're interested, I'll ask my boss for the names of people you should get in touch with. They can tell you more about the process for getting selected."

My brows furrowed. "Why would your boss know?"

Roman grinned. "Eric puts in the bids for doing the city fireworks. Our company doesn't always win the bid, but he knows who plans events and whatnot. If singing is something you've dreamed of doing, it's never too late to start making it a reality."

"Thanks, Roman, that's really kind of you," I said.

He dragged a hand down the side of his cheek. "I wouldn't call it kindness. I suspect your father knows just how great you are, and wanted to hold you back. If I can help you gain some notoriety, it's just another way of sticking it to him."

My head reared back. "I never knew you were so vindictive."

"About certain things, I am," Roman said, and walked away.

Whitney joined us, putting her forearms on the bar and leaning forward. "Hey, prospect, I need another margarita after that!"

"I can't. Mensa doesn't want you here," the prospect said.

"Too bad, she's with Nadia and they aren't leaving. Give her a drink or I'll come back there and do it," Sandy said.

The prospect rolled his eyes and made a margarita.

Whitney smiled at Finn. "What are you going to sing?"

Finn slid his arm around my waist. "I'm not. Riley's done for tonight."

"I am?" I asked, tipping my head back.

He tugged on my waist and I slid off the stool. "You are because it's time to hit my room."

Whitney smiled even wider. "Have fun. Especially since you won't be seeing me out."

Finn nodded. "I'm leaving that to Mensa and Sandy."

Chapter 11

This Is Real, Babe

Finn

The moment he closed the door to his room, Finn took Riley's mouth. He walked them to the bed, while tugging her t-shirt free of her jeans.

"What's gotten into you?" she asked.

He stared into her tawny eyes. "Every time I turn around, I learn something new about you. Watching you sing... it was like watching a bird take flight."

She rolled her eyes. "That's an exaggeration."

He twisted his head an inch. "Not even, babe. Your voice had me mesmerized, but then I had to fight back my anger. I got no doubt you could've been someone, if you'd been trained or taken voice lessons."

Her lips shifted into a skeptical grimace. "There's a whole lot more to it than that, Finn. Like luck and timing... and getting in front of the right people."

His finger traced along the edge of her jeans. "We'll talk about that later. Your voice always turns me on, but you belting out a rock ballad made me hard as steel."

She gave him a coy grin. "Really?"

He swiveled his hips. "Yeah, and I can't wait to fuck you."

Her head turned and she gave him some side-eye. "All because I can sing?"

With a quick yank, he pulled her shirt over her head. "No, woman. Because you're you, and I can't get enough of you."

Riley gently shoved his cut off his shoulders. He tossed it onto a nearby chair while she fiddled with the button on his jeans.

He swatted her hands away. "Take off your bra, I'll deal with this."

"Boy, you're impatient tonight."

He toed out of his boots and shoved off his jeans. "Yeah, so don't keep your man waiting."

Her eyes widened for a second before she tried to hide it. He didn't miss the bob of her throat as she swallowed, either.

"Don't freak out, Riley."

"I'm not freaked, it's just that with everything else going on, I forgot how driven you are," she said, unclasping her bra.

He slid the straps down her shoulders. "You're so damned gorgeous."

She snapped the band of his underwear. "I'm not, and for someone who's impatient, you're taking your time getting naked."

He cupped her chin with his hand. "Don't say that shit. You're gorgeous, Riley. Don't let anyone tell you different."

She nodded once. "Okay, well, you have a gorgeous cock I'd like to suck, so —"

"Not right now," he said, letting her go and getting out of his boxer briefs.

Her tongue peeked out and her eyes roved his body. She took off her jeans and panties. "You have great tats, Finn."

With his hands under her armpits, he picked her up and put her on the bed. "Thanks. Not lost on me that you don't have any ink… that something you've wanted to do?"

"Maybe, one day."

He kissed her neck. His hand glided down her body to spread her legs. He settled between them. She guided his lips to hers and she kissed him hard. His fingers delved inside her warm pussy and he found her already wet.

"You're so slick for me, baby."

She grinned. "You do that to me, Finn."

He lined his cock up with her and slid inside. Nothing had ever felt better. He groaned.

"You okay?" she asked.

"Yeah," he breathed. "You just feel so fucking good."

"So do you, Finn, but I need you to move."

He grabbed her thighs and lifted her legs. Then he raised up on his knees and moved. Slow and easy.

"Finn," she breathed.

"Right here, babe."

Her eyes were warm on him. "You know I don't like it slow."

He lowered his head to her breast and sucked on a nipple. His rhythm staying steady... and slow.

Her fingers drove into his hair. "Finn, I'm serious."

He raised his head. "I know, Riley, but I want to savor this."

She bucked her hips to meet his thrusts. "You're going to drive me crazy."

A thought hit him and he grinned. "You want me to go faster?"

"Yes," she groaned.

"Sing to me."

Confusion washed over her face. "I can't sing and have sex."

He shook his head. "You're right. Promise to sing to me when we're done, and I'll give you what you want."

She grabbed his ass. "Fine. Now fuck me like you mean it."

He didn't fuck her like he meant it, he fucked her like he loved her.

Curled up naked next to him, Riley finished singing the last notes of 'Zero.'

"Where have I heard that song before?" he asked.

"It was in an animated movie a while back."

He nodded. "Oh, yeah. The one where he breaks the internet, right?"

"Yeah. You've seen it?"

He grinned. "Wes loved that movie."

"It's one of Jonah's favorites, even now."

Finn twisted to his side. "You trying to tell me something, singing that to me?"

She shrugged a shoulder. "I feel like you're giving me a way out, but part of me keeps thinking this isn't real at all."

His arm snaked under her and he shifted to his back, pulling her on top of him. "We've known each other for more than a year. I know I put the freeze on you for a while, and that wasn't cool, but this is real, babe. As real as you want it to be." He hesitated. "And I didn't ghost you, so get that out of your head."

Her head tilted. "But why did you freeze me out?"

"Gramps dying hit me hard. I got my cut the next day and all I did was get drunk. It wasn't that I wanted to ignore you that night, it was that I wasn't in a good place."

She nodded. "And me being me didn't help much either."

He shook his head. "No, but don't blame yourself. Shit happens, and I realized I needed to lay shit out for you. No way for me to give you a shot if you don't know what I really want."

"And what you want is a family?"

"Yeah. The question is, do you want the same thing?"

She rolled off him. "Honestly, I don't think about the future much. It's one day at a time for me. I'd like to have my own family, but it won't be easy with Jonah."

He turned on his side and propped his head up on his hand. "Babe, you're making assumptions. Anything worth doing requires work, but Jonah won't make it harder."

"Right. You know, you could have any woman you wanted. Why me?"

A chuckle escaped him. "Riley, you may have come here because it's the safest place you know, but as long as you've been coming here, you get the life."

Her eyes narrowed a touch. "What do you mean?"

He weighed his words. "This is between you and me, yeah?"

She nodded.

"I don't know if you've paid attention, but on some level Brute had to ease Kenzie into this part of his life. Roman, Gamble, and to an extent Block, had to do the same things."

Her chin dipped. "Tiny did, too. Hell, he nearly bit my head off the first time he brought Sierra around."

Finn's lips tipped up. "Yeah, but he didn't know you'd been given your last reprieve."

"Right," she whispered.

"My point is that I don't have to go through that shit. You know we sometimes skirt the law, but for good reasons. Even though you're a judge's daughter, that doesn't bother you. All that means, you aren't skittish because I'm part of the Riot."

She smiled. "No, you definitely don't have to worry about that."

He lowered his chin. "And, I'm starting to think you don't just want to be *an* old lady, you actually want to be mine."

"Yeah. Not gonna lie, it hurt when you froze me out last year because I'd really thought we connected."

He rubbed his hand along her arm. "We did connect. There was more family drama after Gramps died, and it sounds like a lousy excuse, but believe me, Riley, I was shitty company. No way would I have been able to prove to you the kind of man I am."

She turned to her side. "Don't you think I could have helped you not be shitty company? I could've been someone you could talk to about that shit?"

He pressed his lips together and exhaled through his nose. "Hard to say. That night I earned my patch, I saw you hanging on a different prospect and it pissed me off. Made me think I misread the whole damned weekend we spent together."

Her body jerked with a silent chuckle. "Guess that makes two of us because I thought the same thing about you." She traced her finger along his jawline. "But I'm glad we got that sorted out now."

Someone pounded on his door and Riley flinched.

"Yo, Finn! They need you at the bar," Joules shouted.

He knifed off the bed and grabbed his boxer briefs. "What the hell for? Cynic just opened up Twisted Talons!"

"Not that bar, dipshit. The one out here!"

He adjusted his underwear and opened the door a crack. "There's no reason they need me out there, Joules."

Joules aimed a dry look at him. "You're the only one who knows how to fix the fuckin' soda gun since you never shared that info with me or anybody else."

He sighed. "Fine. I'll be right there."

With wide eyes, Joules said, "With some pants on. The rest of us don't want to see you in your boxer briefs."

Finn grabbed his jeans and noticed the concern on Riley's face. "What's the problem, babe? I'll be right back."

She shook her head and cleared her expression. "Yeah, I'm fine. I'm just a little jumpy and the heavy knocks didn't help."

He shrugged on his t-shirt. "Yeah, that reminds me. Joules needs to get his shit together. Pounding on my door wasn't cool since it freaked you the fuck out."

"It's okay, Finn."

"The fuck it is. Stay here."

Riley

The next morning, I wandered out to the common room while Finn groomed his beard and took a shower.

Two-Times found me at a high-top table where I had finished my breakfast.

He dragged a stool out from under the table and perched his skinny frame on it. "Got Finn's text. You sure you want the media in on this shit? My go-to move isn't normally murder, but I'm thinking taking your daddy out would be easier all around. Probably doesn't have his affairs completely in order, house goes to you and your brother, bing-bang-boom."

That might have been the most I'd heard Two-Times say to anyone... ever.

"Um, I'm pretty sure the untimely death of a judge would get a very thorough investigation. Not that all deaths aren't investigated, but —"

He nodded. "I know what you mean. And you're probably right, but I'm thinking that would die down after a while and you'd never have to worry about what he'd do to you ever again. You go the media route, he might get arrested. But he might not, and then he'd still be walking free to take his anger out on you."

I sipped my water. "He would. Thing is, I blame myself for Mom's death. I don't need his death on my conscience, too."

Even first thing in the morning, Two-Times had a shadow of stubble along his cheeks. He twisted his lips. "Did you hit your mom?"

"No, but—"

"Yeah, save it. Not your fault. But I get it. Most civilians are soft like that when push comes to shove. I just wanted to save you some hassle."

A wan smile curved my lips. "Thanks. Sorry I can't quench your blood-thirsty nature."

He chuckled. "No problem. I'm calling Sabrina now, gonna put you on speaker. Sound good?"

"Sure."

Over half-an-hour later, Sabrina said, "Your story definitely interests us, Riley. I need to talk to my news director. If you can come to the station, that would move things along."

"Not happening," Finn said, sitting on a stool next to me.

I shot him a look. "Why not?"

"They can send someone to you," Two-Times said.

"We can," Sabrina said, hesitation lacing her tone. "But that might delay —"

"We'll see what another station can do," Finn said.

"Samuel, tell your friend it doesn't work that way. Anita will want this, but other assignments have been scheduled. We need a day or two unless we can shuffle other stories. Let me get back to you."

"You do that," Finn declared.

"Thank you for helping us is what he means," I said.

Sabrina laughed. "No, he didn't, but that's okay. I'll call you in twenty minutes, sooner if Anita has questions."

Two-Times ended the call.

Finn smiled at me. "Sounds promising, babe. You need to change clothes so you're ready for whatever Cynic has planned."

"It's not even nine in the morning, Finn. Besides, I have an appointment with Smith Wharton at nine-thirty."

"Fuck," he hissed. "Well, you better tie your hair up."

I finished my coffee. "Vickie said she's coming by to take me there."

"Why?" he asked.

I blinked. "Because she knew I rode here with you, and she offered. Plus, I didn't know what you have going on today."

His blue-gray eyes seemed extra steely as he gave me a dry look. "For the next three days, you're all I have going on, Riles."

I shrugged a shoulder. "Well, I'm sure there's room in her car for you and me."

FINN'S FURY

My phone rang and the screen showed a local number I didn't recognize. "This might be Vickie calling from her office now," I said before I answered.

"Riley, it's your dad," Dad said, his voice gravelly and stern.

"Hi," I said, but it came out so high-pitched it bordered on being a chirp.

Finn and Two-Times tuned into the shift in my demeanor, and Finn cocked a brow and mouthed, "Your dad?"

I nodded at Finn. He reached for the phone, but I backed away.

Dad mimicked my greeting. "'Hi.' That's all you have to say to me? Disgusting."

It took effort, but I dug deep and kept myself from apologizing. In retrospect, I *always* apologized to him for things I had no control over.

I took a breath and tried not to have any sass or tone. "Is there something you need?"

Dad's tone turned condescending. "Why yes, daughter, there is something I need. There are no more frozen dinners, and it's been three days since you stocked our refrigerator."

Our *refrigerator. Ugh.*

Times like this I didn't have to wonder why Jonah reverted to calling me Sissy, because Dad still talked to me like I was fourteen. It wasn't lost on me that he almost spoke to me like I was Mom and it creeped me out.

A muscle in Finn's cheek twitched, and if I wasn't mistaken his forearms looked tense, too. Yet, I had to stand up to Dad. "Well, I'm sure you can find more at the grocery store."

Finn's eyes widened with surprise at my response.

Two-Times did a slow shake of his head. "Your woman needs to hang up, man."

"What did you say?" Dad demanded.

"The grocery store is less than a mile from the house, Dad. Grab a cart or a basket and load up on your TV dinners."

"Wow," Finn whispered.

Dad sighed. "If you know what's good for you, Riley Jean Tyndale, you will be home before I am this evening, the freezer will be stocked, and Jonah will be back where he belongs."

The urge to mention the money from Mom's parents overwhelmed me, but I restrained myself.

Instead, I said, "That isn't likely to happen, Dad. Jonah and I are both adults. We don't have to be home because you say so. I mean it, you should reacquaint yourself with the supermarket. You might like to switch it up and have a fried chicken from the deli or something tonight. I've got an appointment soon, so, bye for now."

I wasn't fast enough ending the call which meant Dad's response came through crystal clear. "Your boyfriend isn't as tough as he thinks he is, Riley. If you and your brother aren't in the house tonight, I'll make sure 'your man' pays the price."

Him threatening Finn made my control slip. "You can't do anything to him. You're a judge, not God."

"Stock me up, Riley. And, clean the floors when you get home. There's glass on the floor because you didn't load the dishwasher properly. I don't want Jonah to cut his feet."

My jaw dropped and I heard the double beep of the call ending.

"That fucking sonuvabitch," I muttered.

Two-Times stood. "Told you she should have hung up."

"What did he say?" Finn asked.

I closed my eyes, took a deep breath, and willed myself to ignore the helpless feeling building inside me.

"Babe, you're worrying me."

After a slow exhale, I opened my eyes. "He wants me and Jonah back at home. I'm supposed to stock him up on frozen dinners. It's all he eats – probably thinks I'd poison him—"

Two-Times put his stool under the table with a nod. "That's a great idea if you're up for it."

I chuckled. "No, I can't do something like that."

"Pity," Two-Times muttered and wandered to the bar.

Finn kept focused on me. "Yeah, and you told him to go the grocery store. Did he threaten Jonah?"

"He threatened *you*, saying you'd pay the price if Jonah and I aren't back in the house. And apparently there's broken glass on the floor that I need to clean up."

"Fuck that. You aren't his damned maid."

"I know that, but we have to be careful. I don't want him to do something to you."

Finn shook his head, a strange smile on his face. "Let him. He'll either run out of favors or he'll fuck up and his bullshit will land his ass in trouble."

"Good morning! I brought coffees... and a chai latte for you, Riley," Victoria said.

"You didn't need to do that, Vickie," Finn said.

She smiled. "Yeah, I did because I'm guessing that last night she didn't get a chance to tell you about her appointment."

A soft laugh bubbled out of me at Finn's nonplussed expression.

"She didn't, but how the hell would you know that?"

Victoria scoffed. "You and the brothers came out of church all fired up to talk self-defense. Add Sandy turning this place into a karaoke club with Riley knocking our socks off – I figured it slipped her mind."

"I didn't knock any socks off," I argued.

Victoria tilted her head toward Finn. "You didn't see how he watched you. Believe me, you knocked him for a loop."

I sipped my latte.

"Anyway, let's go. I want to beat Smith's receptionist to the office. She's... closed-minded... if you know what I mean."

I groaned. "Great. I'm not sure Finn can handle anything else pissing him off today."

"Will Dad be notified that the money has been claimed?" I asked at the end of our meeting.

Mr. Wharton shook his head. "Not officially. Your father has plenty of contacts, though, so unofficially he could catch wind of it."

"Don't worry about that now," Victoria said, and from her cautious tone I suspected she wanted to change the subject.

Mr. Wharton's eyes pierced me. "I'm surprised you're coming forward after so long. Did Jack want to wait until you were twenty-five? It's a common age when trust funds are distributed."

"Not exactly," I hedged. "It got lost in the shuffle."

Mr. Wharton nodded. "I can only imagine that's true. Re-elections are cumbersome, I hear. Never had any interest in it myself."

"Right," I whispered.

He pushed a folder across the table to me. "That's everything you need. Albert over at the brokerage was friends with your grandmother. He's taken good care of the money. I checked on it earlier. It's earned quite a bit in the past nine years – even as volatile as the market's been."

I didn't know how much 'quite a bit' was, but I hoped it would last a long time.

Victoria gathered her purse. "Thank you for your time, Mr. Wharton."

His sharp eyes gleamed at her. "Never a problem, Ms. Carlton. I'll see you at the Bar meeting next month," he glanced at me. "Might even see your father there, I'm guessing."

I pasted a fake smile on my face. "You never know, sir."

Back in the car, I let out a sigh of relief. "Thank goodness that's done. Keeping quiet about Dad's violence was much harder than I thought it'd be."

Victoria nodded. "Yeah. I could see that all over your face, which was why I jumped into the conversation."

"What do you mean?" I asked.

"Technically speaking, if Smith, or any lawyer, knows about a crime, they're obligated to report it."

My teeth sunk into my lower lip. "Doesn't that apply to you, too?"

She chuckled. "Not if I'm your representative, which I told Smith's receptionist that I was. Are we off to the bank, now?"

"No," Finn said in the firmest tone I'd heard from him. "She's got to meet Cynic back at the clubhouse, and I'm guessing you got to get back to work, Vickie."

"She's a client, so technically, I'm working, Finn." Victoria glanced at me. "By the way, did you sign that form I gave you?"

I nodded. "It's back at the clubhouse."

"Great."

Chapter 12

That Damn Serious

Riley

Blood rushed to my head and I heard my pulse in my ears while I held Cynic's arm out to his side, my fingers gripping his wrist as hard as possible.

"Whatever you do, Riley, don't break his wrist. I really like what my man can do with his fingers," Fiona said from the front door of the clubhouse.

I burst with laughter at her unexpected words.

Cynic chuckled. "I wouldn't let her break my wrist."

"Then you aren't teaching her very well, honey. Her father or any other attacker isn't going to 'let her' break his wrist either."

Cynic cocked his head to the side. "No, but her adrenaline will play a part too, Fi."

"What time is it?" I asked.

"Twelve-thirty," Fiona said.

I sighed. "No offense, Cynic, but are we done yet? I feel like we've been at this for five hours."

Cynic frowned. "Hasn't been that long. The first half hour was me explaining how to wield the damn knife. One more time and we'll be done."

We repeated the exercise. When the knife clattered to the floor, I grinned like it was Christmas morning. "Holy crap! You just let me do that, didn't you?"

He chuckled. "No."

From the corner of my eye, I caught sight of Fiona at the bar behind us. "You were distracted by —"

"It was all you, Riles," he murmured.

"Wow," I whispered.

A skeptical frown pulled at his lips. "No 'wow' about it. It's like anything else. You practice enough, you'll get better."

Finn brought two platters of barbequed meat out from the kitchen. "What's that smile for?"

"I made him drop the knife! It only took thirty-five tries, but," I threw a fist toward the sky. "Whoo-hoo!"

He grinned and shook his head. "That's good. Hope you want ribs."

"Where the hell did you get ribs?" Cynic asked.

Finn put the platters on the bar. "Tiny left four racks here and I cooked 'em."

"You put that seasoning on 'em?" Cynic asked.

Finn nodded.

Fiona rubbed her hands together. "Awesome. I love that stuff."

I did, too. But I didn't think Finn knew that.

Finn glanced at me and back to Fiona. "So does my woman."

It still hit me strange to hear him call me his woman. A zing swept through me hearing his words. I hoped it never went away.

"All right, I talked to Dr. Verla," Fiona said, drawing my attention and I nodded. "She's willing to examine Jonah if you want, but she also gave me a recommendation for another doctor."

"Why wouldn't she want to do it?" Finn asked.

Fiona's head tilted a smidge. "Essentially for the same reason I didn't recommend using Doc Silverman. Her dad's gonna dig in on whoever examines Jonah and the moment he finds a connection to the Riot MC - no matter how remote - he's gonna use that to his advantage. I figure we shouldn't give him a leg up in any way."

"You got that right," I murmured.

Fiona grabbed a rib off the platter. "One more thing, I don't know if Mensa shared or not, but I met Jonah yesterday."

"Oh, that's cool."

She swallowed her food. "Yeah. You're right, he has moments where he regresses, but otherwise he's capable. I think if his therapy weren't interrupted, he'd be better still."

"Okay. Maybe this is just my default setting, but why do I feel like another shoe is ready to drop here?"

Fiona shot me closed-lip smile. "I told him to get his eyes checked out. He was playing video games, but I noticed how he leaned toward the screen a little more than necessary."

"Right."

"He didn't like me suggesting an eye exam."

My eyes slid to the side and I kept quiet. That wasn't like Jonah.

Finn looked between me and Fiona. "If you saw him yesterday, wasn't Aurora's sister there?"

Fiona nodded.

"What does that have to do with anything?" I asked.

A knowing gleam hit Finn's eyes. "He was probably embarrassed. Most men don't like their short-comings being pointed out in front of a woman they're interested in."

Fiona nodded repeatedly. "That makes sense. When he regresses, he's anxious, right?"

I thought back. "Yes, but I don't know why —"

Fiona squeezed my hand. "You don't have to solve it, Riley. That's a job for the doctors. Knowing what triggers him is a great starting point."

"What's next then? Does she need to contact this reference from your boss to get things moving?" Finn asked.

"Her aunt is already taking care of it."

My head reared back. "Really?"

"Yep. Before I made the mistake of mentioning glasses, I asked Jonah a few of the questions Vickie and I had. He says he gets disability. He didn't know if he was under a guardianship or not. Your aunt didn't think he was, but I'd imagine your dad might keep that to himself."

I gave a small head shake and a smile. "It's like you know Dad."

Fiona grinned, but it held no humor. "I had a narcissist in my life once, too. It sucks."

"That's an understatement," I said, a rib at my lips.

A shrill alarm sounded from Cynic's phone.

"What the fuck? Is that the alarm for the bar?"

Cynic's brows furrowed. "Yeah. Should be a false alarm since it's never gone off before and it's the middle of the fucking day." He dug a set of keys out of his pocket. "Gotta check Block's room see what's on the feeds."

Finn followed Cynic out the common room.

"You look worried," Fiona said.

I exhaled slowly. "I know I shouldn't be, but I've been on edge all week."

Fiona shook her head. "Your situation will be taken care of soon. This is probably a malfunctioning alarm system or something else, like my man said. I know you've been paranoid for a long time, but take a deep breath."

Finn and Cynic rushed back into the common room.

"Where's Two-Times?" Finn asked.

I shook my head.

Fiona said, "He left shortly after you brought the ribs out."

"Shit," Cynic hissed.

Finn ran a hand through his hair. "It's cool man. I'll follow you there. Hopefully this bullshit won't take long, and Riley's safe here."

Fiona caught Cynic's eyes. "What is this bullshit?"

Cynic's knife had been resting on the bar. He tucked it into a holster on his belt. "Looks like a couple people are trying to bust into the bar. Called Block, he's going to meet us there."

Fiona's eyes narrowed. "Why not call the cops?"

Cynic gave her a dry look while he pulled his long hair into a ponytail. "Because this shit happened about a month ago and it took two hours for a cop to roll out. By then, they were long gone. We're tired of this, and it looks like the same assholes."

Fiona nodded. "Be careful, honey."

Cynic moved in and wrapped his arms around her. "Always am, woman."

Finn's hand went to my hip and he swiveled my barstool so I faced him. "Don't go anywhere. Not sure you can since we came here on my bike, but I mean it. Stay here, babe. It'll make me feel better."

I nodded. "I will. Maybe I'll see if Whitney wants to hang out with me."

His eyes widened. "Don't do that. Mensa was ready to kick my ass when he found out I didn't kick her out right at ten o'clock last night."

I bit back my smirk. "He isn't here right now, so what he doesn't know…"

Finn sighed and closed his eyes. "You are trouble. Be good."

He kissed me — longer than I expected, but I wasn't complaining.

"Be careful," I called as I watched him saunter out the door.

Whitney took a sip of whiskey and rolled her eyes. "Riley, that man's moods shift worse than a see-saw during recess."

I twisted the top off the Pepsi One she brought me. "Didn't seem that way last night. He did not want you here."

She chuckled. "Yeah, but if he'd meant it, I'd have been gone right then and there, no?"

My eyes darted to the side.

She laughed. "Admit it now. Any biker wants a woman out of this clubhouse, she's gone no matter what Sandy has to say about it."

I nodded. "You're right."

Her chin dipped. "Yeah. So the fact he didn't run me off himself says everything. He doesn't want me here for some unknown reason. The fact he doesn't *do* anything about it tells me he knows his reasons are ridiculous."

I swallowed some soda. "I feel like that's a stretch, Whit."

She shrugged a shoulder. "Maybe, but I don't think so."

Block barged in through the front door. The moment I locked eyes with him, I knew something was wrong.

His eyes slid to Whitney and his lip curled. "She has to leave." He looked back at me. "Right now, you're comin' with me."

"Finn wants me to stay here," I said.

Block raised his chin for a second. "Yeah. That was before the Biloxi PD arrested him and Cynic for assault."

My mouth dropped open and I struggled to find the right words. "They weren't planning to assault them."

Block chuckled. "Neither of them would tell you what they were planning to do, but they didn't assault the bastards."

"They didn't?" Whitney asked.

Block's eyes shifted to her and back to me. "No. I arrived just as the cops hauled them away. I'm here to see if there's footage of whoever did kick their asses."

I shook my head. "Then why do I have to leave?"

His lips twisted. "There's a chance the cops are headed here, and Finn wants you to be safe. That means we're leaving in five minutes."

My eyes widened. "My gut says Dad's behind this. I don't think going to Finn's is a good idea. Whitney can take me to Aunt Celeste's instead."

Block scrubbed a hand down his face. "Does your father even know Finn's name?"

"I don't think so, but a cop came by Finn's house to tell me to go downtown because Dad pulled a favor and my vehicle was on a BOLO."

"That house isn't in Finn's name. Your dad doesn't know who he is and damn sure didn't know Finn would be headed to Twisted Talons. This is random and unrelated to your issues. As for taking you to your aunt's house, that could work, but your dad already knows your brother is staying there. I'm taking you to Finn's house. That's where he wants you to be."

I fought against my frown. Maybe I was being paranoid, but I knew not to underestimate Dad. He had ways of finding things out. I'd never dug into how he did it, and now I wished I had.

My eyes locked with Block's. "That's great but I don't have keys."

Block smiled. "Lucky for you, I know where he keeps the spare key."

Half-way to Finn's house, my cell rang with Aunt Celeste's ring tone. "Hey, Aunt Celeste, everything okay?"

"Yes, and no."

I chuckled. "That's clear as mud."

"Your brother's fine — if that's why you asked if everything's okay. But I think I messed up."

"How do you figure?"

She sighed. "My brother's always known how to push my buttons, and I should have hung up on him... but I didn't."

My lips tipped up. "Dad has that effect on people. He called me this morning, and someone told me to hang up, but I didn't. In hindsight, I should've ended the call."

"Right. Well, I shouldn't have done it, but your father got me so angry that I let Finn's name slip."

My stomach sank. I hated when I was right about Dad. "His first name or... you don't even know his last name, do you?"

"I do since Mensa brought Finn around last November after he'd lost his grandfather."

"Oh," I muttered.

"And unfortunately when I'm that ticked off, I rattle off everyone's full names. I'm sorry, Riley-bug."

I nodded. "It's okay, Aunt Celeste. When did you let it slip?"

I could hear the smile in Aunt Celeste's voice. "This morning. Seems Jack was on a tear to spread his willful ways. Said you'd be by to pick up your brother to take him home."

"Yeah, that isn't happening."

"You better believe it isn't. It sounds like you're driving, so I'll let you go. Take care of yourself, Riley."

I put my phone back in my purse with a head shake.

"That was your aunt, I gathered. Did she know Finn's last name?" Block asked.

I nodded. "Yeah, and she let it slip to Dad some time this morning." I shot a sideways glance at Block. "So it's feasible that Dad's behind this. Hell, he threatened Finn when he was on the phone with me this morning."

Block parked in Finn's driveway. "Still say it's a stretch, Riles. He may have Finn's name, but how would he know about Twisted Talons? Let's get inside. I can't stick around long because I'm headed to the courthouse to give 'Nic and Finn a ride. Assuming the club lawyer gets the charges dropped."

Inside the house, I tapped out a quick text to Aunt Celeste asking if she'd told Dad about Twisted Talons.

Her response was instant.

> Sugar-jits, I did. Back when Mensa started working there regularly. Maybe three months ago.

Great.

"What's that look all about?" Block asked.

"Aunt Celeste told Dad about Twisted Talons. I think all of this is related, Block."

He nodded. "I'll keep that in mind."

A motorcycle roared up the drive. "That should be Dylan, one of the prospects. He's gonna be here to make sure you're safe."

"Okay, is he coming inside?"

"No," Block said, his tone granite. "He's going to stay outside so he can watch for threats before they get to you."

"Okay-dokes."

"You good here?"

I nodded. "Sure, and I'm guessing Finn's cat needs to be fed."

Block tipped his head to the side. "It was his grandpa's cat. He tried getting Joules and Sandy to take it."

I grinned. "And I bet she thought it'd be good for Finn to have a cat."

Block shrugged. "Don't know. Gotta jet. Later, Riles."

After a quick search of the pantry, I found a few tins of cat food. At the hiss of the blade sinking into the can, Baller came running. While he ate, I searched the guest room and office for signs of a litter box. I doubted Finn trusted a prospect to deal with that.

In a dark corner of the office, I found the litter box. As I stooped over to examine the box, I realized it appeared to have been cleaned.

"Hmph," I muttered.

Footsteps coming down the hall had me jerking up right. I turned and saw Nina standing in the doorway. I splayed my hand on my chest. "Oh God, you scared me."

She gave me a regretful smile. "Sorry, dear. Where's Finn? Did he have to work? That prospect outside didn't know."

I did a circular nod. "You could say that."

She mimicked my nod. "What are you hiding?"

"Nothing. Something came up at the bar, but he should be home soon," I said with a grin that I hoped didn't look too nervous.

Baller prowled into the room toward the litter box.

I looked at Nina. "I'm surprised you're back in town."

Nina's sighed. "I never really left. I found out my brother Steve is on his way into town tonight. He didn't believe the realtor report I sent him, and he's determined to take his own pictures and talk to this hotshot agent in town."

My eyes shifted to the side. "I can't believe he doesn't trust Finn to take care of the house."

A patient smile crossed her face. "It's not about trust, it's about money, sweetie. And frankly, I'm fed up with it. I love my brother dearly, but I care more about family than I do about money, and I've realized it's time to dig in harder on this fight."

"So, it is a fight?" a gruff male voice asked from the hallway.

Nina's face set with the annoyance of a sister. "Steve! You can't just barge inside the house. Finn is living here, you know."

It seemed Finn came by his curls from his mom's side of the family because his Uncle Steve was tall and had a head full of tight silver curls. He leaned against the doorway. "And Finn knows we're looking to sell the house, so he needs to get used to intrusions."

Nina's tone turned truculent. "Not from you he doesn't."

She took the words right out of my mouth.

"Who's she?" Steve asked.

"I...," I trailed off.

"She's Finn's girlfriend," Nina said.

His lips puffed out. "Did he give her that black eye?"

Shit. With everything that happened earlier this morning at the clubhouse, I hadn't taken the time with my eye makeup.

"Of course not, you dolt!" Nina cried.

Steve's lip curled. "Geez, Nina. You act like she's your daughter."

Nina blew out an exasperated breath. "She's a human being. Plus, the idea you'd think Finn would do that... That's enough to make me want to kick you, right there!"

Steve lowered his chin, a contrite look on his face. "You're right. I'm sorry. I'd like to know how she got a black eye." He held a hand out to me and introduced himself.

I shook his hand and told him my name. "As for the shiner, it's a long story, but my dad hit me."

He crossed his arms on his chest. "Is your dad part of the biker gang Finn joined?"

Nina gasped. "Stephen! What's gotten into you?"

He widened his eyes. "I may not know his gang, but it's clear she's a biker bunny. Stands to reason her dad might be part of that."

"She's not a club bunny. That's the last time you disrespect her like that," Finn said from the hallway.

When he came into the room, my eyes lit up. Finn caught my gaze and gave a slight head shake.

Steve focused on Finn. "It wasn't disrespect, it's the truth. Look at what she's wearing."

My lips pursed. I wasn't wearing anything that risqué seeing as I had on my yoga pants and a tank top, but I guess my real nature shined through no matter what.

"I cannot believe you," Nina hissed.

"Why are you here?" Finn demanded.

"Watch your tone, bub. This house doesn't belong to you."

"Until it's out of probate, it doesn't belong to you either. And where were you when Gramps needed to get to his oncologist appointments?"

Steve kept quiet.

Finn dipped his chin. "That's right. You were working your cushy job in Missouri."

"Finneas," Nina warned.

He glanced back to Nina. "What? He gets to come in here, bad-mouth my woman, and you expect me to take it? I'm paying rent, taking care of this house, and he damn well knows Gramps would have wanted me to live here rather than sell the place just because the market's hot. Gram and Gramps valued *family* far more than they valued money."

Steve scoffed. "You're wearing rose-colored glasses. Dad taught me to always sell high and buy low. Market isn't gonna bring a better price, and we gotta act fast."

As subtly as I could, I shifted toward the door.

Finn slung an arm around my shoulders. "Don't let him bother you, babe. It's all good."

"I'm not bothering her," Steve muttered.

"Her dad's been hitting her for over a decade, Uncle Steve. Confrontations make her nervous and I can tell you're making her antsy."

Steve's irritation dissipated for a moment. His eyes glittered at Finn. "Sorry to hear that, but she can leave the room if she's uncomfortable."

From the corner of my eye, I saw Finn's jaw clench. "Like she won't hear you? Are you staying here tonight?"

Steve stared at Finn for a long moment. "No. I'm staying at one of the casinos. I can't check in until after four. Figured I'd take some pictures so I'm ready to hit the realtor's office in the morning."

The way Finn's grip on my shoulders tightened, I worried he wouldn't be able to control his temper. "You know I'm livin' here, right?"

Steve's eyes widened. "Yeah. You shouldn't let yourself get so attached."

Finn scoffed. "It isn't a matter of getting attached, Uncle Steve. It's the fact you *know* I want to buy the house, and you'd sell it out from under me."

A shifty smile curled Steve's lips. "Then pay the going rate, Finn. Or don't you make enough at the biker bar you work at?"

The urge to punch this man ate at me. I felt and saw Finn's chest rise with his deep inhale. "I make plenty, Uncle Steve, but it's good to know you're greedy enough to fuck over your nephew."

"Language, Finneas! I'm serious."

Finn let me go and tossed his hands out. "Mom, if ever there were a time to curse, this is it. I'm gonna have to find another place to live, and my uncle doesn't fuckin' care about that. My uncle doesn't care about keeping the house in the family."

Steve rolled his eyes. "This is no time to be sentimental. Hell, even Dad wouldn't have been this sentimental about shit."

Finn sighed. "Maybe not, but he'd honor the lease I signed *and* he'd consider selling to me first instead of being so greedy."

Steve's eyes narrowed. "Don't be so sure about that. And that lease says we can shift to month to month any time with advance notice. Consider this your thirty day notice."

Finn

The way Uncle Steve spoke to Riley had Finn seeing red. Hearing how fast Uncle Steve wanted to change the terms of the lease made his blood boil. Worse than that, he'd lost respect for his uncle.

Finn knew money messed up family relationships, but being in the middle of this sucked. He didn't want to lose his uncle over this, but he didn't tolerate people who were that greedy and didn't have any empathy.

Uncle Steve stalked out of the office, Mom hot on his heels.

Finn turned and wrapped his arms around Riley. "Why were you all back here?"

She sucked in a breath. "Well, I'd planned to clean out Baller's box, but then your mom scared the bejeebers out of me. Not long after that your uncle showed."

"And he talked down to you the whole time?"

She made a high-pitched non committal sound. "Not initially. He thought you had hit me, which set your mom off."

"Oh, fuck no," he breathed.

She put her hands on his chest. "It's —"

"Don't say 'fine,' Riley. It's anything but fine or okay."

She nodded. "No, but it's over. Is everything okay with you? How did you get out so fast after being arrested?"

"You got arrested?" Uncle Steve almost yelled.

Finn's eyes flared at him. "I wasn't arrested. Charges were dropped since it was a set-up – and a bad one at that."

Uncle Steve glanced over his shoulder at Mom, who was right behind him. "Hope you're proud of your boy, Nina."

"It was a set-up," Mom said.

"That's what all the criminals say."

Riley crossed her arms and jutted a foot out at an angle. "My father's a judge and manipulative enough to set Finn up. He threatened him earlier this morning."

"Maybe that's a sign you should heed."

Finn's control snapped, and he stepped toward Uncle Steve.

Riley moved in front of him. "Let it go, Finn. He's never suffered at the hands of a narcissist and it shows."

A smile threatened at the edges of his lips and he choked on laughter. This was what drew him to her. Time and again at the clubhouse, he'd hear her say things that were subtle yet snarky. The way she stared up at him, clarity hit him. This was one of the many reasons he loved her.

Uncle Steve said, "This is the kind of woman your son brings home, and you still don't see she's a —"

"I told you she's not a club bunny, Steve," Finn said.

"That's Uncle Steve to you."

His brows arched. "You'll be my uncle when you show my woman the basic respect she deserves, what anyone deserves."

Uncle Steve's head reared back. "You'd cut out family over her?"

Finn gave a curt nod. "Yep. I'm that damn serious about her."

Uncle Steve's brows arched. "Then why does she look so surprised?"

Riley scoffed. "Because nobody's cared about me like that before. I'd think you'd care about your nephew the same way. Not hurl insults and make assumptions about him and the people he cares about."

With a headshake, Uncle Steve turned around and trudged down the hall.

Mom shot wide eyes at Finn, but he pushed past her and followed his uncle. He didn't want to confront the man any further, but he needed to leave.

"Are you leaving?" Finn asked.

Uncle Steve frowned. "Not until I take pictures."

Finn crossed his arms. "You can't move forward with the house tied up in probate. Besides, your realtor will want to take their own photos. And if they don't want that, then I'd have to wonder if they're the hotshots you claim them to be."

Uncle Steve's lip curled. "You need to get to packing. Thirty days goes quick."

"Stephen! I can't believe you just said that! I'd never do something so heartless to your kids."

Uncle Steve gave Mom a pointed look. "He's not a kid any more. Be at the law firm at nine tomorrow morning, Nina."

As soon as the door clicked shut behind Uncle Steve, Finn turned to Mom. "What's happening at the law firm?"

She sighed. "More run-around if I had to guess, but Steve swears the will is coming out of probate."

Finn closed his eyes. This fucking day couldn't end soon enough for him.

"Don't worry about it, honey," Mom said. "I'm not going to let Steve toss you out."

He opened his eyes and nodded at Mom. "I know. Just sucks seeing how... money-hungry he is, and how judgmental, too."

Mom nodded. "You're right, though I don't think he's that judgmental, down deep. He's angry, Finn. Nothing about this is easy. Even if it's been a year since Dad passed, it's hard being back here. Show him some grace."

"Will he do the same, Nina? Something tells me he won't," Riley said.

Mom turned her head and Finn saw a hint of shame cross her face. She faced them. "I've got to get going. Don't be surprised if your uncle drops by with a realtor tomorrow morning."

"I'm sorry, Finn," Riley said.

He fought a frown. "What do you have to be sorry for?"

"For bringing up the cops and stuff. If I'd kept my stupid mouth shut, your Uncle Steve wouldn't know that happened."

He wrapped his arms around her. "Listen to me, Riley. Don't blame yourself for this shit. I'm serious, don't do it. He'd have found out one way or another – you can count on that. You got it?"

The smile she shot at him seemed placating. "I got it."

He dipped his chin. "Riley. I'm not an expert on this, but I got no doubt you blaming yourself for my Uncle Steve's reaction comes from your dad's abuse. It's gonna take work, but we're gonna break you free from that habit."

Sincerity filled her eyes. "Thanks, Finn. And thanks for telling your family you're that serious about me. It felt nice, even if you were stretching the truth a bit."

He put his hands on her cheeks and stared into her eyes. "I didn't stretch the truth at all, babe. You're my woman, and I want a future with you. Are you having second thoughts about that or some shit?"

She blinked. "No, I'm not. But it's not unusual for people to change their mind about me, especially when their family members point out my flaws."

He slid his hands down to her neck and then her shoulders. "Flaws? If you're talking about you looking like a club bunny even though you're wearing yoga clothes, that isn't a flaw, woman. The way you dress turns me on, and always has."

She gave a breathy scoff. "Always has, huh?"

He nodded. "Damn right. Couldn't do much about it as a prospect, wanted to make sure I earned my patch."

Her head tipped to the side with her nod. "I can see that."

"Right. Now why do you think your dad was behind this set-up?"

Riley broke free of his hold and sat on the couch. "I hate to tell you this, but Aunt Celeste goofed and gave Dad your last name. Before that, she'd mentioned Mensa working at Twisted Talons, so it stands to reason that —"

He joined her on the couch. "No. Your dad wouldn't half-ass shit like this."

She frowned. "Why do you say it was half-assed? It got you taken downtown."

With his arm around her shoulders, he pulled her to him. "Yeah, but that's just an inconvenience. If he's the least bit smart, he knows there are cameras on the building. The footage is the reason I'm not being processed right now. Your dad wants to come after me like that, he's gonna make sure charges will stick."

She wrapped an arm around his waist. "Can't argue with that."

"Love it," he murmured.

Her head jerked up, those brown eyes wide with concern. "You love what?"

He took a deep breath. "I love that you won't argue with me... about that, anyway. But I love that you heard me out and decided to back down because I could tell you wanted to make a case for your dad being behind all this."

She shrugged a shoulder. "Part of me still thinks he *is* behind this, but between what you said and Block being so adamant that I was wrong, I guess I'm seeing reason."

He slid his free hand up her thigh to her hip and maneuvered them both so he lay on top of her. "I'd rather make you see something else right now."

She spread her legs and wound her fingers in his hair. "Really? What do you want me to see?"

He took her mouth in a long kiss. "Stars."

Her eyes locked with his. "Stars?"

He grinned. "Yeah, because I'm going to make you come. Only question is do you want it here or in the shower?"

She laughed. "I'm not fussy, Finn. Either one works for me."

Chapter 13

We're Tough

Riley

"Thank you for sharing your story, Ms. Tyndale. It takes a lot of courage to speak out against an attacker, and even more when they're family," Anna St. Claire said.

Anna was a lead anchor on the news, but she also covered politics and elections. She and Sabrina had come to Finn's house to interview me and Jonah.

"Their faces will be blurred out, right?" Finn asked.

Sabrina smiled patiently. "Yes, Finn. We're going to protect their identities as much as we can." She looked at me. "If either of you have social media accounts, I'd make sure you set your privacy settings so only trusted people can see your profile. That should cut down on the number of crazies coming for you. Hate to say it, but there are zealots out there who are going to hunt for you online. More you, Riley, than Jonah."

I nodded. "Right. Jonah doesn't use social media, but I'll update mine. Do you know when this will air? Tomorrow? The next day?"

Anna chuckled. "I think we're shooting for tonight's six o'clock, unless my boss needs to send it up to our corporate legal department."

Sabrina zipped her messenger bag. "Right, then it might air at eleven, but with the election right around the corner, we're aiming to get this on as soon as we can."

Anna grinned. "Promotions can't wait to get a sound byte from us, so you might even hear your voices on the radio later this afternoon."

My brows drew together. "You can put something together that fast?"

Sabrina tilted her head. "The ratings period starts today, and this is an exclusive. Management likes to make the most of stories like yours."

"This better not put her or Jonah in more danger," Finn said.

Anna shook her head. "It shouldn't."

"Yeah. Nobody's going to harm me other than Dad."

Finn sighed. "As far as we know, but it's those zealots I'm worried about."

Sabrina hiked her bag on her shoulder. "I'm sorry I said anything about that. Really, they're just internet trolls. As long as you can withstand their nasty vitriol online you'll be fine."

Even though Sabrina and Anna missed it, the low growl from Finn told me he wanted to protect me from all of it.

Sabrina grinned. "Wipe that look off your face, Finn. It's all good. If this were likely to bring her more problems, I'd have told Samuel as much yesterday."

"Right," he drawled.

I patted Finn's bicep. "It's going to be fine."

Jonah grinned. "Yeah, Finn. We're tough, and Sissy's the toughest person I know."

Aunt Celeste stood from her spot at the dining room table, her lips set in a firm line. "Jonah, dear, we've got to get moving. Your therapist will be at the house in half an hour."

After everyone left, my phone dinged with a notification.

Finn pulled me close to his body. "We're staying at the clubhouse tonight."

"But —"

He shook his head. "Nope. Even though I don't think he set me up yesterday, your concerns aren't far-fetched. He knows where I live. This story is going to piss him off. I'd feel better if we stay at the clubhouse. At least there we got cameras and my brothers to vouch for whatever happens if he shows." After a moment, he muttered, "And there are more guns."

I chuckled. "More guns?"

His head tilted. "Like you don't know that."

My eyes slid to the side and I frowned. "Yeah, but I don't want anyone getting arrested because of me."

He chuckled. "Darlin', it's too damn late for that. We're gonna do whatever it takes to keep that asshole from hurting you ever again."

The thought of my voice being on the radio hit me again.

Yeah, Dad was going to blow a fucking gasket.

I glanced up at Finn. "Is Mensa or someone going to be around to make sure Dad doesn't go after Jonah? The more I think about it, there's no way Dad isn't going to lash out at somebody."

He nodded. "Yeah. Mensa's gonna be around. Block and Tiny are splitting shifts when Mensa can't be there."

I smiled. "Good. Tiny will scare the pants off, Dad."

Finn's lips tipped up. "Yeah. That's the idea. Let's get our shit packed, babe."

I followed him to the bedroom, pulling my phone from my pocket as I went. My feet stilled when I saw the text message from Dad.

> Disobedience is a sin, daughter.

I exhaled hard.

Finn looked over his shoulder at me. "What's up?"

I peeked up at him. "Dad texted. Guess he didn't like me and Jonah not being home last night."

He did two nods with his lips pressed together. "Might feel like we're running, but that's another reason to be around the brothers."

We arrived at the clubhouse after a late lunch.

Cynic stood at the stove stirring what smelled like a pot of chili. "What are you doin' here?"

"Hiding out," I said reflexively.

That got me Cynic's distinctive side-eye. "She serious?"

Finn snorted. "Yes and no. She and her brother did the news interview. They're moving faster than I'd expected with that, so I'd rather be here if Tyndale decides to overreact."

Cynic laughed. "Overreact. Haven't met the scumbag, but I'm guessing that's his default."

"Facts," I muttered.

Finn tipped his head toward the stove. "That for dinner tonight or are you eating late?"

Cynic's lips pushed into a slight pout. "It's *my* dinner. Willing to share if you make the damn cornbread... from scratch."

"Done," Finn said.

He guided me to his room where we dropped off our bags.

I put my purse next to a nightstand and turned to Finn. "I have to say Finn, I'm feeling antsy being off work for the past week."

His lips quirked in a half grin. "And yet, this week you found out you're a millionaire. I'm thinking you're doing just fine not working."

With a sigh, I sat on the edge of the bed. "You know that money isn't really for me. I'll need all of it to care for Jonah."

Finn shook his head. "Gotta change that way of thinking, woman. At least a third of that needs to be for you because you don't know what Jonah's care really costs. He isn't hospitalized. He might be dependent on you from now on, but his care shouldn't set you back like you think. Especially now that you know he's getting disability payments."

I thought about it for a second. "You're right."

His reminder about the money brought back a fleeting thought I'd had yesterday afternoon.

After a deep breath, I said, "You aren't going to like this, but —"

He shook his head. "Babe, if you know I'm not going to like something, let's save it for tomorrow. Shit's been stressful enough."

"It's about your Uncle Steve."

His face twisted with confusion. "What about him?"

I grinned. "Yesterday before you came home, it struck me that I could buy the house and keep your uncle from doing you dirty."

His expression went blank to the point of stoniness. After a long moment he relaxed. "As much as I appreciate that, Riles, it won't work."

"Won't work or you won't let it work?"

He shook his head. "Doesn't matter, babe. I can't let you do that for me."

I sighed. "I'd be doing it for both of us."

His brow went up. "You freaked out on me the first time you walked in the door."

My hands twisted up. "Yeah, because it reminded me of my grandparents' house, which I hadn't been in since I was seven years old. Those same grandparents are the ones who left me the money, by the way. I feel like it's a sign."

He chuckled silently. "Not sure it works like that, Riley."

"Fine," I chirped, deciding to let it go.

For now.

His left eye narrowed at me. "I'm onto you, woman. That 'fine' doesn't mean anything is *fine*. It means you're biding your time." He paused and then both his eyes narrowed. "And if it means you're gonna do what you want behind my back, that's a damned problem, woman."

I loved and hated that he could see right through me.

With my head tilted to the side, I asked, "Is it really a problem if I buy the house? Especially if that means you're free to use your nest-egg to start your own business like you'd originally planned?" I threw my hands up for a split second. "I know my parents weren't a shining example, but that doesn't change the fact that in a decent marriage it's all about the give and take, Finn."

His eyes looked past me and I knew he was thinking about it.

I kept at him. "Besides, how great would it be to sit across the table from your uncle rubbing his face in the fact that you wound up with the house anyway?"

His chin dipped. "*You* would end up with the house. We aren't married yet, so my name wouldn't even be on the deed."

My mind tripped over the word 'married', but the word 'yet' really threw me for a loop.

"You want to marry me?" I blurted.

"Yeah, why wouldn't I?"

I shrugged. "Some bikers are cool with just putting a cut on their ball and chain."

He blinked and gave me a dry look. "I'm not 'some bikers'."

I nodded. "Right, but if we're getting married at some point why not let me buy the house? It would completely throw your uncle off his game."

He turned and paced away from me. "Don't do it, Riley." He whirled back to me. "I'm dead serious. If Uncle Steve is willing to sell that house to me, then I want to know it outright. We're family, for fuck's sake. I shouldn't have to sneak around behind his fucking back to buy a house that he should want to keep in the family."

"He seems pretty —"

Finn's hands ran through his hair. "Riley, just don't. This shit has me stressed enough. I'm going out back to work out."

He grabbed a pair of sneakers from under his bed and stormed out.

"That might have been our first fight," I whispered.

I sent a text to Aurora asking what she was up to and suggesting she join me at the clubhouse. Then I wandered out to the common room.

It was the middle of the afternoon and most of the brothers were working day jobs or doing other things. I settled on the end of the couch near another club bunny named Dahlia.

She looked up from her phone. "Hey. Long time no see."

I nodded. "Yeah. Lot of crazy things happening these days."

Her chin lifted slightly. "Heard you're with Finn now, that true?"

Again, I nodded.

She twisted her lips. "I'd say congratulations, but really, it was already slim pickings around here. Now it's even slimmer."

Heidi and Victoria came in through the front door having an animated conversation.

Victoria pointed at me. "Just the woman I want to see!"

Dahlia's eyes cut to me and she stood. "I'll see you around, Riley."

Heidi watched her slink away and a sly smirk twisted her lips. "We don't bite, believe it or not. You don't have to leave because of us."

I debated sharing with them, but Daliah had long legs and the same build as Victoria. If I wasn't mistaken, she'd been with Gamble more than once before Victoria came along.

I shot Heidi a small smile. "She's doing you a favor by leaving, Heidi."

"Really?" she asked.

"Yeah. It isn't comfortable being around the old lady of a biker you've been with, unless you're the type who likes causing drama. That's what makes Dahlia cool. She doesn't do drama unless another woman drags her into it."

Heidi toyed with one of her hoop earrings. "So she was with Block?"

I blinked twice and said, "Sure."

Victoria laughed. "I'm not that sensitive, Riley. I'm also not that dense. If she weren't blonde, she and I'd look very similar to one another."

"Right," I whispered.

Victoria sat down between me and Heidi. "Anyway, I wanted to let you know that I've filed a complaint with the state Commission on Judicial Performance."

My stomach churned. "Are you sure that was a good idea?"

She grinned. "I filed it anonymously, no need to worry."

Heidi leaned forward. "On the way here, we heard a radio commercial for an exclusive interview about a scandal involving a local judge. If you ask me, the timing couldn't be more perfect."

Victoria chuckled. "I think Shirley Calhoun would have preferred the complaint to be filed a few weeks earlier, but *c'est la vie*."

I nodded. "That's going to take a while, I'm sure."

Heidi's head cocked to the side. "Don't sound so defeated. Progress is progress, no matter how slow it moves."

Victoria's eyes examined me. "Something else is wrong. Are you worried about being on TV?"

With a half smile, I shook my head. "Yes and no. I... I think Finn and I had our first fight." My eyes slid to the side and I grimaced. "I shouldn't have shared that with you two."

Heidi laughed. "That's what the brothers want you to believe. Forget that. Spill."

Victoria grinned. "She's right. Besides, Finn's so easy-going I doubt it's as bad as you think it is, so let's hear it."

I shared my plan to buy the house and Finn's reaction.

Victoria leaned back into the couch cushions. "That would be a great idea, but I also see his point of view. All these men are so headstrong about providing for their women and stuff like that."

Heidi gave her a sideways glance. "Heaven forbid that street runs both ways, though. I mean, I should be able to provide in ways other than in the bedroom."

Victoria nodded. "You are not wrong. Add in biological family, though, and this takes on a different dynamic."

At the dry look on Heidi's face, I braced for what she had to say.

"I'll take your word for it since my biological family is almost as dysfunctional as Riley's."

"Gee, thanks," I muttered.

Heidi chuckled. "You're welcome. We can't all come from families like Vickie's."

Victoria's eyes slid to Heidi. "Mom's in therapy, you know."

Heidi's brows shot up. "Yeah, mine won't even contemplate an hour long A.A. meeting, so you got one up on me right there."

Joules sauntered out from the hallway and stopped in the middle of the common room. "What are you girls arguing about down here? I can hear you all the way down the hall."

A gleam hit Heidi's eyes and she smiled. "Injustice," she said in a relishing tone. "And we're not arguing, we're discussing."

His eyes widened behind his glasses. "Well, discuss a little quieter, hear?"

After he sauntered to the bar, Heidi asked, "What got into him?"

I caught her gaze. "He's a retired school teacher. He doesn't like when women get too loud – or men – but for some reason, women really get him riled up."

"I never noticed that before, but you're right," Victoria muttered.

A prospect barged inside, I realized he was the same person who brought my car to Finn's. "Hey, Joules. There's a cop at the gate, should Joe let them inside?"

"They got a warrant?"

He shook his head. "Don't think so. We didn't ask."

"Well ask, dammit," Joules snapped.

The prospect scurried back out. Joules blew out a beleaguered sigh and set down a bottle of rum.

He went to the front door, pointing his finger at Heidi along the way. "Call your man. Gonna need more brothers here if there's more than one cop out there."

Heidi grabbed her phone and put it to her ear.

I looked at Victoria. "Why didn't he tell you to call Gamble?"

Her head tilted side to side. "Pretty sure he's trying to protect me. Even though just telling Gamble to come out here isn't aiding in a crime."

Heidi looked to me. "Block wants to know where Finn is."

I jerked my head toward the backdoor. "He's working out."

She repeated what I said and nodded. "He says to go out back to the workout shed. You should hurry."

Victoria stood when I did. "I'm going with you."

We hurried out to the shed. The door opened just before I reached for the doorknob. Sweat dripped from Finn's face to his neck and down his bare chest. Lust swirled through me.

"What the hell, Riley?" he asked.

Victoria said, "Cops are at the gate. Block wanted her to come out here, I figure it's better for me to be with her, too. I'm her lawyer, after all."

"Shit," he muttered, shifting his t-shirt to his right hand. He held out his cut. "Hold this, Riles."

I took the cut and watched as he shrugged into his t-shirt. This was no time to get carried away by my hormones.

He grabbed his cut and put it on, then pointed at the workout room. "Lock yourselves inside. Don't open it for anyone - the brothers all have keys. Got it?"

Victoria nodded and Finn left.

Finn

Finn crossed the backyard of the clubhouse at a rapid clip. Block's kelly green Harley rumbled through the back gate and he parked close to the concrete slab patio. Finn waited for Block to dismount.

"You know what's goin' on?" Block asked.

"No, just that cops are here and my woman and Victoria are in the —"

"Yeah," Block said. "Let's hit the gate. Joules probably needs our help."

At the gate stood the same officer who came by Finn's house.

He aimed a pointed look at Finn. "I'm looking for Riley Tyndale. She needs to come with me."

Finn opened his mouth to speak, but Joules said, "Like I told you, she isn't here."

The officer's brown eyes cut to Joules and back to Finn. "Her car is parked in his driveway, but there's nobody at the residence. It stands to reason that she's here with him."

"Most people have jobs, officer," Block said.

"Is she under arrest?" Finn asked.

The officer shifted his jaw. "No, but she is needed for questioning. Her brother is missing."

Block turned his hands up. "Well, you should have said so."

The cop glowered at him. "I told both of these men why I need to speak with Ms. Tyndale."

"Riley and I had breakfast with her brother this morning. He isn't missing," Finn said.

The officer shook his head. "His family has reported him missing this afternoon. He's disabled with special needs. Ms. Tyndale is one of the last people to see him. She's needed downtown for questioning."

Finn bit back his anger. "I'll give Riley a call. I'm sure she can call his family and clear this up."

The officer gave him a hard stare. "She's needed downtown."

Finn gave a curt nod. "I'm sure she and her lawyer will be downtown in half an hour tops."

"She doesn't need a lawyer. It's just questioning."

Finn pulled his phone from his back pocket. "I'll let her know, officer."

Joules rubbed his hands together. "Welp, seems that's sorted. I'll head back inside."

The officer watched Joules amble back to the clubhouse for a moment before he huffed out a breath and went back to his cruiser.

Finn didn't leave the gate until the tail lights on the officer's car formed two red dots in the distance.

"You were telling the truth. Her brother's not missing, is he?" Block asked.

Finn scoffed and started back for the clubhouse. "He was at my house for the interview at eight-forty-five this morning. Didn't want that cop to know there *was* an interview because Tyndale doesn't deserve to be tipped off."

"What a bastard," Block muttered and fell instep with Finn.

"Looks like I'm headed back to the fuckin' police department for the second time in twenty-four hours."

"Sorry, man."

"Yeah, at least Vickie's here to make sure shit doesn't go sideways."

Disbelief washed over Riley's face. "This really can't be cleared up by having Aunt Celeste and Jonah call the police?"

Victoria gave a couple short shakes of her head.

Finn said, "Babe, I got a feeling this is part of a bigger plan of his."

"I think Finn's right, and if it is part of a scheme, then the more you cooperate with the authorities the better," Victoria said.

"This sucks," Riley wheezed.

"Yeah, but the sooner we get down there the sooner we can hopefully get out. I need to call my boss, and I'll drive us," Victoria said.

Riley stood in the middle of the workout room with her arms crossed and a look of sheer disgust on her face. "Isn't there anyone else we can report this to? Like the FBI or something? I mean, I appreciate the filing with the judicial commission, but this is bullshit. Claiming someone to be missing when they aren't is a serious crime."

Finn shook his head. "Doesn't matter, babe. Even if there is, your dad will feign ignorance and beg forgiveness. Let's get this shit done, I'll follow you two on my bike."

On the steps of the police station, Victoria said, "I know you want to be with her, but they aren't—"

He lifted his chin. "I'm gonna be in the lobby, Vickie. I don't care if this is some kind of trap. Tyndale isn't putting hands on her."

She nodded. "Fine, though he's most likely at the courthouse, and there's no way he'd hit her in front of the police."

He opened the door and followed them inside.

A uniformed officer who couldn't be more than twenty-two years old made eyes at Finn. "Sir, you're going to have to remove your vest."

Finn bit his lower lip.

An older cop was working the front reception also and he narrowed his green eyes at Finn. "No gang colors in here."

He stifled his sigh and shrugged out of his cut.

Victoria explained to the younger cop why they were there. The cop's eyes shot to Finn and back to her. "He can't go back with her."

Finn sat down on a cold plastic chair. He watched Riley walk away and he hoped Tyndale would show his face. Wasting everyone's time like this... that should have been a crime, too.

His phone rang with his Mom's ringtone. "Hey, Mom."

"I hate to tell you this, but we met with the lawyer. I'm stalling as long as I can, Finn, but the house is going on the market by next weekend."

Shit. He had to make a decision. Let go of his grandparent's house where he'd thought he would start his family, or wait even longer to open his own business.

He could try to do both, but his credit rating would take a beating. Most of all, he wouldn't be able to give Riley the ring he wanted to put on her finger when the time came.

"Are you there?" Mom asked.

"Yeah. It's been a crazy day, Mom."

"You're not wrong, son."

He wiped his free hand down his cheek. "Uncle Steve going with that realtor he mentioned?"

"Strangely enough, he's using the one we saw."

Finn let that sink in and his eyes wandered to the lobby window. A news van had parallel-parked near a hydrant. He spotted an SUV for another news station circling the block. That wasn't unusual since crime happened and it made headlines, but Finn's instincts were on high alert.

A tall, slim, older man with graying hair pushed inside and strode to the desk. Finn stared at him. His suit pants were creased so sharp it looked fake. He acted as though he owned the room. Finn caught snippets of the conversation. It sounded as though this man were name dropping, then again he seemed the type.

After a moment, a female officer came out and escorted him to the back.

The older cop chuckled at the younger one. "That your first time dealing with Tyndale, rookie?"

The rookie grunted. "Yeah."

He nodded. "You did good."

Finn stood, drawing the attention of both cops. The door opened and they looked that way, frowning.

The older officer said, "No. You know the drill. No press inside here. Front steps only."

A blond-haired, blue-eyed reporter smiled at them like they were friends. He wore a shirt and tie with khaki pants and brown hiking boots. He stepped closer to the desk. "C'mon, Officer Faust. We just need to shoot some b-roll. Besides, what's Judge Tyndale doing inside, anyway? Is his wife's case being re-opened?"

The older officer rolled his eyes. "If it were, it'd be an *ongoing* investigation and we wouldn't talk to you about it anyway. Now, out on the steps." The cop's eyes darted to Finn. "Feel free to go with him."

Ordinarily that would have Finn settling back in for the long haul, but at least three other news crews were gathered outside. By the time Riley was done, it would be a madhouse trying to get down the steps, and one of those reporters was likely to figure out who she was.

Not happening.

He followed the reporter out and put on his cut. The reporter turned curious eyes to Finn, but he hurried down the stairs and around the block. Earlier, he'd followed Vickie into a small parking garage. It wouldn't be safe for them to go out the front in that sea of reporters, and he didn't want them going out the back alone and trying to get to the garage on foot.

He slung a leg over his bike and motored around the block to the alley that ran behind the police station. It was risky doing this since cops wouldn't like him loitering out back, but he'd be damned if Riley or Vickie got accosted by Tyndale or reporters.

Chapter 14

Same Song, Different Day

Riley

I'd never been in a police interrogation room before, and after today, I didn't want to be in one ever again. Even though there was an obvious two-way mirror, the whole room felt cramped and triggered my claustrophobia. No doubt that was by design to get people to spill their guts that much quicker, but when there was nothing to spill, it sucked being stuck in here.

Victoria had nodded at every question the officer threw at me and I answered. He proceeded to ask all those questions a third time and I wanted to ask Victoria why we were going over this so much. I knew that wouldn't look good, so I didn't complain.

"Is there anything else, Officer?" she asked.

Officer Gatlin stared at Victoria while he twisted his lips. "No, I need to check something. It'll only take a minute."

"What are you checking? My client has been nothing but cooperative. A simple phone call will clear this right up. We don't have all day."

Oblivious to her comment, he left, and *my freaking father* slid inside before the door closed. "You're right, Ms. Carlton. A phone call would solve everything, which was what I did in the beginning. My disappointing daughter failed to heed my warnings."

I shook my head. "I told you I wasn't going to come home —"

Victoria put her hand on my forearm, and I fell silent.

Dad arched a brow at Victoria. "What they say about you seems to be true, Ms. Carlton. You're exceptionally intuitive."

"Would you care to elaborate, Judge Tyndale?"

His eyes held Victoria's and he *almost* smiled. "No." He frowned at me. "A strange thing happened today, Riley. My secretary tore into my office insisting I take a call from Anna St. Clair. She wanted to ask me about an exclusive interview she'd conducted pertaining to me covering up a crime."

By some miracle, I held myself perfectly still and kept eye contact with him. "Okay."

He rolled his eyes and shook his head. "I gave her a piece of my mind and she refused to answer my questions. My PR firm, on the other hand, found out that the interview is with my daughter... in fact, I heard your voice on the radio during my short drive over here." He leaned toward me. "Are you stupid enough to think I wouldn't catch wind of this?"

I bit the side of my lip and glanced at Victoria. She tipped her head just enough to let me know it was my call about what to share... or not.

Dad's voice rose. "Answer me."

I squared my shoulders and looked him in the eye. "I'm more interested in Shirley Calhoun catching wind of it."

The way his expression fell was like watching a balloon deflate. "You don't know what you're talking about."

Victoria scratched her neck. "If I may, sir, what is the point of all this? It appears to be an elaborate ploy to corner your daughter and intimidate her, only you didn't expect her to have a lawyer on hand."

"I have to wonder why Gower and Gower can spare you for a simple round of police questioning."

"We take our clients' rights very seriously, sir. Out of curiosity, did you tell the officers that your son isn't missing? It's my understanding Jonah has called you three times in the last hour to tell you where he is and that he's not in danger."

Dad looked at Victoria like she was a child. "I can't trust that with his head injury."

Victoria grinned at Dad in the most coy and devilish way. "Jonah also called the lead detective of the Missing Persons division. I thought that might have been what the officer was checking on when he left, but I was apparently mistaken."

My admiration for Victoria grew to the point it bordered on being a girl-crush. What I wouldn't give to be that confident and assertive when shit hit the fan.

Dad aimed a condescending look at Victoria. "You're too green to understand this, Ms. Carlton, especially since you've never had to run for an election, but public opinion is everything. Controlling the narrative, as they say, is key to winning an election."

Victoria's eyes slid to the side, then she did a dramatic nod. "So it's a twofer. You get to corner and intimidate your daughter while also attempting to discredit her."

"This isn't an attempt, Ms. Carlton. The fact she's been in here for an hour is discrediting enough." He speared me with his eyes. "Get your scrawny butt back home and bring your brother with you."

My mouth fell open, but Dad stormed out of the room.

Victoria rose and grabbed her purse. "Let's go. This has been a total sham. If only the damned cameras had been running, we'd have evidence to submit to the CJP."

I grabbed my wristlet and followed Victoria out of the room, back the way we came. Only Victoria stopped short, and I bumped into her.

"Sorry, I didn't mean to—"

Victoria whirled around, her expression resolute. "You aren't going that way."

I swung my head to the side and immediately understood. Dad had made it two steps out the door before reporters swarmed him.

In a weird twist of fate, a tiny sliver of me felt bad for him. That sliver of me who remembered him being nice when I was six years old and had the role of a Christmas angel in the church Christmas pageant.

Victoria stepped past me, but grabbed my hand. "Let's go. There's a back way out. I just don't know if they'll let us use it."

We were ten feet from the back door when an officer lumbered into the corridor. He had to be six foot three inches tall, and with his lumbering gait, he'd probably played offensive line on his high school football team. His lips pursed and he glowered at us until he focused on Victoria.

"Miss Vickie?" he asked.

Victoria's shoulders relaxed. "Officer Remy! It's so good to see you. I know we aren't supposed to be back here, but could you possibly help us use the back exit? There's a sea of reporters out front and —"

He waved a hand at her. "Say no more. They're like vultures. Be careful goin' out this way, though. You never know who's out there."

We stepped outside to find Finn stubbing out a cigarette and standing next to his bike.

"Isn't he a smart one?" Victoria muttered.

I smiled, but kept quiet.

Finn came to me and put his hands on my shoulders. "Did he threaten you? Touch you?"

"Not really and no," I said. "He wants me to come home and bring Jonah with me. Same song, different day."

With a seething exhale, he shook his head. "I should have stuck around just to punch the asshole." His eyes slid to Victoria. "Sorry, Vic, but I can only take Riley on my bike. Mensa's on his way to get you back to your car."

Victoria pulled a face as though the idea didn't sit well with her.

Finn's eyes widened. "You're not walking back to that garage."

"Damn right," Mensa said strolling around the corner to join us. "Besides, it's a two-block ride, you'll survive and Gamble would rather you be safe than dealing with the press."

Finn's hand rested at the small of my back and we stopped at the door to Blue Moon Bayou Pizza. The sign was flipped around to say they were closed, but we could see Joules, Heidi, Block, Gamble, Cynic, and Fiona sitting at a long table.

Sandy wandered up to the front door and opened it. "Hey, you two. About time you got here."

I did a double-take as we crossed the room. Whitney and Aurora were sitting at the far end of the table, which had been out of sight of the windowed door.

My eyes caught Aurora's. "What are you doing here?"

"Good to see you, too," Aurora deadpanned.

I shrugged. "Don't you have work?"

A small smile played at her lips. "I did. I finished early today. Your dad's a real piece of work."

"Piece of shit is more like it," Finn muttered.

Cynic cocked a brow. "You didn't even see him on the news. He's trying to spin shit."

"Just like a politician," Block said.

From the doorway, Mensa's demanding voice filled the room. "What is she doin' here?"

Sandy glared at my cousin. "I invited her. Lose the chip on your shoulder. We're here for Riley, and Whitney's our girl's friend."

Two empty chairs sat next to Whitney. She pulled out the one next to her and I settled into it. I acted as though I were getting situated and leaned toward her. "You sure about this? I could offer this seat to Mensa."

She aimed a sly smile at me. "But you wouldn't, because you hate confrontations."

I shrugged. "Things are changing. Watching Victoria spar with Dad has me rethinking many things."

"Don't forget, you gotta crawl before you walk," Whitney said.

I narrowed an eye at her in question.

She grinned. "Victoria verbally spars with people for a living. You need to work up to it. Especially where your pops is concerned."

My friend suddenly sounded like a New Yorker. Almost as though her accent slipped, the way mine did when I got angry.

Mick – the owner and Victoria's godfather – brought out two large pizzas and some chicken wings.

Everyone quieted when Mick turned up the volume on one of the televisions. I hadn't realized the time until now, but it was ten after six.

Oh, hell.

I looked to Sandy and then Finn. "I didn't plan on watching this."

Finn squeezed my upper thigh. "Figured that, but try to be strong, Riley. You got this."

I widened my eyes at him. "It's Jonah I don't want to see, Finn. It was hard enough reliving it with him this morning."

He nodded. "You can go to the bathroom if you want, but I think it's better to see how they're portraying this."

Victoria came in and sat across from us. From the wry look on her face, I knew she'd heard Finn. "He's right. It's good to hear the 'narrative' and everything."

A tray with glasses of red wine sat in the middle of the table. Sandy grabbed a glass and put it in front of me. "Here. Sip on that. It'll be fine, doll-face."

I laughed silently.

Finn's lips brushed against my ear. "You *are* a doll-face, woman. Don't go laughing as if that's crazy."

Between his words and the glass of wine, I was distracted enough that it took a minute for me to realize the interview had started.

Rather than watch the story, I watched everyone at the table. The Riot brothers had their eyes pinned to the screen. Seemed I was right, my abuse angered them. All six brothers had their jaws clenched, and looked like they wanted to tear somebody limb from limb. The women paid close attention to the screen, too. Then Heidi shifted her head and her eyes met mine. It wasn't pity in her eyes, but possibly sympathetic understanding.

I cast my eyes across the room and saw Mick staring at me. He looked as angry as Finn did when I'd first shared my story. His eyes darted back to the flatscreen; the segment appeared to be over. After a moment, he aimed the remote at it, and the screen went dark.

"You answered like four questions in that whole story. What the hell?" Aurora asked.

I shrugged. "She asked me like twenty others. I guess they wanted to focus on Jonah."

Joules tipped his beer bottle at me. "And did the cops inform your father that lying about a missing person is illegal?"

My lips pressed together.

He widened his eyes. "That was rhetorical, Riley. I know they didn't. It's a wonder you and your brother survived his garbage."

Aurora paused with her wine glass halfway to her lips. "Wait a minute, what's this about the cops?"

My head tilted. "We just came from the police station."

"They didn't tell me that!"

"Sorry. I figured you knew," Sandy muttered.

I recapped my afternoon visit downtown.

Aurora grabbed my forearm. "Shut up! He arranged to corner you at the police station? Who does that?"

I grinned. "Nobody that I know of, but it was pretty great to take the wind out of his sails when I mentioned Shirley Calhoun would love hearing the story."

"I bet that was epic," Whitney muttered.

Finn's phone rang. "Hey, Mom. If you haven't eaten you should come down to —"

I turned my head when he stopped talking.

"You are shitting me," he bit out.

The rest of the table tuned into Finn's vibe at that moment.

He stood. "Yeah. Be there soon."

Finn

Finn stared down at Riley. "Your car's been towed. My neighbor across the street came out and talked to the tow truck driver because she thought he was towing my car. He said the owner set it up. Guessing that car's in your dad's name since you don't have a decent credit rating, right?"

She nodded. "Yeah. Good thing I don't have to go back to the hardware store until next week."

Victoria sent Riley a reproachful look. "Riley."

She widened her eyes. "That's for Jonah, not me."

Sandy turned a hawkish expression on Riley. "What's for Jonah, but not you?"

Satisfaction washed over Vickie as she cocked a brow at Riley. "Tell them. They won't judge, but they'll set you straight."

She looked up at him. "Can we go now?"

He hesitated and Gamble pointed a chicken wing at them. "What's she hiding? It almost sounds like she's sitting on a pile of money or some shit."

Riley glared at Victoria.

Finn lowered his lips to her ear. "Don't blame Vickie. She'd never share that with Gamble."

Riley nodded.

"Well?" Sandy demanded.

"Sandra," Joules chided.

Riley sighed. "My mother's parents left me and Jonah a large sum of money. They did it in a way that prevented Dad from getting it. He conveniently never mentioned it to me when I turned eighteen either.

Victoria found out about it and got the ball rolling for me to claim it. But really, that money is all for Jonah."

From the far end of the table, Mensa said, "Bullshit. You need a car of your own, and Jonah is going to need somewhere to live. He's good at Mom's for now, but no matter what Mom says, that's gonna take a toll after a while. Use the money to set yourself up right, Riles."

Whitney nodded, drawing Riley's attention. "He's right."

Victoria's eyes darted between the two of them. "I'm confused. If her car's already been towed, why are you going home? It's not like you can change anything, Finn."

Finn shook his head. "No, but my instincts say he's gearing up for more bullshit. I'd rather not be blindsided if I can help it."

As he and Riley crossed the room, Mick whipped a dishtowel over his shoulder. "Young lady, any time you come here, you get whatever you want. On the house, you hear?"

Finn hadn't ever heard the man speak with such conviction. Riley sniffed, and from the press of her lips Finn suspected she was holding onto things by a thread.

She smiled at Mick. "You don't have to do that, sir."

"No, but I insist." Mick's serious eyes caught Finn's. "Go give 'em hell, biker."

Mom and Uncle Steve's cars were both parked in the driveway, leaving Finn with nowhere to put his Harley unless he rode up the yard. Riding his Harley on the yard Gramps had doted on for so many years was the last thing Finn intended to do.

That left him parking his bike at the curb.

His neighbor, Helen, bustled outside and across the street to them. The woman was seventy-three years old but acted like she was thirty-three.

"Thank heavens you're finally back. I thought for sure that was your car they were towing. Did Nina tell you that?"

Finn nodded. "Sure did, Helen."

Helen twisted her head and shot Finn a furtive look. "Well, I didn't tell her this part. While I was talking to the tow truck driver, the so-called owner of the car came up and yelled at me to mind my business."

"He *what*?" Riley yelled.

Finn slid his arm around Riley's shoulders. "Chill out, Riley. Did this man threaten you, Helen?"

Helen's smile held a certain snide innocence. "He tried. The tow truck driver was having none of that — though I could have held my own against him."

"Ma'am, no offense, but I wouldn't be so sure," Riley said.

Helen stared at Riley for a long moment. "You sound familiar."

Finn said, "I'm glad he didn't threaten you outright, Helen. If you see him again, stay away from him. Can you do that for me?"

Helen wagged a finger at him. "Don't you take that tone with me, young man. I can handle myself."

Finn took a calming breath.

Riley stepped closer to Helen. "He's not a good man, Miss Helen. You have to steer clear of him."

Helen's lips pursed. "You're the one who was driving that car. Why did that man get it towed?"

Riley turned her hands up. "It's not a big deal, to be honest. It had all kinds of engine issues and it was at least five years past its prime. I'm not going to get mad about it. He probably did me a favor."

Helen shook her head. "I know a fib when I hear one, young lady. But I'm letting it go." She speared Finn with her eyes. "Tell Nina to call me before she leaves town. I want a word with that brother of hers."

He would not *be telling Mom to call her.*

"Sure thing, Helen. Good night."

They watched Helen cross the street and waited on the sidewalk until she'd closed her front door behind her.

Riley wrapped an arm around his waist. They walked together up the front sidewalk to the stoop when Uncle Steve came outside.

"Nina told you the news, right?"

Finn nodded.

Uncle Steve smiled. "Better start boxing your shit up, Finn."

With effort, Finn kept himself from frowning. "I'll keep that in mind, Uncle Steve."

"What the hell?" Uncle Steve asked when a car pulled into the drive behind Mom's car.

"He can't be serious," Riley muttered.

Judge Tyndale cut the car engine, and unfolded from the small Mercedes sedan. Finn exhaled, willing his temper to die down. The fact Tyndale drove a recent model Mercedes, but let Riley take her chances on the road in a run-down Toyota boggled Finn's mind.

Then again, it didn't.

"Leave, Tyndale. You're not welcome here," Finn said.

Tyndale advanced on them. "I'll leave when my deceptive daughter gets in the damned car where she belongs."

Uncle Steve looked at Riley. "He's the man who hit you?"

Riley's chin lifted ever so slightly.

Finn said, "Don't wade into this, Uncle Steve."

Uncle Steve chuckled derisively. "You're not the only one who doesn't like women getting beaten, Finn."

"She hasn't been beaten. She was disciplined," Tyndale said.

Finn's vision blurred. "She's twenty-five, she doesn't need discipline from anyone."

Tyndale glared at Finn. "You don't understand our way of life."

Finn loosened his hold on Riley and lowered his voice so only she could hear him, "Go in the house."

Riley edged away from him, but hadn't left his side.

"Your way of life?" Uncle Steve asked, disdain dripping from his words.

Tyndale gave two short shakes of his head. "Christianity. It's clear neither of you are God-fearing men."

Uncle Steve scoffed. "More like you got a God-complex, forcing your flesh-and-blood to fear you. That's messed up."

Tyndale's eyes lit with something Finn couldn't place. From the corner of his eye, Finn saw Riley take two steps backward toward the house.

Suddenly Tyndale threw a punch. Finn's body stiffened for a moment before he realized Tyndale had hit Uncle Steve.

"Steve!" Mom yelled from the stoop and stormed down the walk.

"Get inside, Mom! And call 911!" Finn yelled.

He gripped his Uncle by the arms and pulled him away from Tyndale.

"Let me go, Finn," Uncle Steve bit out.

"Not a chance. You aren't getting arrested tonight. He assaulted you, and the cops are on the way."

A Biloxi Police Department cruiser sped up the road and stopped at an angle on the driveway – half in the road, half on the drive.

A burly officer lumbered out of the car. "There's a report of assault here." His eyes traveled between all three men, then settled on Finn. "I need you step over there."

Uncle Steve started explaining the situation.

Tyndale cut him off. "That's a lie. I'm here for my daughter. She needs to get away from the Riot MC thugs." Tyndale pointed at Finn. "He hit his uncle."

"That's not true," Finn bit out as he shifted away from the men.

"If I may," Miss Helen interrupted from the end of the driveway. "I videoed this from my porch, Officer." She tipped her head toward Tyndale. "That man threatened me earlier and now he's hit Steve."

Miss Helen ignored Finn's reproachful look.

The officer nodded at her. "I'll talk to you in a minute, ma'am."

Tyndale squared his shoulders. "I'm a judge, Officer..." he trailed off, fishing for a name.

The cop's hard eyes cut to Tyndale. "Officer Remy."

Tyndale lifted his chin. "I have no reason to hit anyone, sir. They're trying to set me up."

Officer Remy glanced down and then up to Tyndale's eyes. "Why are your knuckles bleeding?"

Surprise and guilt washed over Tyndale's face and he brought his right hand up, then jerked it down to his side as though realizing his mistake.

Another squad car pulled up to the curb and two cops exited the vehicle. Officer Remy spoke to them for a minute. Once Officer Remy led Uncle Steve across the yard, one of the other cops took Helen aside and the third officer stood talking to Tyndale.

After a while, an officer spoke to Finn, asking him the same question many different ways. Meanwhile, Officer Remy watched Helen's video.

He lumbered over to them. "The sound on that video doesn't pick up the conversation leading to the altercation. You didn't do anything to provoke Judge Tyndale, did you?"

Finn took a deep breath. "No, sir."

He nodded. "We're taking him downtown. Should be gone in a few minutes, you can head inside if you want."

"Thanks. I'll make sure my uncle is good to drive first."

Finn joined his uncle and Helen in the drive.

Helen watched as an officer put cuffs on Tyndale and read him his rights. She put her cool hand on Finn's forearm. "I heard he's your lady friend's father. I'm going inside to make sure she doesn't see him being put in that car."

Finn wheezed out a chuckle. "Miss Helen, she's twenty-five and I think she'll enjoy watching him be taken away."

Helen leveled her stern brown eyes on him. "No child should see this, Finn."

"You're right, Miss Helen. Thanks for shooting that video and bringing it by, but I mean it, don't do that again. It's going to get you in trouble," Finn said.

Her dry look told him she would do what she wanted.

Finn pulled out a cigarette and lit it. Both squad cars left and Uncle Steve stood in the drive staring at the Mercedes sedan.

"How the hell are we supposed to move that asshole's car?" he asked.

Finn heard footsteps behind him. Riley wandered up with a grin on her beautiful face. "I have his spare keys. I can move it."

"Sweet," Finn said.

While Riley moved the car, Mom joined him. "She really cares about you, Finn."

He nodded. "That's good, seeing as I love her."

Mom returned his nod. "Easy to see why."

Chapter 15

A Little Psycho

Riley

As I walked up the driveway, Steve gave Nina and Finn a half-hearted chin-lift before he got in his car and drove away.

A wide smile split Nina's lips and she rubbed her hands together. "Well, that wasn't very much fun, but at least he's been arrested."

I bit my lower lip. "I hate to say it, Nina, but it isn't going to stick."

Nina chuckled. "Sure it will. Three witnesses when it happened, plus Helen and her nosy ways getting the whole thing on her cell phone. It's going to stick, Riley. Have faith."

Life had taught me early that faith didn't do much for me. With a wan smile, I nodded.

Helen came out of the house, tucking her phone in the pocket of her windbreaker. "I have to get back home. I'll be keeping my eye out for that man."

Finn ran a hand through his hair. "Miss Helen, please don't."

I nodded. "Yeah, besides he's going to have to come back to get his car, but hopefully he won't do anything crazy."

"I won't hold my breath, dear," Helen said, and wandered away.

Nina sighed. "I'm going to get out of your hair, too. Have a good night."

Finn pulled me to his side while Nina backed out of the drive. "You might have silently agreed with what Mom said earlier, but I can read you. Why don't you think the charges are going to stick, baby?"

I blew out a breath, wrapped my other arm around him to press my front to his side, and tipped my head back to look into his eyes. "I'm not saying Dad's above the law – though, I'm sure he thinks he is – but I expect he's going to worm his way out of this. At a bare minimum, I doubt he'll spend the night in jail."

Finn chuckled. "Babe, I don't think you or your dad understand how slow shit moves in the legal system – even if your dad is a judge. You get arrested, it takes a shitload of time to get out."

"If you say so. I'm starving. Can we make dinner?"

He shifted his body so we were chest to chest. "Yeah, babe. We'll make something quick because I'm exhausted."

My head tilted. "You are?"

He nodded. "Yeah, but don't worry. I'm not too exhausted to take you to bed."

I grinned. "Good, because after this long day, I could use an orgasm or two."

He returned my grin with a devilish gleam in his eyes. "Should be more like three or four for you, babe. I love making you come and at least once tonight you're gonna do it on my face."

A wave of desire rolled through me and I shifted my legs. "Keep talking like that, Finn, and we can just skip dinner."

He lowered his lips to mine for a quick kiss. "Nope. Gotta keep my woman well-fed."

Maybe it was because I was so hungry, but the fajitas Finn made tasted so good I'd stuffed myself silly.

"I'll handle the dishes, you put the stuff away, babe," Finn declared, grabbing my plate.

I sealed up the bag of shredded cheese and closed up the salsa and sour cream containers. When I shut the refrigerator door, I turned to see Finn putting each component of his Ninja Foodi in the dishwasher. It hit me that the water hadn't been running in the sink.

"You didn't rinse anything," I said.

His eyes cut to me. "Nope. Don't need to." He closed the dishwasher door. "The dishwasher kicks off with a steady rinse cycle before the soap gets loose. It's cool."

My eyes widened. "Finn, that's how you end up with baked-on, caked-on grime."

From the quirk of his lips, he was biting back a smile. "Riley, that's what the soap companies tell you."

I spluttered for a second. "You think we're going to bicker about Pepsi versus Coke, but *this* is what we'll really bicker about."

He tipped his head back to laugh long and loud, and it was contagious.

I always enjoyed watching him laugh any chance I got, but I loved being the one who made him laugh.

Come to think of it, I loved him.

He wrapped his arms around me. "Babe, it's Coke versus Pepsi because the winner is always named first. But the dishes will be fine without rinsing."

My lips twisted. "You aren't the one who'll be scraping food bits off the plates at the last minute."

He lowered his chin. "I will if you want me to, woman."

"Really?" I muttered.

He grinned. "Yep, and I'll hand you a Diet Coke to drink while you watch."

I smiled. "I just bet you will."

"Yep," he murmured, brushing his lips against mine. "And you'll love it."

He laid a soft, warm kiss on me before I could retort. I slid my hands up along his arms and crossed my wrists behind his neck. He leaned into me, his tongue delving into my mouth. I pressed closer to him.

His hands traveled downward. He splayed his fingers and gripped my ass. His grip became more of a tug and he lifted me up. I wrapped my legs around his hips.

Finn carried me to his bedroom. I expected him to lay me on the bed, but he put me on my feet, breaking the kiss.

"Get your clothes off, Riley."

I yanked my t-shirt out of my shorts. "After that kiss, I'm surprised you aren't doing it."

He reached behind his neck and tugged his shirt over his head. "I get that. I'm in a hurry to get you naked because I'm gonna take a long time making you come."

I unbuttoned my shorts. "Why would you do that? Take your time, I mean."

He pulled off his boots. "It's been a long-ass day and we both need this. Normally, I'd get us a bottle of tequila, but we gotta stay sober. So, you're getting it slow tonight." He stared at me. "And wipe that calculating look off your face, woman. You're not gonna change my mind."

He'd read the look on my face all right, but I could read him, too. He had an ulterior motive for going slow, but I couldn't put my finger on it.

With a warm look in his eyes, he prowled to me in his boxer briefs. His warm, calloused hands cupped my cheeks. "Do you know how much I care about you?"

My head tilted. "Pretty sure I got a good idea, Finn."

He stared at me, that warmth building. "Not so sure, babe, because if you did, you'd call me out right now."

I felt one eye squint at his words. His body crowded me and he walked us back to the bed. I sat down. His hands fell away for a moment. Then we were laying down and he held my face in his hands tenderly.

Reverently.

Like I was his.

"I—"

He shook his head. "No, Riley. I'm gonna show you, but I still need to tell you this."

When he paused, I whispered, "What?"

"I love you."

Butterflies gathered in my belly. I glided my fingers along the close-cropped hair on the side of his head. "I love you too, Finn. More than I—"

My words were cut off by Finn's mouth taking mine. This kiss wasn't slow or easy. It was fast and rough. I squirmed and rolled him to his back.

I lifted away from him with a grin. "You are notorious for telling me one thing, like you're going to take a long time with me, but then doing the very opposite, Finn O'Halloran."

A sexy, sly smile stretched his lips. "Not true, babe. Just not every day a gorgeous woman tells me she loves me too. Good thing you don't have to be anywhere in the morning, because it's gonna be a long night."

In the morning, my chipper demeanor shattered when I peeked out the blinds and Dad's car wasn't where I'd parked it last night.

I looked over my shoulder at Finn, who stood by the coffee maker. "I told you!"

"Woman, it's too early to tell me anything. What are you worked up about?"

As I crossed the room to him, I kept my face neutral. "Dad's car is gone. I told you the charges wouldn't stick."

The sight of Finn's tattooed hand dragging down his face mesmerized me.

He sighed and shook his head. "You never know, woman. He's got an administrative assistant, doesn't he? Maybe he called her to get his Merc."

My head dipped toward my shoulder. "That feels like a stretch, but you might be right."

He gave two short, quick nods. "Right. Let me get my java and I'll make breakfast."

Finn made us a huge breakfast of pancakes, bacon, sausage links, poached eggs, and cheese grits. I'd insisted on doing the dishes. While I scrubbed grits from a pot, I marveled at how much my life had changed in a week.

Jonah was getting the therapy he needed.

I'd learned my grandparents had left me and Jonah a huge sum of money.

It hadn't been easy, but I'd finally told people about what Dad did to me.

And not least of all, I had a man who loved me – which was also the best thing of all.

It had been a whirlwind, that was certain.

Still.

I felt restless. Working at the hardware store wasn't a career, but it made me feel productive and that gave me a sense of fulfillment.

"I know grits are a bitch to get off the pot, Riley, but what are you thinking about so hard?" Finn asked.

I rinsed the pot under the tap with a sigh. Once I knew it was clean, I rested it in the strainer and turned to Finn. "I'm thinking about how much has changed, and yet... even though I know you don't want me to, I still feel an urge to go to work. It gives me a sense of purpose, no matter how small that might be."

He wrapped his arms around me from behind. "I get it, babe, but it'd be good if you wait a couple more days."

"Okay," I said, slipping a skillet into the soapy water. "Let me finish these up and we'll get on with our day."

I had finished the dishes and had downed two sips of my Pepsi One when my cell rang. A number I didn't recognize lit the display. My gut said to let it go, but the number was local so I answered.

"Hello?"

"Riley Tyndale?" an older female voice asked.

"Yes," I said hesitantly.

"This is Lyssa Wallace, I'm your father's publicity manager."

My body froze. She wasn't just Dad's publicity manager. Her husband was an upstanding member of the church. The first time Dad ran for election, he'd had a rare moment of open-mindedness and gave her a chance at handling his campaign media. He'd won and the rest was history, as they say. After I did the interview yesterday, I'd considered how Shirley Calhoun's people might reach out, but I hadn't given much thought to Dad siccing his people on me.

"Are you still there?" she asked.

"Yes," I whispered.

"Good. I have to say, you've put your father in a bad situation."

I did a long blink. Had I heard her correctly?

Dad was in a bad situation? As if.

With a head shake, I got myself together. "I'm guessing you've seen the news story and that's the 'bad situation' you're referring to."

"It's no news story, Riley. It's slander."

My eyes widened. "You're..." I trailed off. Then said, "You can't possibly believe my brother could commit slander."

"With coaching, I'm sure anything is possible."

Finn came to me and put his face in mine so I could read his lips. "Hang up," he mouthed.

I shook my head. There was no way I could do that. Like rubbernecking on the interstate, staying on the line was a compulsion. "What do you want, Ms. Wallace?"

"Ideally, I want you to retract your interview with Anna St. Claire. If you can't find it in yourself to do that, then I'll release a statement that questions your veracity as well as your brother's, not to mention it will implicate your boyfriend."

"What?"

"Finneas O'Halloran is a known member of the Riot MC and it's also known that a producer at channel six is related to Samuel Samuels, another Riot MC member."

"Babe, hang up," Finn whispered.

I straightened on the sofa. "Do your worst, Ms. Wallace. All of that will backfire on you."

After delivering that, I hung up.

"What's going to backfire on her? And seriously, Riley, you gotta hang up sooner."

I stood and took my phone to the charger. "Her plans to discredit me and Jonah are going to backfire."

Finn's tone dripped with disbelief. "She's going to refute your story?"

I nodded and walked back to the sofa. "Yeah. Unless I retract my story."

He sighed. "Whatever. Let her. You shouldn't have engaged, though."

I crossed my arms. "Yeah, I'd have been down with that until she threatened to drag you, Two-Times, and the Riot into this. That's not happening."

His head tipped back and I admired the column of his throat. When he righted his head, those steely grey-blue eyes widened at me. "You don't need to protect us, babe."

My hands went to my hips. "Finn, that woman intends to accuse me of slander and coaching my brother to do the same thing. Her threatening you in *any* way was a bridge too damned far."

His chest puffed out with his inhale and his lips parted.

No matter how much I knew he had something to say, I was on a roll. "And like it or not, I'm *done* taking whatever the damned world dishes out to me. Between you opening my eyes, and hearing how Victoria handled Dad yesterday, I know I can handle way more than I give myself credit for."

"Right, but you can't let someone threatening me get to you."

My head twisted and I gave him a look. "I'm sorry, what?"

He stepped closer to me. "She pressed your buttons with those threats and no offense, babe, but you gave her the upper hand by reacting."

My head dipped toward my shoulder. "You would've kept your cool if someone threatened your brother Wes?"

His chin dipped. "I get where you're coming from—"

"I don't think you do," I muttered.

He tilted his head as though seeking patience. Luckily he cut it short and met my gaze. "I need you to get this, babe. Anybody threatens to drag me into this shit, I can handle it. The club can definitely handle it."

"I know that, Finn."

He stepped into my personal space. "Okay, then I'll be more clear. If you know that, then when someone threatens me, you need to be cool as a fuckin' cucumber and rest easy in knowing it's handled."

The telltale signs of a headache were gathering along my brow line. "Why are you harping on this?"

His arms wrapped around my waist. "Gonna let the 'harping' comment slide, but I don't want anything getting worse for you because someone used me against you."

Finn

"What do you mean?" she asked.

He arched his brows. "She knew mentioning Jonah would goad you. She *didn't* know how you'd take it when she threatened me. Now you've given that away. That's something she didn't have and it could make things worse for you."

She gave him a deep nod. "You have a point, honey. But nothing like this will happen again."

His eyes went wide. "You think so? The club operates on the right side of the law, but a jackass tries to take down brothers in the club or whatever, it could absolutely happen again. Some idiot tells you that I'm going to jail if you don't...do what they want, they've got you. It could absolutely happen again, and I need to know you can keep your shit tight when it does."

She shook her head "Those things aren't connected, Finn. I can keep my shit tight in your hypothetical scenario because it won't involve my brother and the man I love. Call me crazy, but having the two most important men in my life threatened all in the same breath makes me a little psycho."

Her words hit him deep.

Most important men in my life...

"Fuck," he whispered, raising his hand to her cheek, letting his fingers brush along her eye where the blackness had finally receded. "That's the first time you've said I'm important."

Her tone softened. "That happens when you love someone. They become really important."

His lips quirked. "Well, make sure you don't allow someone to manipulate you because you love me."

"I won't," she said, leaning into his touch.

He kissed her forehead at the same time someone knocked on the door.

"Fuckin' A, that better not be Mom or Uncle Steve," he muttered.

She swallowed and her lips pressed together hard as if she were holding back laughter.

Finn opened the door. "Whitney? What are you doing here?"

Riley whirled around to them.

Whitney shot her a wave. "I'm here to give Riley a break from you. And before you balk about keeping her safe and all that stuff, it's all over the news that her Daddy's been arrested. She isn't working right now, so she's free to go to the shop with me and do lunch later."

He shook his head. "The news doesn't always get it right. He's got enough money and clout, he undoubtedly posted bail."

Whitney scoffed and pushed inside. "I don't think so, Finn. The news made it clear he was in hot water."

Finn shut the door and crossed his arms. "I don't trust it, lady. His car was left here last night, but someone came and got it in the past twelve hours. Might have been a lackey, or it might have been him."

Whitney shook her head. "He got his car back, that doesn't mean he knows who I am or where I'm taking Riley. It'll be fine."

Finn opened his mouth, but Riley sidled up to him. "Honey, it would be good for me to get out with Whitney. Dad knows I'm hanging with the Riot at this point, but he doesn't know that I'm friends with Whitney. And it's highly unlikely he knows about the leather shop where she works."

A devious smile twisted Whitney's lips. "You're welcome to come with us, Finn."

He stared at Riley for a long moment before he blew out an exasperated sigh. "No. You go with her – but I'm meeting y'all for lunch. I'm not normally a killjoy, but I don't trust anything about Tyndale at this point. The only reason I'm relenting is because this isn't your typical routine."

She smiled so bright he nearly missed her excited little hop before she wrapped both hands around his neck and gave him a hard kiss. "Thanks, honey! I love you."

Had it not been for Whitney standing there, he'd have bent her backwards over his arm and kissed her silly. Instead, he grabbed her hips to get her attention. "I love you, too, babe. But seriously, be fucking careful."

Not long after Riley left, Finn fed Baller and then took a quick shower. He rode over to Har's custom bike and body shop. Unlike other brothers, he didn't visit the shop often because he didn't want to waste Gamble or Har's time. This wasn't a random social call, though. Finn wanted to customize his bike and he planned to peruse Gamble's portfolio, since he did most of the custom art work.

Finn had put it off because Julie had been such a relentless flirt. He couldn't deal with that since he'd been thinking about Riley for so long - it wasn't fair to either woman or himself.

Deep down he didn't want to manipulate the situation, but if Julie pressed her luck with him it might be the perfect way to get Riley into a job where she'd be safe. Plus, it would put Finn's mind at ease.

Finn parked his bike next to Gamble's and put his kickstand down.

Har tucked a rag into his back pocket and strode out from a garage bay. "Tell me you aren't here to shoot the shit. We got five bikes that need to get done before Sunday."

Finn shook his head. "No, I'm here to look at Gamble's sketches. Want my bike customized, I'm just not sure what I want done."

Har nodded. "Gotcha."

Finn looked around the shop. "Where's Gamble? Is he dealing with Julie?"

A grimace crossed Har's face. "More like dealing with her mess. She quit this morning."

Something in Har's tone put Finn on alert. "Why is there a mess? She seemed pretty organized."

Har's brows jumped. "Yeah. Except when I said she'd only get paid for her existing hours, she 'spilled' coffee all over her calendar, invoices to be sent out, and the damned receipt book."

Finn lowered his voice to take the sting out of his question. "You don't use PayPal to invoice customers?"

"No, Finn, I don't, and it wouldn't have mattered much seeing as Julie hadn't put shit in the system for weeks. I'd be screwed if Gamble hadn't been right there with a sponge."

"What a bitch," Finn muttered.

"Yeah. She burned a bridge, that's certain."

"Damn right. Might be too soon to suggest this, but —"

Har nodded. "Gamble already mentioned Riley. Is *she* interested, or is this your idea?"

"Maybe both."

Har chuckled. "If there's one thing I know about women, it's that you're better off when it's *her* idea. Especially when it's job-related."

"True."

"Though our hours wouldn't interfere with her singing career."

Finn chuckled. "She says that's not her goal."

"Goals change all the time, man. If she's interested, tell her to be here Monday at seven-thirty."

"Cool," Finn said.

Har led him to the open garage bay. "Gamble's book is over here. Let him finish up in the office, pretty sure he'll be done soon."

Gamble trudged out of the office ten minutes later. "That shit is whacked. Why'd she have to spill coffee?" He caught sight of Finn. "What are you doing here?"

Finn held up the three-ring binder with Gamble's sketches. "Figuring out what I want you to do to my Harley."

Gamble looked out to the parking area and back to Finn. "Where's Riley? You haven't left her side all week."

Finn nodded. "She's with Whitney at the leather shop."

"Is that wise?" Har asked, wiping down a bike with a gleaming fresh coat of wax.

Finn met Har's gaze. "Her dad has no idea who Whitney is or what leather shop we use."

Finn's phone rang and he saw Riley's name on the screen. "Speak of the devil." He hit the green 'answer' button. "Hey, Riley."

"Hey, we're going to The Fillin' Station for a late lunch."

"Are you sure that's a good idea? That place is close to the courthouse."

"Dad always eats at eleven-thirty, and Vickie texted me. Dad's court dates have all been postponed because of his arrest. Besides, I never go there because it's so close. Today seems like the only time I can do this."

"Yeah, I can see that, babe. I'm at Har's body shop, it isn't far from The Fillin' Station. I'll meet you there."

Gamble gave Finn a hard look. "Hey... we haven't had lunch yet either. Do you want company – since it's close by and the courthouse is right there?"

Finn paused mid-headshake. "That's not a bad idea, now that I think about it. She's gonna have Whitney with her."

Har cleared his throat. "Gamble, you go ahead. I got a client coming in about twenty minutes."

Gamble gave Har a chin lift. "Got it, boss. I'll bring you back a Po' Boy."

Chapter 16

Best Laid Plans

Riley

I forgot how the best laid plans often went to shit. Whitney and I expected it to be a breeze to find parking close to the Fillin' Station. But, no.

We found a spot four blocks away and much closer to the courthouse than I liked.

"Wipe that worried look off your face, Riley. Finn just parked his bike across the street."

At the sight of Finn dismounting, I smiled – big and cheesy I was sure. I was also sure I didn't care.

"Gah, you've got it bad," Whitney said, opening her door.

"Sue me," I quipped before I unfolded from the car.

Finn dashed across the street to us. He claimed me by wrapping his arm around me and laying a kiss on me.

"Hi," I whispered when he pulled away.

"Hey," he murmured. To Whitney, he said, "How's it goin', Whit? Hope you two don't mind, but Gamble's joining us. He parked illegally so he could make sure we get a table."

The three of us walked toward the restaurant. Once we were within view of the patio dining area, Gamble threw his arm up in a wave.

"You cool with sitting outside?" Finn asked.

I nodded. "Yeah. I feel like I've been inside for days, it'll be great."

Whitney greeted Gamble, and I got the impression that he didn't hold the same grudge against her that Mensa did. I made a mental note to ask Finn what was going on there. Sometimes I thought Finn had the same chip on his shoulder, and I wanted to know more about it.

Seconds after we sat down, our server came for our drink orders. I didn't know if she was nearing the end of her shift or what, but she wasted no time coming back for our food orders.

The moment she departed, Whitney nodded at me. "In the car, you mentioned needing to find the restroom. I gotta go, too. You want to come with me?"

I nodded and stood.

Finn's hand darted out to grab my wrist. "Be quick, Riley. I'm not trying to scare you, but don't waste any time, okay?"

I nodded.

The concern etched on Finn's face brought it home: the shit with Dad had to end. This was hitting Finn harder than he would admit to me and I didn't like it.

The Fillin' Station was an old gas station from the 1920's that had been outfitted into a restaurant. There were seven tables inside, but a bar dominated the majority of the space. I followed Whitney inside and we wove our way through the close-set tables toward the women's room at the back.

A man sitting at the bar swiveled on his stool, reached out, and grabbed Whitney by the wrist. "Hey, Whit."

I collided with Whitney's back. As I stepped back, I realized how focused they were on each other. Focused with animosity and disdain, from the vibes I caught.

My instincts from my childhood reared up, but I fought against the urge to bolt. For all I knew this guy was a total stranger, but Whitney jerked her wrist free of his hold.

"You aren't supposed to be here." Over her shoulder, she glanced at me. "Hit the restroom ahead of me, sweetie. I'll be there in just a moment."

I took in the hulk of a man who stared at Whitney like she amused him and annoyed him in equal measures. *As if they're related*, a little voice said in the back of my mind. Yet, I'd never asked Whitney if she had siblings. He had a very authoritarian air about him like he'd been in the military, or might be an undercover cop.

"You sure?" I whispered.

The man smiled, and I suspected he'd charmed many women. "Yeah, she's sure. I'm not gonna hurt her."

With the din of conversation and other restaurant noise, I couldn't be sure, but I swore Whitney growled.

"Be there in a sec, Riley."

"Okay," I said and stepped past her.

The restrooms were at the end of a lengthy, dim corridor.

As I veered right toward the door for the ladies' room, a closet door to my left opened.

Dad stepped out and waved a small pistol at me. "God is good. When Saul Demps asked me to have lunch with him today, I declined, but he talked me into it. And the Lord has provided."

I shook my head and my heart raced. I took a step backward.

He stepped forward and raised the pistol. "It's time to go home, daughter."

I opened my mouth to scream, but his free hand covered my mouth. "Nobody is going to hear your feeble scream, Riley. Time's up. We're going to get Jonah and go home."

He moved his hand from my mouth to grip my bicep. I widened my stance and planted my feet against his pull.

He chuckled. "I will throw you over my shoulder and carry you out, if I have to."

"As if. You're in your fifties and I'm not that light."

He put his face in mine. "Stop. Arguing."

"I'm not going to help you get Jonah. He's staying with Auntie Celeste. And I'm not going with you."

"I can't believe you've been around those bikers. That man has tattoos on his hands," Dad spat.

"Better than blood on his hands, like you."

He released my bicep and backhanded me. Hard. Not only was that going to leave a mark, but Finn was going to be so pissed. Hell, I was pissed.

Even with my mind reeling with pain, I pivoted and lunged away. Dad anticipated my move, though. He locked an arm around my waist, yanking me back.

I struggled against him, gripping his wrist like Cynic had taught me, but it didn't help.

Dad grunted and jerked me backward. I collided with him. The momentum made his footing slip, and he backed into the emergency exit.

The door opened and the high, shrill alarm blared through the building. He pulled me out into the alley, then he hauled me around to face him. "You're going to pay, Riley. Everything's your fault. From your mother's death, to the fact I'm out of work right now. And your report to the judicial commission won't work, either."

As he spoke, he dragged me along the alley.

"That isn't true," I muttered.

He jerked my arm. "It is, and roping your brother into that stupid interview! You're the reason I'm being pressured to drop out of the race."

We hit the mouth of the alley. His Mercedes was parked a few feet away. He shoved me against the vehicle, putting the muzzle of his pistol on my chest to keep me in place. With his free hand, he grabbed his keys. The car chirped and the lights blinked when he unlocked it.

"For once in your life, be smart, Riley. I know it's hard, but you can do it. Now get in the car."

The restaurant alarm stopped and I heard men shouting. If I could stall, somebody might help me.

Dad raised the pistol and aimed it down the street away from the restaurant, and he fired a warning shot. "Get in the car now, Riley." He wrenched the door open, then gave me a shove, and I sat in the car.

My body trembled with anger and fear. Dad had never snapped quite like this. I couldn't let him take me anywhere.

When I saw Dad was halfway around the hood, I opened the door. After just three steps, he fired the gun. Searing pain ripped through the top of my shoulder.

Dad dragged me back to the car. "So stupid, Riley."

He shoved me back inside the car. I felt woozy and I willed myself to ignore the shoulder pain. The problem was, I could hardly keep my eyes open.

Dad floored it. The car peeled away from the curb and raced down the road.

I took a deep breath, fighting nausea.

"Don't even think about getting out of the car again."

"No, sir," I lied.

My plan was to make a run for it at a red light.

Ahead, a traffic light turned yellow. The way Dad loved his Mercedes, I expected him to stop.

He didn't.

He sped through the intersection. An oncoming tractor trailer barely missed us.

If his abuse didn't kill me, a car wreck would.

At that thought, another wave of nausea hit me. "Slow down, you're making me car sick."

Dad's tone became even more condescending. "Too bad. The sooner I get you home the less you'll bleed on the seats."

My shoulder still hurt. It also felt abnormally warm and I realized blood had soaked through my t-shirt.

In the driveway, Dad took the winding route faster than normal. He hit the garage door clicker, pulled inside, and cut the engine. As if he expected me to run again, he hit the clicker and closed the door.

Rather than fight with him, I trudged inside the house.

"You'll start with the floors. Might hurt that shoulder, but you brought that on yourself."

I ground my teeth together to keep my temper in check at his audacity. My mouth dropped open when I took in the kitchen. 'Utter shambles' was the only term for it. Broken glass and shattered plates littered the floor.

"As you can see, the house falls into disarray when you're gone," Dad said, slapping me on my wounded shoulder.

Intense pain overwhelmed me. My vision blurred, and then I collapsed.

Finn

Finn watched Whitney and Riley weave between tables. As he scanned the patio, he saw the two men who'd come to the house to 'discipline' Riley.

"Oh, shit," he muttered.

"What?" Gamble asked.

He locked eyes with Gamble, then tipped his head at the men sitting across the patio. "Those assholes came to the house for Riley. That can't be coincidence. Something's up."

Gamble gave a single nod. "Calm down, Finn." He gave the men a cursory glance. "They don't know we're here."

He shook his head. "Man, my gut tells me something's wrong."

Gamble twisted in his chair to get a better look at the men. "I hear you, Finn. I'm keeping an eye on them. Whitney won't let your girl get into —"

From inside the restaurant, an alarm pierced the air. Finn recognized it as a security alarm.

"That isn't right," Gamble said.

"No shit," Finn replied, striding toward the building.

The men from Tyndale's church stood and blocked Finn.

"Now where do you think you're going?" the one with the thick glasses asked, Finn couldn't remember their names.

"Get out of my way. Riley's in danger," he bit out.

The other man scoffed. "Danger? That's just a security alarm malfunctioning."

Gamble stepped forward. "Let him through, if it's *just* some malfunction."

The distinct sound of gunfire rang out, but it wasn't inside the restaurant. Finn locked eyes with Gamble.

Gamble nodded. "I'm on it."

Only his Riot brother didn't get far because a police cruiser pulled up to the patio.

Whitney scurried around the two men from the church. "Where's Riley?"

Finn's stomach dropped while his mounting anger turned to rage. "What do you mean? Why aren't *you* with her?"

Whitney's face paled and she gave her head a short shake. "Someone I know stopped me. We were two feet from the ladies room. She went on without me... she should be back."

Finn lost control of his volume. "He took her in that amount of time, dammit!"

The more-fit looking church leader crossed his arms. "Who would have taken her?" His tone was skeptical and condescending.

Finn ignored him and stared at Whitney. "Mensa's right. Something about you ain't right."

"What are you saying? That I had something to do with this?"

"Yeah, because you had nothing do with keeping her safe!"

Another gunshot sounded. Finn bolted toward the side patio exit.

The tubby man stepped in front of him with a police officer at his side. "He thinks a woman is missing, officer."

A woman.

Finn's eyes widened at Demps or Coleman – he didn't care which one it was. "Her name is Riley Tyndale and her father took her out the back exit."

"You don't know that —"

The police officer interrupted the church elder. "Did you witness that, sir?"

"No, but nothing else makes sense."

Finn heard the faint sound of tires screeching. He bit his lip and thought of the best way to get out of answering the police officer's questions.

As if he could read Finn's mind, Gamble clapped him on the shoulder. "Hey, just got a text from Vickie. Riley's meeting her at the office."

Finn let fake relief wash over his face so the cop would buy Gamble's ruse. He pasted a sheepish smile on his face. "Sorry, officer. Guess my imagination got carried away with the fire alarm."

Whitney started to say something, but Finn aimed a quick, quelling look at her. She nodded. "That's right. She told me she couldn't stay long."

"Good," the officer nodded, and ambled away.

"Now why would your tune change so fast?" the tubby man asked.

Finn ignored his question and hurried to his bike.

Most days Finn lived by the biker adage that 'loud pipes save lives.' This afternoon, though, he couldn't afford for Tyndale to hear him roaring up the drive to Riley's rescue. He parked his bike at the curb near a neighbor's house. The first time Finn had been here, he hadn't realized that the lots were four-acre parcels.

He opened a saddlebag and grabbed his gun, tucking it in his waistband. An iron fence lined the front of the property. Between the slats, he saw an empty driveway and the garage door was closed. The house seemed empty, but Finn couldn't imagine where else Tyndale would take Riley.

The church was a possibility...
No, he couldn't second guess himself now.

He heard the sound of a motorcycle approaching from down the street. Gamble hadn't followed him. Finn prayed Gamble hadn't texted a bunch of brothers to come take his back.

Then he realized none of the other brothers knew where Tyndale lived.

Except Mensa and Cynic.

The rider came into view and Mensa gave a nod before pulling his bike to the curb and cutting the engine.

Relief and anger warred inside Finn. On the one hand he was grateful for the backup, but on the other hand he didn't want anyone else getting involved – even if Mensa was family.

"What the fuck are you doin' here?" Mensa demanded, striding to Finn.

Finn shook his head. "Don't need the attitude, man. Riley and I went to lunch. She went to the bathroom, shit went down, and we were separated. I'm pretty sure her Dad took her."

Mensa's chin dipped at an angle. "Why do you say that?"

"Two men from the church were there – same men who came to my house to get Riley to come home. They kept me from checking shit out."

"They kept you?" Mensa asked.

Finn gritted his teeth together. "A security alarm was already going off. They were in my way. I should have shoved them aside to get to her, but then I'd be sitting in a squad car."

"Right. You followed Jack here?"

"No. There were gunshots and... Christ, Mensa, I need to get in the house. Not answer your questions."

Mensa chuckled. "Yeah, Uncle Jack has security and then some, Finn. Knowing about Riley and Jonah, all that makes sense now. Bottom line, you can't just walk through the front gate – even if it's wide open."

Finn sighed. "He's got her. I feel it down to my bones, Mensa. I can't just hang out at the fence with my thumb up my ass."

Mensa grinned and it looked maniacal. "Yeah, that's why we're gonna go through the side. He's got a blind spot in his security and a loose fence panel."

Finn squinted at Mensa. "How do you know that?"

He widened his eyes. "I haven't been sitting around with my thumb up my ass either, man. This past week, I've been watching him, and when I knew he was at work, I scouted the property. That's how. But if Riley's in there, we gotta get her out. This way."

Finn followed Mensa to the edge of Tyndale's property. They trudged through the neighboring woods. After fifty feet, they stopped. For some reason a wooden fence lined this side of the property. Through a gap in the wood, Finn saw the side of the house and the back deck. The backyard was extensive.

In a low voice, Mensa said, "Riley mentioned Uncle Jack roams the yard every evening because of neighbor dogs digging under the fence."

"What does that matter?" Finn asked.

Mensa opened the fence panel a few inches. "Seeing as Denver told me about this loose panel she uses to sneak in and see Jonah, my guess is she digs those holes."

Finn shook his head. "I understand Riley having to sneak around, but why can't Jonah's friend use the front door?"

"I'm thinking Jonah doesn't want Uncle Jack to know how important Denver is to him. But, then again, who the hell knows why Uncle Jack is the way he is? Bottom line, his preoccupation with those damned holes has probably covered their secret gateway."

"Right."

Finn wondered if Riley knew about these secret meetings between her brother and her best friend's sister. Then he figured the less she knew the better.

Mensa moved halfway through the makeshift gate, paused, then held a hand out to stop Finn from following. "Somebody's here... looks like an unmarked car."

"Shit," Finn hissed. "Whitney better not have called the cops."

Mensa's head cocked to the side. "Okay, never mind. I've seen that woman before. She works for Jack." He pulled a gun from a shoulder holster. "If you don't have your piece with you, I got one you can borrow."

"No, I took care of that before you rolled up, but we're not shooting if Riley's in the way."

"Yeah. Let's get moving."

They sprinted across the side yard and pressed their backs to the siding on the house. Finn focused on regulating his breathing. He had to be quiet once they got inside.

Mensa jerked his head toward a side entry. "He's probably in his office on the other side of the house. We'll hit the garage side-door, here."

Mensa grabbed a spare key from under a flowerpot, then Finn followed him inside the garage. He trailed his finger along the hood of the Mercedes. The heat of the car told him it hadn't been in the garage very long.

The light in the garage shifted and Finn saw Mensa had opened the door in complete silence. How Mensa did shit like that, Finn would never know. Stepping through the doorway, Finn found himself in the kitchen. It seemed Tyndale hadn't lied. There were glass shards everywhere and probably a broken plate or two from the looks of it.

He caught sight of blood streaking the floor and his stomach lurched.

"Keep your cool, Finn," Mensa whispered, so softly Finn had to read his lips.

They took their time moving through the kitchen. One false step and the crunch of glass would give them away.

Finn bit his lip in an effort to quell his anger. It wasn't that fuckin' difficult to vacuum. Who lived with glass and ceramic shards on the floor? That man didn't need to wait for Riley to show up to clean it. Especially when he was the asshole who created the mess anyway.

He felt Mensa's eyes on him, and Finn realized he'd been making noise low in his throat.

Finn nodded, and Mensa shot him a look to say he understood but still showed his annoyance.

Then they heard the conversation coming from the office.

"You need to get her checked out, Jack." A feminine voice said.

"She's fine."

"I'm not blind. She's bleeding through her shirt. If you want to kill your daughter, you're well on your way to success."

"I don't like your tone."

"I don't like dead bodies, and she could bleed out from a flesh wound."

"Stop being so dramatic, Lyssa."

"It isn't dramatic when your car is on multiple traffic cameras speeding through intersections, and that trail goes right back to where a false security alarm happened at the Fillin' Station."

"What of it?" Tyndale demanded.

"I'll tell you what of it, there's also blood on the sidewalk adjacent to where your Mercedes left skid marks on the road. I can cover plenty of political indiscretions —"

"Then do that," Tyndale barked.

Lyssa sighed. "But I can't cover murder or attempted murder."

"I haven't committed murder."

"Not yet. But that assumes that you're right and it's just a flesh wound."

"Where is your loyalty? You work for me. I call the shots, dammit."

There was a loaded pause. Lyssa's calm tone impressed Finn. "Logic trumps loyalty, Judge Tyndale. Especially when someone's life is at stake, and if she gets an infection – then her life is on the line."

Finn clenched his fists and brought one up in the air, but he didn't let it fly. No matter how badly he wanted to do it.

"Her life isn't on the line here. Do your job and get me an interview with Morris Ackerman at channel five. I played golf with him last spring, and from what he said about Anna St. Clair – he'll be eager to refute her piece."

Finn leaned to the side and caught sight of the woman tipping her head back in exasperation. "I'll get right on it, sir. I'm headed back to the office. Will you need anything else?"

At that, Mensa pointed to the kitchen. Finn led the way, careful not to step on any glass.

Once they were back in the kitchen, he realized Tyndale had kept quiet for a long moment. Finally he said, "No. Make the interview happen ASAP."

Lyssa's footsteps could be heard coming down the hallway on the hardwood floors. Mensa and Finn crouched so they were hidden behind the kitchen island.

The front door opened, but they didn't hear it close.

Then Lyssa said, "I thought you were only listening in on the conversation. I wore the wire and did what you asked."

An authoritative male voice said, "His daughter is in there, bleeding. I'm obligated to get her out. Go to your car."

The door closed, and silence filled the house. Yet Finn knew the man had to be inside.

Finn made eye contact with Mensa and raised his brows in question. Mensa shrugged and shook his head – worry filling his eyes.

Chapter 17

A Classic

Finn

Turned out, Finn was wrong.

Lyssa hadn't left. Her hissing whisper cut the oppressive silence. "This isn't what I agreed to, Agent Heston."

"Too bad. This situation changed the moment you mentioned his daughter bleeding through her shirt. Introduce me to him, and you can go." The agent spoke in a conversational tone, as though he wanted Tyndale to come out of the office.

"Lyssa? Are you still here?"

Lyssa's voice quavered. "Yes, sir. Someone was at the door."

"Send them away," Tyndale called.

"It's a little late for that, Judge Tyndale. I'm Special Agent Ben Heston with the FBI."

From the shifting direction of Heston's voice it was clear he had moved down the hallway. Finn heard the front door close. He peeked around the island. Lyssa wasn't in the living room.

He heard Tyndale telling the FBI agent to leave. Mensa stood and trudged out of the kitchen.

"What's the plan?" Finn whispered.

Mensa paused at the front door and whispered, "Uncle Jack's gonna lose his shit. Much as I don't like it, we gotta have this special agent's back."

Mensa knocked on the front door, then immediately opened and closed it. "Uncle Jack! It's your nephew, can I come in?"

"Don't move," Tyndale yelled, but Finn knew it was directed at Agent Heston.

The tone of Tyndale's voice was off. It had the same edge of hysteria as last night. Finn darted past Mensa and into the office with his gun raised. At the sight in the room, Finn's body froze and he felt his blood drain from his face.

Tyndale had an arm locked around Riley's neck and upper chest. Finn focused on Riley. His eyes sought hers, but she appeared to be having a hard time keeping her eyes open. Letting his gaze drift lower, his teeth clenched at the sight of her wound. Her shoulder was a shock of deep blood-red. No wonder she struggled to keep her eyes open.

"Let her go," Finn bit out.

Tyndale's eyes darted from Finn to Agent Heston and then to Mensa. "Leave. All of you. Right now, or I shoot her."

Finn had never felt so helpless in all his life. He concentrated on keeping his gun steady on Tyndale.

"Put the weapons down – both of you," Agent Heston ordered.

"Get an ambulance here," Mensa said.

"Goddammit, Tyndale, let her go," Finn said.

"If you want her safe, get out of this house and let me handle this," Agent Heston said.

Finn turned it over in his mind for a long moment. As crazed as Tyndale looked, something told Finn the bastard would take Riley's life without a backward glance. It wasn't good for Tyndale to feel trapped. Finn took a step backward. He wanted to rescue Riley, but he wanted her safe more than anything.

In a low voice, he said, "Don't fuck it up, Agent Heston."

Tyndale heard him and laughed. "Now that's rich. The fuck-up is asking the FBI agent not to make a mistake."

Finn took a deep breath, willing himself to keep calm.

Agent Heston said, "Put your weapon down, Judge. Riley needs medical attention. Co-operate and it'll look better for you."

Tyndale shook his head twice. "I'm a judge. It never looks better for anyone — co-operation or not."

"You could be the first," Heston offered.

"All of you leave, and I'll let her go."

Heston seemed to consider it. Finn couldn't believe the agent even had to think about it, because sure as hell, Tyndale was lying.

Riley's eyes met his for a fleeting moment before she closed them again. If she was out of it, Tyndale gave no sign of exerting extra effort trying to hold her up. Finn saw her throat bob with a swallow and he itched to rush to her side.

"Do you remember when Jonah wanted to be a judge — just like you?" Mensa asked out of nowhere.

"You need to leave," Heston clipped out, turning his head an inch toward Mensa without losing eye contact with Tyndale.

"I do, Kenneth," Tyndale spat. "Then my sorry excuse for a daughter messed it all up."

"Wasn't Riley who hit him. She didn't leave him injured for life. Something that could have been prevented, but crushed Jonah's boyhood dream regardless. How can you live with yourself after all that?" Mensa asked.

Finn had a guess on what Mensa was trying to do... work Tyndale up into a frenzy. And Finn didn't like it.

"Brother," he drawled.

Agent Heston spoke, "Judge Tyndale, your daughter needs help."

Tyndale nodded. "You're right. She needs help only an expert can provide."

That strange tone had returned to his voice.

Heston gave a quick nod. "Right, let Finn or Kenneth take her—"

"The expert is the *Lord*, Agent Heston."

Finn's stomach sank a moment before all hell broke loose.

Multiple gunshots cracked the air around him. Finn had never believed in out-of-body experiences before, but he suddenly found himself across the room, prying Riley's listless body off Tyndale's.

"Get her to the ambulance," Heston yelled.

Finn carried her out of the house.

Her head turned when he stepped out onto the front stoop. "Finn," she breathed.

"Yeah, baby. I'm here. Save your energy."

Two paramedics crowded around him and helped him lower her to a stretcher. They paid him no mind as they strapped her in and moved the stretcher to the waiting ambulance.

Finn paced in the ER waiting room. The ambulance had arrived well before he had, but nobody could tell him squat about where they'd taken Riley.

A man stood against the wall watching Finn. In a vague recess of his mind, Finn thought the man seemed familiar, but he chalked it up to seeing the same face for the past half hour or more.

Mensa wasn't there. Part of Finn wondered at that, but his only concern was for Riley. Come to think of it, he had no idea if Judge Tyndale had been shot dead or not. If the man was dead... Finn might jump for joy, but that might also explain why Mensa hadn't arrived.

The outside double doors slid open and Whitney bustled inside. Her eyes lit on Finn and she looked relieved. "Finn, is she okay?"

Finn stopped, shoved his hands in his back pockets and stared at Whitney. "I don't fuckin' know since nobody will tell me shit. I'm not family."

The man standing against the wall cleared his throat, and it almost sounded natural.

Whitney turned her head toward the man standing against the wall. "Wyatt?"

"Whit," Wyatt said, his voice deeper than Finn expected.

Whitney fidgeted as though she were uncomfortable. "Why are you here?"

"Pretty obvious, isn't it? I'm waiting."

Whitney looked to Finn. "Sorry, that's my brother. I have to talk to him for a sec."

Finn took a hard look at Whitney's blue eyes and her oval face. He shifted his eyes to Wyatt. The family resemblance between them was uncanny.

The double doors slid open again and Mensa strode into the waiting room.

"What's the story?" Mensa asked.

"No clue. Just told Whitney, they're only talking to family."

Mensa dipped his chin. "Let me see what I can find out."

A few minutes later, Mensa sidled up to him. "They're still examining her, but in a few minutes they'll allow someone to see her – I'll make sure it's you, if she doesn't insist first."

Finn nodded.

Mensa's gaze moved about the room and locked on Whitney, who was having an animated conversation with Wyatt. The sheer disgust on Mensa's face forced Finn to re-examine Wyatt. He had a large badge on his belt.

Shit. He should have caught that earlier.

Mensa noticed the badge also. "I fuckin' knew something was off about her. Why the hell is she having a conversation with a cop? And we had her in the clubhouse multiple times. Christ."

Whitney wandered back to them. "Have they said anything?"

Mensa narrowed his eyes at her. "Doesn't matter. Don't ever come to the Clubhouse again."

She squared her shoulders. "Why?"

Mensa lowered his voice. "Seems you're a snitch...chattin' it up with a cop over there."

Her head tilted a touch. "He's my brother, and he works in security. You shouldn't make so many assumptions, Mensa"

A nurse called Mensa's name and Finn followed him to the desk. "You can go back. She's at bay four, but your friend will have to stay —"

"He's her fiancé. He's the one who needs to head back there."

The nurse arched a brow at Mensa's lie, then gave a short headshake. "Fine. I'll buzz you through."

Finn snuck behind the curtain. A small chair sat next to Riley's bed. Her shirt had been replaced by a hospital gown. She had her eyes closed, and an IV in her arm.

A nurse in blue scrubs was adjusting the IV. "Once this transfusion finishes, she should be discharged. The doctor doesn't want to keep her overnight."

He nodded and the nurse left. Through all of that, Riley's eyes stayed closed. He figured she was sleeping, and he sunk into the bedside chair as quietly as he could.

For months, he took Gramps to his cancer treatments inside a hospital. All those visits left Finn with a hatred of hospitals.

Gramps had tried to change his mind. "Ought to love 'em, Finneas. Whole lotta people wouldn't be here without 'em."

Strange how that memory of Gramps brought Finn comfort now, when he'd so easily dismissed it at the time.

"What are you doing here? You hate hospitals," Riley rasped.

He grabbed her hand, dismayed at how cold her fingers were. "Wherever you are, that's where I'm gonna be, Riley."

A small smile curled her lips. "That's sweet."

"Not sweet, woman."

"They're letting me out soon, I think."

"Yeah. Once your transfusion's done."

Her brows drew together. "How'd you know?"

"I was here. You were asleep."

"No, I was resting my eyes."

He chuckled. "Sounds a whole lot like sleeping."

"Smartass." She closed her eyes for a moment and opened them again. "Where's Dad? Did he survive?"

Finn pressed his lips together, fighting his knee-jerk response that he hoped Tyndale bought it. "Haven't heard."

She gave a short nod. "Be nice to know if I need to worry."

He squeezed her hand. "Honey, he held you at gunpoint, in front of an FBI agent. If he survives, he can't spin or cover that."

"I was so out of it in the house, Finn. He kept hitting my wound or squeezing it to make me hurt worse. I collapsed in the kitchen, then I woke up in his office. How did the FBI get in?"

Finn turned his head so she wouldn't see his raw anger at hearing Tyndale made her gunshot wound worse. He turned back to her. "Seems Lyssa had an agreement with Special Agent Heston."

"How do you know that?"

"Mensa got us in through the garage. We overheard her and your Dad. He kept her from helping you, and we had to hide in the kitchen when she left. Only, she was wearing a wire and Heston came in to get you out."

"Wow," Riley murmured.

"Wow is right," a chipper nurse said, sliding the curtain back with a whoosh. "You are done with the transfusion. Eat these crackers, and I'll get your discharge papers from the doctor." The nurse removed the IV, bandaged the infusion site, and left.

"Wonder who will clean up all that glass?" Riley asked.

"Does it matter?"

She widened her eyes at him. "If your uncle tosses you out and you won't let me buy the house then, my man, we're gonna need somewhere to live. Besides the clubhouse, obviously."

He huffed a humorless chuckle. "And you would want to live there?"

"With Dad out of the way, sure. If Dad's still free, then no."

"Let's take it one thing at a time. I'll have a couple prospects clean the kitchen. But I'm hopeful Uncle Steve will... open his mind."

Riley

"I'm sorry, Ms. Tyndale. Your father passed away," the doctor said.

Three tears streaked down my cheek. More were brimming in my eyes.

The doctor seemed concerned as though I might be a volcano ready to blow.

I was stunned I had any tears to cry over Dad. I thought I'd hardened my heart to Dad a long time ago, but I was wrong. Even with all his abuse and vitriol, his death hurt.

Likely because a naïve part of me clung to the hope that Dad would change his ways.

Auntie Celeste wrapped me in a fierce hug. "I'm so sorry, sweetheart."

I returned her hug. "I'm sorry, too, Aunt Celeste."

She pulled away from me, her eyes brimming with tears. "What for?"

"That you lost your brother. Wrong as it might be, I'm relieved. It's Jonah I'm worried about. He's going to be devastated."

Her lips pressed into a thin line and tears streamed down her cheeks. "That just makes me so angry. He should have cared more, done something to get himself the help he needed."

I shook my head. "We can't change any of that."

She sighed. "No. We can't. If you don't mind, I think we should tell Jonah in the morning."

I nodded. "Yeah. That's a good idea, especially since you said he's having a good day today."

Her head tipped to the side. "I feel sure Denver coming by for a visit had everything to do with that."

"You're probably right," I whispered.

She nodded and put her hands on my shoulders. "If you need anything, call me. Anytime. I don't care how late or how early. If you don't want to handle his…" She sucked in a hiccupping breath and continued, "Last wishes, I can help you with that."

"Okay," I said, a sense of overwhelm crashing over me.

Agent Heston stood nearby. Once Auntie Celeste left, he moved closer. "Judge Tyndale was under investigation for disability fraud and embezzlement from his church. Do you know anything about that, Ms. Tyndale?"

"No, I honestly don't."

Agent Heston nodded and for a moment his eyes focused beyond me, and I suspected it was on Whitney, who had hugged me after I first came out of the ER. Then she moved to the other side of the waiting area, and the doctor found me and Aunt Celeste.

I aimed a small smile at the agent. "Will Jonah and I have to sell the house to deal with the crimes?"

Heston raised his chin, his lips quirking up. "It has to be determined how long he's been defrauding the Social Security Administration. Then the money would be taken from his bank. If that's insufficient, the house and other assets could be seized."

I glanced up at Finn, who stood at my side. "We better work on your Uncle."

Finn's eyes closed for a moment. Those gray-blue eyes held humor when he opened them. "Babe. Seriously, one thing at a time."

"Fine. Let's get some food. I'm starving."

We were sitting outside at Sonic. Finn set his soda on the metal-grate style tabletop and sighed. "We should have taken a cage, Riley."

I widened my eyes and reared my head back. "I'm gonna tell the brothers you said that! What kind of biker suggests such a thing?"

"This biker. The one who wants his woman to heal up. Not mess up her bandages on her gunshot wound."

"It's a flesh wound."

His eyebrows rose and he pointed a tater tot at me. "All wounds are serious, Riley."

"Yes, well, I needed some food, Finn. Besides, I didn't feel like being with anyone else but you."

He sighed. "This shit's never happening to you again, so we'll table this argument."

I tipped my head toward his food. "Are you finishing those tots?"

He slid them my way. "Are you sure you're okay? Never seen you eat so much. It's almost like you're pregnant."

I laughed. "No, I'm not pregnant. It's late, I didn't get to eat lunch before Dad took me, so I haven't eaten since you made that big breakfast at nine o'clock or whatever."

"I'll take your word for it."

I swallowed a tater tot. "Plus, I love Sonic. The only downside is that they serve Coke."

He smirked. "Is that why you got a shake?"

I grinned. "Not really. I was hungry. Any other time, I order the cherry-limeade."

"A classic," he said, leaning his forearms on the table. "What do you want to do with your life, Riley? Leave Jonah out of it. Do you want to stay in Biloxi? Keep hanging around the clubhouse?"

"Not to quote you, but one thing at a time, Finn."

He shook his head. "What I'm asking is, do you love it here? I want to start a business—"

"And a family," I muttered.

"Yeah, but if you've dreamed of living... up north, out west, whatever, you could do that now. Completely get away from the bad memories."

I sipped my shake. "They aren't all bad memories. And I can't leave Jonah out of my decisions, but I get what you're saying. What would I do if I could? I love the Riot, and even if we moved to another town with a

Riot MC chapter, I'd still want to be here. Jonah loves it here, it doesn't snow, and—"

He grabbed my hand. "You could sing professionally, Riley. Nashville or Los Angeles—"

I shook my head. "No, Finn. I'm not interested in touring and all that, but Roman's idea seems doable."

Finn nodded.

"Why do you ask? I feel like you have an agenda."

He let go of my hand, sat back, and stroked his soul patch. "It takes money to start a business. I need to know you won't regret staying here. Moving yourself is one thing. Uprooting a business, that's a whole other deal."

I shook my head. "Why didn't you just say so?"

He grinned. "I didn't want to sway your answer. Wanted you focused on yourself. Thinking you haven't done much of that – other than focusing on surviving."

"Right. Where are we staying tonight?"

"Your call, Riley. Clubhouse or my place."

I smiled. "Your place, honey. I need a quiet night."

We got back to Finn's at quarter to ten. His uncle stood from a chair on the front porch.

Great.

He met us in the driveway. "Quite the story about your father."

Finn tucked his helmet under his arm, and slung his other arm around my waist. "Uncle Steve, it's been a long day."

"Yeah. In the morning, let's talk. The real estate agent says the market's slowing down. Laurie and Nina have convinced me that selling to one of the big firms might not be the best move."

I felt Finn's body relax. "Surprised they made you see that."

Steve clapped Finn on the shoulder. "We'll chat in the morning."

Inside the house, I leaned against the couch while Finn locked the door. If I sat down, I didn't think I'd get up again and I wanted to sleep next to Finn. The moment he turned around, I said, "Am I wrong? That sounds like good news."

Finn shrugged a shoulder. "It should be good news." His eyes went wide and he lifted his chin for a moment. "Jesus! That reminds me. Julie quit this morning."

"Julie — Har's assistant?"

Finn nodded and smiled. "Yeah. Har said to show up at seven-thirty on Monday if you're interested. Gives you the weekend to think about it."

"Are there benefits?" I asked, without thinking.

"Probably," he muttered, his brows drawing together.

Victoria's words came back to me. I didn't need to be in a hurry — except for insurance for Jonah. My hunch was that any coverage he had ended with Dad's death.

"What are you thinking? Normally I can read you, but that look on your face is a new one."

I shrugged. "I guess it's just hitting me that I've got money. The only issue is health insurance. Otherwise, I could take my time figuring out what I want to do."

Finn nodded. "That's true, but I don't think you'll find a better boss than Har."

That was likely true. Julie had said something similar — though I'd suspected she took advantage of Har's good nature.

My cell rang with Jonah's ringtone. For the first time, a sense of dread hit me knowing I'd be talking to my brother. "Hey, Jonah, I'm sorry I haven't called, but —"

"It's your Aunt Celeste. You could have told me you were shot!"

I thought back to seeing her at the hospital. It felt like days even if it had only been three hours ago. Finn and I had found Aunt Celeste in the waiting area after I was discharged. Since Whitney had loaned me a spare long-sleeved shirt she had in her car, Aunt Celeste hadn't seen me in a hospital gown and hadn't realized *I'd* been injured, too.

"Young lady," Aunt Celeste prompted.

"I'm sorry. I didn't want you to worry, and it's all good. Nothing serious."

She spluttered. "'Nothing serious!' I don't know who's worse, you or Kenneth. He talks about people getting shot like it's old hat."

"I'm sorry, Aunt Celeste. They discharged me and it's good. I'm fine, just a few stitches."

She couldn't hide her harsh exhale. "You better be here first thing, Riley Jean. Dean and Kenneth had to talk me out of coming over there."

"Mensa's over there? Is that how you found out about the gunshot wound?"

She barked out a laugh. "No! Phyllis Demps dropped by to offer her condolences on behalf of Jack's church. She 'inadvertently' let it slip about you being in the crossfire."

I opened and closed my mouth. Mom had always told me to keep mean things to myself. For once I followed her advice.

It hit me that Steve would be here in the morning. "Aunt Celeste, I can't be there first thing. Finn has a family issue we have to deal with—"

"Uncle Steve can wait," Finn said. "Your brother can't."

God, how I loved Finn.

"Okay, never mind. We'll be there first thing."

"Good. I knew I liked Finn for a reason."

I chuckled. "Me, too, Aunt Celeste. Me, too."

In the bedroom, Finn watched me plug my phone into the charger. "You want the shower first... wait, no. You got bandages on your shoulder."

"I'll do a sponge bath or something in the morning. You go ahead."

While Finn showered, I put on my pajamas, careful of my bandages. A shower would have been nice, but I legitimately didn't have the energy.

My phone buzzed with an incoming call. Seeing Aurora's name on the screen, I pulled the phone off the charger to take the call.

"Hey, Aurora."

"Hey," she said in a strange tone, part concerned, part questioning.

"I should have called you sooner."

"Yeah... I'm rethinking whether I like Finn for you."

I chuckled. "It isn't his fault it took me so long. There were FBI agents and I had to get stitches."

"Stitches? What?"

I gave her a quick run-down of my eventful day.

"Oh God," she breathed. "Denver didn't tell me all that."

"Yeah, we haven't told Jonah about Dad yet. We're doing that in the morning."

"Ugh. Do you want company for that? Denver and I can —"

I grimaced. "No, it's better if it's just me, Aunt Celeste, and Uncle Dean. Given the seriousness of this news, having Denver there might make Jonah more agitated."

"We can swing by after if you need us."

"Thanks, Aurora."

"No need to thank me, Riles."

We both were quiet. After a moment I said, "At least you don't have to cover for me any more."

"Riley..."

"What?"

She sighed. "I shouldn't speak ill of the dead, but you sound so cavalier."

I shook my head. "I wouldn't say that. Like I told Aunt Celeste, I'm relieved."

Her tone became serious. "Anyone from the FBI offer you grief counseling?"

My face fell. "Aurora —"

"No, Riley. Maybe not right now, but at some point I think you're gonna need it. Your relief is probably covering something else."

"Elation, maybe?"

"I'm being serious here."

I yawned. "I know. It'll be serious enough tomorrow when we tell Jonah."

"Yeah, that won't be fun, so I'll let you go. Just saying, I love you and I'm grateful as can be that you're still here."

"I love you, too, Aurora. I'll call you tomorrow."

Finn opened the bathroom door. He wasn't wearing a shirt, so his muscular, tattooed chest was on full display as he used a towel to dry his hair. A pair of black pajama pants in a beer mug pattern hung from his angular hips.

I suddenly felt thirsty.

Finn tossed the towel into a hamper, his eyes on me the entire time. "Not tonight babe. I'm beat, you've got to be exhausted, and this damned day needs to end... though I love how you were starin' at me."

I nodded and put my cell back on the charger. "You make a decent point. I'd probably fall asleep in the middle of a blow-job. That's not cool."

He climbed under the covers, laughing. "Damn right. That sounds like a nightmare." His arms came around me, he pulled me close, and laid a long, tender kiss on me. "I love you so fucking much, Riley. Hated how helpless I felt hearing about your wound, then seeing how much blood you lost. I'm grateful as all fuck God spared you today."

I stared into his eyes. "Are you getting religious on me?"

His eyes widened. "I'm being serious here, Riles. Haven't prayed in a long time, but I damn sure did today. I love you."

"I'm grateful your prayers were answered. I love you, too, Finn. "

Chapter 18

Enough

Riley

Uncle Dean opened the door to me and Finn. "Riley-bug, you need a hug."

Those words from my childhood made me feel loved and I wrapped my arms around him. Then he and Finn introduced themselves, and my eyes cut to the sofa across the living room. Fiona sat next to Jonah and on his other side was Aunt Celeste. I noticed Cynic leaning against the breakfast bar that wasn't far from Fiona's side of the couch. Mensa sat on a barstool next to him.

I hadn't expected anyone from the Riot to be here besides Finn and Mensa.

Fiona stood and joined us. "Hey, I didn't mean to horn in or anything, but your aunt thought having me here would be a good idea."

I nodded. "I'm sorry we're ruining your Saturday."

Fiona put a hand on my bicep. "Riley, you're not ruining anything. You're part of the Riot."

Jonah sat rubbing his hands on his fleece pajama pants. He knew something was up, so I hurried over and took the seat next to him. "Morning, Jay."

He kept moving his hands on his legs, but he looked at me. "Auntie Celeste said you got hurt."

I nodded. "I did, but it's okay."

Aunt Celeste put an arm around Jonah. Once she had his attention, she made short work of telling him about Dad's death.

I tried to zone out because his muffled sobs were a sound I'd never forget.

I rubbed his back, while Aunt Celeste rocked him. He turned away from her and gave me a fierce hug.

"I'm sorry, Jonah," I whispered.

After a long while, Jonah collected himself. He backed away from my hold, and his watery eyes met mine. "Crying sucks."

I hugged Jonah again. "It sure does."

"Do you miss Mom?" he asked, blindsiding me.

"Every damned day," I croaked.

With bloodshot, watery eyes, he stared at me. "Me too, but I don't think I'm gonna miss Dad. Not like that."

Out of everything, *that* broke my heart. And it's when I lost my shit.

Suddenly I was squeezed closer to my brother as someone wedged in behind me on the couch. Then Jonah let me go, my body was shifted and Finn held me tight to his chest.

Someone had picked up donuts from a mom-and-pop shop. Mensa brought me a powdered, blueberry-filled donut (my favorite), but I could only stomach half of it.

Auntie Celeste was explaining to Jonah about the FBI, and how he'd have to be evaluated by a doctor.

"Is that happening today?" Jonah asked.

Fiona smiled. "No. Sometime this coming week."

"Monday?" Jonah persisted.

I lifted my chin at Fiona. "He likes specifics." I patted Jonah's knee. "Probably Thursday would be my guess."

He nodded. "Thursday is good. I like Thursdays, they're my favorite."

"Why's that?" Cynic asked.

I bit back a laugh, wondering if Jonah would remember. He bumped his shoulder into mine. "Because Sissy says Thursdays are the shit."

Cynic's brows furrowed. "I'm not following."

Jonah looked him in the eye. "Because you get to be 'So Happy It's Thursday.'"

Everyone but Mensa chuckled. He just shook his head. Then again, he'd been the one to tell me about the little acronym.

Jonah glanced at Aunt Celeste and then at me. "Can I go home now?"

My eyes widened for a moment before I schooled my expression.

"There's probably going to be media outside the house today. It'll be worse if they know someone's home," Uncle Dean said.

Aunt Celeste said, "You're more than welcome to stay here, Jonah."

Jonah nodded. "I just wondered…"

From behind me, Finn said, "Gotta get somebody to clean up the kitchen, but you could go later this afternoon if you want, man."

My head twisted slowly to Finn, and I aimed a pointed look his way.

"He probably wants his own space, Riley," Finn murmured.

Jonah heard him. "I want the good internet."

I hung my head and quietly chuckled.

"Boys and their toys," Aunt Celeste muttered.

Uncle Dean cleared his throat. "I think you should sleep here tonight, though, Jonah."

Jonah nodded, surprising me.

I caught Jonah's eyes. "That means you'll have to stop around seven to get back here and go to sleep."

He rolled his eyes to the ceiling. "I know."

Mensa glanced up from his cell. "Dylan's swinging by for the house keys, him and two other prospects are gonna take care of the mess." He locked eyes with Jonah. "I can take you over there after lunch. We'll go in through the back to avoid any media. Cool?"

Jonah grinned. "Cool."

As we straightened from the turn onto Finn's street, I glimpsed the news van on the curb outside his house. Nerves and anxiety welled up inside me.

Uncle Dean said Dad's story had made the national news. Yet, I hadn't expected to see one of the local stations back at Finn's place.

Luckily, nobody else was there. I'd fully expected his Uncle Steve to be waiting for us.

Anna St. Claire slid out of the passenger side of the van and stalked up the drive to us. "Riley, I'm so sorry to—"

Finn moved in front of me. "No. You're done."

"I beg your pardon," Anna said.

Finn crossed his arms on his chest. "You got your exclusive... but then you went and called her father—"

"Good reporting covers both sides—"

"It got her pulled downtown and gave that scumbag the chance to terrorize her. All because you wanted a juicier story. No. You are done." Over his shoulder he said, "Go in the house, babe."

I didn't know how I was going to get in, but then he reached behind his back to hand me the keys. One of my goals was to start asserting myself more, but this was one confrontation I didn't want to have, so I made my way into the house.

As I walked away, Anna said in a calm tone, "I just want to chat with her."

Finn said, "That's what phones are for. You want to put her on camera again. Not happening. Leave."

A wild hair hit me as I moved further into Finn's house. I pulled my cell out and dialed Lyssa Wallace.

"Hello?" she answered.

"Lyssa, this Riley Tyndale. Would you do me a favor?"

"Uh, Riley? What kind of favor?"

I took a deep breath. "Call Anna St. Claire. She's here right now, and—"

Lyssa interrupted me, and her tone sounded relieved. "Say no more. I've got it handled."

Finn came inside a moment later, a scowl puckering his lips. "Should've just taken you to the clubhouse and told Uncle Steve to meet me there. Got that woman to go back to the van, but they aren't leaving."

I shot a wry grin at him. "For once, being my father's daughter paid off. I got Lyssa Wallace handling it."

Finn's head tipped to the side. "Don't take this the wrong way, but I'm not sure that woman could handle a damn thing."

My head wobbled. "She stood up to Dad when it counted."

His eyes widened. "Wrong. The time to stand up to him was when the abuse was clear. I don't know how long she's been working for him, but that would've been years ago."

I nodded and stepped into his space. "You're right. Still, she's going to do what she can." I slid my hands under his cut and up his chest. "Wanna make out?"

His teeth sunk into his lower lip. "There's no such thing as making out with you. It's like you have no 'off' switch and we'll be fucking on the couch in no time. Not doing anything to mess with your wound. I'll kiss you, but that's it, babe."

I tipped my face up and his lips met mine. Maybe he was right because five seconds into our kiss, I had my body pressed close to him and I wanted to hike my leg up alongside his.

A knock at the front door cut things short.

"Your uncle really does have lousy timing."

Finn tilted his head back and laughed.

Finn

Still smiling, Finn opened the door to Uncle Steve.

"You're in a chipper mood," Uncle Steve said, stepping inside.

Finn closed the door. "Not really. Riley's funny, that's all."

Uncle Steve went to the dining room table.

"You sure we couldn't handle this over the phone?" Finn asked.

"I'm sure. Have a seat. Riley, too."

Finn's body went tight. "Riley, too?"

Uncle Steve sat back in his seat. "I heard from Nina that she's coming into some money. I've seen where her father lives."

"Enough," Finn bit out.

Uncle Steve arched a brow. "Buy low, sell high, your grandfather ingrained that into me."

"Not at the price of family, he didn't. Thought you'd had a change of heart last night."

"My heart doesn't pay the bills."

Finn took a breath. "My woman isn't buying the house."

"Then sit down and tell me how much you'll give me," Uncle Steve said.

Riley came to Finn's side, her eyes on Uncle Steve. "Just you? What about your sisters?"

Finn heard the front door open.

"I'm negotiating the best deal for all of us," Uncle Steve said.

"Oh, I do not think so," Mom said.

"Now, Nina—"

"Don't 'now, Nina,' me. Laurie and I didn't agree to this."

Uncle Steve tilted his head toward Riley. "She's gonna be rich. You said he plans to marry her. It's a win-win. We won't have to sell to an investment firm, and he gets to stay in the house he's so sentimental about."

"Not sentimental —" Finn started.

Uncle Steve leaned forward. "Oh, that's right. You got business plans. Probably going to use the house as collateral for a business loan, right? We're doing you the favor here, and I intend to make it worth my while."

Finn sought patience, which was in short supply after his stilted sleep last night and the stress from this morning. His thoughts were a jumbled mess coming at him rapid-fire. He *did* plan to use the house as collateral for his business loan. If that didn't work out, then he might approach the club for backing his business. Overall, though, he wanted to make a go of it on his own, but this bullshit play had him rethinking everything.

Living in the same house as Gramps and Grandma would be cool, but after yesterday it wasn't a dealbreaker any more. He and Riley could live in a tent and he wouldn't give a damn as long as she was there by his side, healthy and happy.

He pulled a chair out, turned it backward, and straddled it. "You got a file folder with you, so you must have some figure in mind. Let's see it. Then I'll have my real estate agent call yours."

"Finneas, that isn't —"

Finn looked up at Mom. "The sooner he tips his hand, the sooner he can leave, Mom. It was a rough night last night, a rough morning, and I'll be damned if I don't have a smooth afternoon today."

"A rough morning," Uncle Steve muttered.

Finn narrowed his eyes on his uncle. "Did you watch a man find out his father was dead this morning? Listen to him say he wouldn't miss his dad – not like he missed his mom – then watch those words tear *your* woman in half? No? Then I'd say you don't get to fuckin' judge how rough my morning's been."

"You sound angry," Uncle Steve said.

"What's your price?" Finn asked.

Uncle Steve slid a manila folder across the table. "It's in there. Call me when you're ready to accept." He stood and brushed by Mom. "I'll call you later, Nina."

"I knew things sounded too good to be true last night," Riley muttered after the door closed.

Finn clenched his fists and pounded one into the table. He stood and whirled to Riley. "And *that* pisses me off even more. From now on, you should expect nothing but good things, Riles. No more waiting for the other shoe to drop or any of that negative bullshit."

Mom moved past Finn and grabbed the folder. "Oh, he did not."

Finn snuck a peek inside the folder before Mom closed it. Three hundred thousand dollars for a fifty-five-year-old, twelve hundred square foot house. "Yeah, that isn't happening. I never knew Uncle Steve wanted to fleece his own family."

"Me, neither, honey. I want to say he isn't trying to fleece you, but a figure that big, yeah. He's gotten very money-hungry and I don't like it. Something else must be going on."

"College is expensive," Riley said.

Mom shook her head. "This feels like more than that." She patted Finn's shoulder. "Now, I heard what you said about the past twenty-four hours, so I'm gonna get out of your hair. I'm leaving on Tuesday, so carve out some time to have dinner with me." She glanced at Riley. "Both of you, but maybe you can pick some place those church ladies don't like."

Riley laughed. "You got it, Nina."

He had Riley naked and on top of him, hands down his favorite position with her, since he could watch her eyes as her orgasm built, and then he could watch his stiff cock slide in and out of her warm, wet pussy.

Yeah, definitely his favorite.

Her straight, brown hair hung over her shoulders, but it wasn't long enough to cover her tits. She had enough of it that the edge of bandage was hidden, though.

She lifted up and slammed down on him fast. He put his hands on her hips to slow her tempo.

"Finn," she whined.

"Slow, baby," he murmured and captured her nipple in his mouth.

Her back arched and she sunk down... slowly this time. He let his fingers glide around to her pussy, finding her clit, and he gave it a cursory stroke.

"Tease," she breathed.

With his hand at her hip, he encouraged her to lift up. She did and he let her set the pace, while he sucked hard on her breast and rubbed her clit.

"Oh, yeah," she moaned.

He let go of her nipple in order to concentrate on bucking his hips. He'd noticed that when she picked up speed, she would demand he fuck her harder. This time he intended to deliver before she asked for it.

"Yes, Finn. It's about time."

The urge to toss her to her back and pound into her ate at him. He gripped her hips tighter, his breathing turned to grunting.

"Love how you fuck me," she breathed.

"I love fucking your juicy cunt, Riley."

She reached up and tweaked one of her nipples. "Keep talking..."

A moment after she stopped speaking, he felt her pussy spasm around his cock. His orgasm wasn't far behind. He picked up his pace, knowing he should loosen his grip on her, but he couldn't. She made him lose his mind when they had sex. Four more strokes and he blew his load inside her with a groaning exhale.

His eyes closed and his hips bucked twice more. He wished he could recover faster.

"I love you," she said.

He opened his eyes. "I love you. Want to do this all fucking night if I could."

Her eyes lit. "Sounds like a plan to me, baby."

He chuckled. "Yeah, but my cock doesn't harden at your command. At least, not when I come like that."

She kissed a path along his neck. "I do love a challenge."

He guided her face to his and kissed her. There was so much tongue action, he thought she might get him hard again.

He broke the kiss. "Not today, woman. We need to catch a nap, which means I'm cleaning you up."

Ever so slowly, she slid his cock out of her slick heat. "I can handle that myself, Finn."

He shifted them both to their sides. "I want to do it, baby. Puts me in the perfect position to eat you out when I'm finished, give you another orgasm, and then we'll rest."

"You have the best plans," she said, smiling. "But I'm getting my hands on you at the same time."

"Nope. It's all about you, woman. Love you so damned much, and yesterday —"

Her fingers came to his lips. "We aren't talking about yesterday any more, dammit."

He kissed her fingers, then kissed her lips. "Now who has the best plans?"

She acted as though she were contemplating it. "Pretty sure it's still you. Hurry up with that washcloth. I'm exceptionally horny."

Chapter 19

Decision

Riley

I smelled Julie's strong perfume before I heard her snide words.

"Oh, *you're* here."

For a Monday, today had been going rather well. I'd arrived at Har's shop at seven twenty-seven. He led me inside the lobby-slash-office area, which smelled like a blend of paint fumes, coffee, and a hint of exhaust.

He'd thrown an arm out at the desk. "It's all yours. Gamble did what he could with it, seeing as Julie went out of her way to douse everything in coffee before she left."

"What?" I whispered.

Har looked at me. "Yeah. Figured Finn would have shared that."

My eyes slid to the side. "No. Who does that?"

"Pretty sure I asked the same damned thing," Gamble said, coming out of what I assumed was a small bathroom, since I heard the post-flush sounds of a toilet.

"Anyway, your salary amount is listed inside that folder along with a form for taxes and direct deposit. That book on the desk is the schedule.

She supposedly had things set up on a Google calendar, too. I'm starting to doubt that."

"Or she sabotaged that in advance," Gamble suggested.

Har tossed his hands up for a second. "Either way, do what you need to do to get organized and keep us on track. Ask Gamble if you got any questions. If he can't answer them, find me."

And that was the last I'd seen of Har or Gamble all morning.

Now that Julie was here, I was stunned they hadn't seen her in the parking lot.

I glanced up at her. "Yeah, I'm here. I think it's crazy that you'd take your chances slinking in here like this. But, really, why are you here?"

"To get my final paycheck."

I tilted my head. "Funny. Har told me I get paid with direct deposit."

Her head reared back. "Wait, what? You're... *working* here? I figured you only worked on your knees."

"You feel like pulling her hair out, I won't stop you, Riley," Har said from the back of the room.

I aimed a closed-lip smile at Har. "Can't waste my time like that, sir. Besides, she'd enjoy it too much."

"What's that supposed to mean?" she demanded, her eyes glittering at me.

Gamble trudged in from the garage bays. His eyes went wide, seeing Julie.

"What do you want?" Har asked.

"I want my final paycheck. I'm entitled to my unused vacation days."

"You used all your days," Har said.

She scoffed. "I didn't. It's in the calendar on the desk."

Har nodded. "That *is* where we note used vacation and sick days. After you spilled coffee all over it, I had to take the time to record it all on computer. Which is how I know you used all your days."

"You're serious?"

"Very," Har said in a tone that scared me even more than Dad on his worst day.

She scanned me in an up-and-down once over, then she looked Har dead in the eyes. "It's just like I said to Cynic last spring, at least I can see you *can't* do better than me."

She turned and flounced out the door.

Gamble's voice was laced with anger. "What a —"

"Save it," Har interrupted. "Thinking Riley's right. She isn't worth your time or energy."

"Time for lunch?" Gamble asked.

Har nodded, but kept his eyes on me. "Depending on how slammed we are, Mondays and Fridays are long-lunch days. As much as you can, schedule shit like your dentist or doctor appointments on those days."

Gamble frowned. "You know, Julie never did that."

Har's head tilted. "Doesn't mean she didn't get the same message. A lot of shit she didn't do, but should have."

"That's the damned truth. We taking Riley to lunch?" Gamble asked.

My eyes went wide. "I actually brought —"

Har smiled. "Yeah, I noticed that you had a cooler with you when you got here. Friday, we'll take you to lunch… though my guess is you don't want to go to The Fillin' Station anytime soon."

I shrugged a shoulder. "It's actually one of my favorite places, that I only went to on weekends because of Dad. I'm not going to let him ruin that for me."

"Good," Har said. "We'll be back around two."

The entire front lot could be seen from my desk and I watched them ride off in opposite directions.

Gamble had been right earlier. If Julie had set up a computerized calendar, she'd deleted it, because I couldn't find any trace of it. The hard copy of the schedule went out through June of next year and I was up to March on the new Google calendar. I got back to putting in spring appointments. Once I finished that, I'd stop and eat lunch before getting acquainted with Quickbooks.

The front door opened and Finn strode inside. He locked the door, flipped the sign in the window to the 'Closed' side, and twisted the blinds in the front window to block out the light. Then he went to the door to the garage and locked that one.

"Hey... Was I supposed to make it look like the shop is actually closed?"

He turned to me with a huge grin. "Fuck if I know. I did it for privacy."

"Privacy?" I asked as he stooped over and kissed my neck.

"Um-hmm."

I stood. "While we eat lunch? I brought the leftovers from dinner with your Mom, and —"

He turned and sat in my vacated chair, pulling me onto his lap. "Not here for lunch, Riley."

Everything clicked and my mouth fell open. "We aren't having sex in here, Finn. On my first day? You've lost your mind."

He chuckled. "They aren't gonna care. Hell, they won't even know, if you stop asking me questions."

I wiggled out of his hold and planted my butt on the edge of my desk. "Finn, this is crazy. They'll fire me."

His lips twisted with skepticism. "You are a former club bunny. They've probably both seen you doing far worse around the clubhouse and they won't care. Hell... for all I know they might want to watch."

My head reared back and Finn chuckled. "I'm kidding. They wouldn't do that, but it's good to know you got a hard limit."

My eyes went wide. "And you don't? You said you didn't want to share me, now you want people to watch. I'm not buying that, Finn."

"No, I don't. But I like nooners. Figure that's the other upside to you working here. You'll be around two men who won't let you take any shit, and on long-lunch Mondays, we can have quickies."

"At the house," I deadpanned.

"Thought you liked to try new things?" he asked, skating his hands along my thighs and up my skirt.

"Finn," I admonished, but it held no venom because his fingers had slid inside my panties.

He grinned. "You're so wet. Something about this turns you on."

"Being near you turns me on."

"Then really get near me, baby," he said, being a total flirt.

I pointed a finger at him. "I'm not gonna let you manipulate me like this all the time, mister."

"Really?"

I launched myself off the desk and straddled his lap. He chuckled like he'd won a game, and I put my lips to his neck and bit him playfully.

"Oh, yeah. Mark me, woman. Let's see what you can do."

I pulled my face from his neck. "You can't be serious. No man likes when women do that."

His eyes rounded. "I do. Hell, I wanted to mark you last week, but wasn't sure how you'd take it until you reminded me of our first weekend together. Then I realized that I didn't want your dad to have any ammunition to say I was abusing you or some shit. So, give me what you got, Riley. I want everyone to know I'm yours."

I wanted everyone to know that, too, and it set me off. With my lips back at his neck, my hands went to his jeans, only he'd already unbuttoned them. Talk about being prepared.

"That all you got?" he asked, his voice husky.

I pulled away, raised my hands to cup his cheeks and kissed him as hard as I could.

He yanked at my panties, and I lifted up so he wouldn't tear them. I felt the tip of his cock brushing my folds and I moved to line him up with me. Then, I sank down on him and I felt it. Not just the fullness of having him, but how very right it felt.

"We're going to hell, Finn. This is so wrong."

He grinned. "The hell we are. I'm a biker and so is your boss. He wouldn't care if I shove everything off this desk to fuck you on it as long as I don't spill coffee all over it."

I chuckled. "You're right. So get to fucking me."

His eyes flared and I found myself bouncing on his cock. Between the thrill of potentially getting caught and Finn's general excitement, my orgasm built stronger and faster than usual. He came not long after I did and he held my body close to him in my office chair.

"I'm gonna think of this *every* time I sit in my chair."

His finger traced my cheekbone. "I know. All part of my plan, baby."

Even for being as fast as we were, I'd broken out into a sweat. "Oh no," I whispered.

"What?"

"They're gonna smell the sex in the air."

I spied the small mark I'd made on his neck when he tipped his head back with laughter. His eyes met mine. "Woman, we'd have to have a three-day fuckfest to obliterate the smell of paint and exhaust in here."

I shook my head. "You're a smoker. Your sense of smell isn't as strong."

His body shook with silent laughter and he tipped his head back even as he shook it. "It's gettin' deep in here."

I gave into temptation and lowered my mouth to his neck.

His body stopped shaking and he cupped the back of my head. "You trying to get caught, woman?"

Slowly, I backed away. "No, but I love seeing my mark on you."

"Keep talking like that and I'll fuck you again."

I smirked. "You say that like it's a threat, when baby, it's anything but."

He lifted me off him and set me on my feet. "You hit the bathroom first."

I straightened my skirt. "I'll be quick."

Finn

Ten minutes later, he'd dragged a chair out of Har's office. He sat next to Riley's desk while they split her leftover shrimp scampi and pasta.

Her lips twisted to the side. "I suppose it wasn't a good idea to bring seafood for lunch on my first day."

A mischievous thought hit him and he grinned. "Or it was brilliant since it'll mask the scent of sex in the air."

"Right," she drawled.

He took a swig from his Coke Zero. "I made a decision."

"About what?"

"The house. I'm not gonna buy it."

Her eyes widened. "Finn! You're kidding. It's all you've been talking about for like six months."

His head turned and he aimed his side-eye at her. "How would you know?"

One of her brows went up and down. "You may have noticed how I looked at you, but you didn't pick up on how much of a lurker I can be. I kept myself in earshot of you any time I could... without being noticed much. I listened to you go on to Gamble, Mensa, and Joules about how much you wanted that house. I just hadn't realized how much of it was because of your Gramps."

He sighed. "For all the damned good it does me. Uncle Steve's fucked it all up."

She tossed her hands up. "But Finn, it doesn't have to be like that. If you're serious about me and want to marry me, then what's mine is yours and vice versa, right?"

"Not the point, Riley."

She tossed her plastic fork in the Styrofoam container. "I'm gonna have to find a place to live... my guess is you don't want to live with Jonah in Dad's house."

"You're assuming it doesn't get seized."

"You're assuming they find Jonah one-hundred-percent competent. If they don't, the amount of fraud lessens. But my point here, is that if I spend any of the money I've been given on myself, it's only going to be for a car and a place to live. The rest is for Jonah and his care. Why *shouldn't* we use my money to buy the house? I didn't see your uncle's price, and I'm guessing it's too much. Get over the manly pride, call the realtor, and force your uncle to make a fair deal. It sounded to me like he needs money fast — which would also explain his greed."

"Would it though?" Finn asked.

"It might, if something else is going on, like Nina suspected Saturday morning."

"He's just greedy, which is disappointing as fuck."

She leaned forward, her blouse falling open. He forced himself to keep his eyes on hers. "Bottom line, *we* buy the house, you won't have rent or a mortgage. You can use all the money you have saved when you apply for a business loan."

"I'll keep that in mind, but the more I think about it, the more convinced I am that we'll outgrow that house. I don't want all our kids to have their own rooms immediately, but... if anything happens where we need to take Jonah in, we're gonna need space."

He saw her warring with herself. "I want to argue with that, but I can't. At the same time, part of me thinks you're reacting to Saturday's argument with him. Whether that's true or not, please be sure, honey. It's a big decision and it's clear it matters a lot to you."

He nodded.

"Did you tell your Mom about your decision?"

"Was gonna do that tonight when I make dinner for her."

The key scraped in the lock and Gamble came inside with a confused expression. "What's the big idea locking the — wait, don't tell me..." His eyes shot to Finn's. "Seriously?"

Finn shook his head and blanked his expression. "No. Riley turned the open sign around before I got here. I just encouraged her to lock the doors since she's here alone."

Thanks to his years of prospecting, Finn withstood Gamble's dead-eyed stare.

Finally, Gamble shook his head. "I wasn't born last night, motherfucker. Least you could do is —"

"You said 'Wait, don't tell me,'" Riley said.

Gamble gave a growly sigh, dropped something in Har's office, and went out to the garage.

"Well, I'm mortified," Riley muttered.

"He doesn't give a shit, babe. He's more irritated it's me who got laid and not him."

"Still embarrassing, but I'll get over it."

He grabbed the empty container from the desk and took it to a large trash can at the back of the room. "You got any special requests for dinner tonight?"

She shrugged a shoulder, "I'm not fussy, Finn. Make something your mother loves."

He nodded, then pointed a finger at her. "Don't make plans with your aunt and uncle for Thanksgiving. I'm taking you and Jonah to Mom and Dad's. You'll get to meet Wes, and Jonah will probably love hitting Atlanta."

"Obviously. He's a big Georgia Tech fan... do you know if they're playing in Atlanta this year? It would blow his mind if he got to go to that."

He chuckled. "I'll find out. And just to say, babe, you better pack your Pepsi One because Coke's headquarters —"

"Are in Atlanta. I know. Dad dragged us there the first time he took us to a Georgia Tech game. Only thing that made it worth it was how much Jonah loved it, especially the part where you get to sample sodas from all over the world."

Finn did a slow nod. "Now it makes sense. You love Pepsi to spite your Dad. Another damned thing he fucked up."

"Believe it or not, we can't blame Dad for that, since it started long before then."

He smiled. "Noted. I love you, and I'll see you at home soon."

Mom set her wine glass down, and Finn realized it was her second glass. He should have paid closer attention to that.

"First of all, Finn, Steve isn't the executor of the estate, I am. He likes to think he's in charge, but the fact is nothing moves forward without me."

"Mom," Finn started.

"Nope. You don't have kids yet, so you can't understand this, but parents know their kids."

"You don't say," he deadpanned.

"Young man, what I'm saying is that I know making Wes the executor of my estate is a heap of responsibility that would be better suited to you. However, asking Wes to deal with being my caretaker is a better choice because he's more... peaceful."

"He's seventeen, Mom."

She grinned. "Right, but those personality traits already shine through, honey. My point is that Dad knew I would weigh things in regard to selling the house. As you mentioned a moment ago, your uncle is money-hungry. That clouds judgment, which leads to bad decisions. Riley's right. Have your realtor get in contact with his. In this case, there's something to be said for having third parties involved."

Finn nodded. "I'll consider it, Mom."

"All right, let's have dessert. I'm going to get rolling first thing in the morning, and Riley has her new job, so we aren't doing breakfast."

At the weekly session of church on Friday, Block ran down the club finances. His eyes darted around the room. "Even if there's money in the coffers, all of our bills have been going up. We should consider other revenue streams now, so we can keep the club in the black."

Gamble tipped his head toward Finn. "I hear Finn wants to open his own AC business."

"That's several months down the road, Gamble."

Gamble shrugged a shoulder. "It takes months for us to back a business, too."

Har nodded. "If you're interested in having us back your business, you need to talk to me, Block, and Brute. Cynic, too if he's free – otherwise, we'll fill him in."

Finn nodded. "To be honest, I'd hoped to go it alone since there are programs out there for veterans who are starting a business."

"Cutting out your brothers?" Gamble asked.

Finn shook his head. "Not really. Two of our new prospects are going through trade school right now. I'll most likely hire them once they earn their patch and things are up and running."

Gamble's lips tipped up. "You can't steal our new admin. She's done more for us in five days than Julie did in five months."

Finn gave a slow head shake. "She and I already agreed we aren't cut out to work together."

"Can't imagine why," Gamble muttered with a sly grin.

"Let's stay focused," Brute said. He caught Finn's gaze. "Every so often people call Meg thinking we do full overhauls of duct work and AC issues; I'll be sure to have her put your business at the top of her referral list."

"That'd be cool, but I gotta get things up and running first."

Mensa leaned forward. "Are we moving onto a new subject?"

Har nodded. "You got an issue?"

"We need to find a different leather shop. Nadia's nephew is an FBI agent."

Block shook his head. "That isn't necessarily a bad thing."

"Well, I don't think they should be in the clubhouse in the future."

"Whitney isn't the problem you think she is," Finn said, looking at Mensa.

"Riley's got you —"

"It's got nothing to do with Riley, man."

"Did you forget how she let Riley go alone and —"

"No, but you see your sibling for the first time in months, you'd get distracted, too."

Brute tapped the table with his finger. "We aren't doing anything illegal any more."

"We don't always allow the law to get involved, either," Roman countered.

Mensa nodded. "Right, and that's the point. We all know to keep our shit tight outside the clubhouse, but brothers get loaded in the common room and Whitney or Nadia's around to overhear it... who the hell knows what happens next? It makes sense to keep them out."

Joules cleared his throat. "We don't have to hunt for a new leather shop for this. Nadia's been here maybe five times in the past twenty years we've worked with that shop. No reason we can't keep her niece at arm's length, too."

Har nodded. "My thoughts exactly." He turned to Cynic. "Inform Sandy and the prospects: unless they're told otherwise, Nadia and Whitney aren't to be here."

Finn didn't envy Cynic, he could only imagine how Sandy was going to blow when she heard this news.

Epilogue

Behind Me

Riley

Three months later...

"I'm right chuffed about this," Whitney said from the other side of the room.

My head swiveled ever so slowly to her, side-eye in full effect. She looked stunning in her navy blue, halter-style sheath dress and with her blonde hair swept up off her neck.

She grinned. "What? I've been binging that British baking show."

I stared at the wall behind her.

"You don't believe me?"

I looked at her fully. "I can't say I made an art of lying to my dad, but at the same time... I did it so much, I'm no slouch either. Every bit of what you said reeks of falsehoods."

"Falsehoods?"

"Don't change the subject. What are you so pleased about?"

"The fact I'm in your wedding, and your cousin doesn't know it yet because his lazy ass missed the rehearsal last night."

"Oh, he knows," Aurora said, a large foundation powder brush in her hand. "Why do you think he skipped out?"

Whitney rolled her eyes while she applied some lip gloss. "Men. So damned immature."

Beside me, Vickie chuckled. "Or just paranoid. He did say you'd never be back inside the clubhouse. Why do you think we have to get ready out here in this..." She circled her hand around in the air. "...Workout shed?"

Whitney's head wobbled with attitude as she said, "Well, he won't keep me from the reception."

Victoria raised her chin. "Which is why there's a tent out there."

"What a jerk," Whitney said, putting her make-up away.

I shrugged a shoulder. "You probably should have come clean about being related to an FBI agent, Whit, instead of claiming he works in security."

"*Would* you stay still!" Aurora admonished as she applied eyeliner to my eyes. "Denver, get me a bobby pin. I forgot how difficult her straight hair can be."

Denver rooted around in Aurora's bag and came up with a comb and a bobby pin. "Here. And just to let you know, Jonah texted. Says he's never seen Finn so nervous."

"Really?" I asked. "You'd think making me his property would have cured him of that. Plus, getting married in the eyes of the law is all he's talked about the since Christmas. That and starting a family. It's like he wants everything to happen, and it needs to happen immediately."

"Men are rather crazy like that," Victoria said.

Aurora smiled. "Does he know about your gift?"

I tried not to shake my head since she still had the eyeliner pencil in hand. "Not yet, but it was a close call yesterday morning."

"What's the gift?" Denver asked.

My eyes slid to her. "I got a tattoo."

Denver's eyes lit up. "Really? Where?"

I moved my robe a couple inches to show her the heart with Finn's name in the center.

"That is a choice," Denver said.

"Denver!" Aurora said. "You just turned eighteen, but I swear you still act like you're eight."

"What? Some people are superstitious and think inking someone's name on you could lead to bad luck. Plus, it's already over her heart, that seems redundant."

I laughed. "You're not wrong, but I liked the way this looked compared to just a scrolling script of his name."

There was a knock at the door, and I righted my robe.

Since she stood closest to the door, Whitney opened it a crack. "What's the password?"

"Has she been drinking?" I whispered to Aurora.

"Just the shot we all had an hour ago."

"Man incoming," Whitney announced, and Uncle Dean stepped inside.

He wore a crisp, navy-blue pinstriped suit with a shiny, lime-green tie patterned with minuscule stars. I hadn't realized, in choosing navy-blue dresses for Victoria, Whitney, Aurora, and Denver that it made it easy for a man like Uncle Dean to match them.

The smile I gave him was wry. "I thought we agreed you weren't going to dress up. Wes and Jonah aren't suited up because none of the Riot brothers are going to wear suits."

Uncle Dean grinned and shook a finger at me. "I met a man named Sam out there. He's a biker's father, but I like what he said best." He paused and shoved his hands in his pockets. "It's the bride's day, but sometimes the men have ideas about the big day, too. He was referring to the groom, but by God, I'm not giving you away wearing jeans. This day is important, and I want you to know I'm taking it serious."

Moisture gathered in my eyes.

Aurora spotted it and shook her head, grabbing a tissue. "Nope, nope, no, we aren't crying. Not now, and hopefully not later, either. Now, I'm almost done, so no more talking."

Victoria led my friends out of the small shed and I stood.

Uncle Dean put his hands on my shoulders. "You look radiant, Riley Jean."

"Thank you, Uncle Dean."

"You're not going to regret this."

I tilted my head. "Is that a question or a statement?"

He smiled. "A statement. I can see that you and Finn have quite the bond. Taking this step isn't something you'll regret. That's clear as day from the way you two are with each other."

"Yeah," I whispered, nodding.

He stared at me for a loaded moment. "Your father missed out on so many good things where you're concerned. Celeste and I wish we'd recognized your troubles sooner."

I shook my head. "Don't beat yourself up like that. I'm pretty good at hiding things."

He nodded. "Right. Well, a word to the wise from an old guy like me who's been married for over thirty years: *don't* hide anything from Finn."

I smiled. "Yeah. I wouldn't dream of it. Besides, he's good at seeing through my bullshit anyway."

He returned my smile. "I've noticed. That's how I know he's good for you. Let's not keep him waiting; he was sweating bullets when I saw him last."

We stepped out of the shed into the mild early-February sunshine. An archway had been set up fifty feet away with rows of chairs lined up on either side of a long white runner. Finn's side of the aisle had tons of people, mine... not as much. Though, Two-Times, Sandy, and Nadia were seated on my side, which made me smile. Joules wasn't seated at all because he was marrying us.

I had informed Finn that I didn't want music playing when I walked down the aisle to him. After a lengthy discussion, he'd agreed.

Except it seemed he'd agreed the same way Uncle Dean had agreed to my no-suit edict.

We took two steps on the white runner, and "Woman, Woman," by AWOLNATION started playing.

Finn turned his head and his gaze locked with mine. I widened my eyes and he simply shrugged.

His lips mouthed the word, "Listen."

I took the time to listen to the raspy lyrics, and Aurora's declaration of 'no crying' went out the window. In my mind, the chorus had it backward. Still, the message was clear, hit me deep, and in the end it was right. The worst was definitely behind me.

Finn

The sight of Riley in a lacy, short-sleeve mini-dress made his heart pound. He fought his dick getting hard, but there was nothing for it. He couldn't conjure other thoughts at this moment. He couldn't tear his eyes from her.

The music started right on time and he loved the annoyed look in her eyes.

"Listen," he whispered.

Her expression relaxed as she did... then he noticed her lips press together and her eyes shone in the sunlight. A couple tears streamed down her face. It made him feel like a jackass that he'd essentially done that to her, but brides cried when they walked down the aisle, regardless. At least he knew she understood how he felt about her.

No doubt about it, after this day – the worst of everything was behind them.

Finn's realtor had advised him to let his grandparents' house go. The price was exorbitant, the termite bond had lapsed (Finn didn't know anything about this, though records indicated Uncle Steve did), and the roof was close to ten years old. Finn losing interest in buying dismayed Uncle Steve, since he thought it would be a quick sale. Instead, they moved into Riley's Dad's house, in part to make things steady for Jonah, and in part because it was closer to the clubhouse and Har's shop.

Jonah's therapy was going well, but he still needed help on occasion. All three of them wanted to get out of Tyndale's house, and Brute had tipped Finn off to a vacant duplex. Riley and Jonah loved the building on sight, and Finn relented on Riley buying the home where he and his woman would live.

Riley had been right. It stung his pride to have her buy their house, but this property was ideal. Jonah would have the privacy any man at twenty-three should have, but they were literally right next door if something went wrong.

The closing was scheduled for the week after Finn and Riley came back from their honeymoon in Nashville. His woman claimed she didn't want to chase the dream of professional singing, but Finn wanted her to be damn sure about that. She wasn't going to wake up at sixty or some other age wondering 'what if?'

Not on his watch.

"When can I start prospecting?" Wes asked.

Any other day, that would garner Finn's full attention, but today he muttered, "Not any time soon, and your ass doesn't even live here."

"No, but I want to find a woman like her. She's hot."

Finn exhaled. "Are you trying to get punched?"

Joules chuckled. "Focus. You only get this moment once, brother."

Aurora, Sandy, and Whitney had balked at Riley's musical choices for dancing with Jonah and then dancing with Finn. Since he'd been in the room during that meeting of the minds, the quelling look he aimed at them ended their criticism.

Now, he stood next to Mensa watching his woman and brother-in-law dance to the fast-paced song, "Zero." Jonah had declared he wouldn't dance to a slow song because that was boring. Finn hadn't seen such a huge, bright smile on Jonah's face since he'd met him a few months ago, and in turn Riley's laughter held more lightness and joy than he'd ever heard from her.

"You better make her happy," Mensa said, putting a beer bottle to his lips.

Finn shoved his hands into his jeans pockets. "No way I'm gonna fuck her over after all the shit she's been through."

Mensa nodded. "I'm just saying, you better not."

Finn rolled his eyes.

"Encourage your woman to cut this party short."

Finn glowered at Mensa. "Why the fuck would I do that? I've never seen her so damned happy."

Mensa's eyes cut across the tent to where Whitney stood with Nadia, Joules, and Sandy. "The sooner we get that bitch out of here, the easier I'll breathe."

Finn locked eyes with Mensa. "Put yourself out of your misery. Go hate-fuck her and be done with it."

Mensa's body shifted toward Finn. "Say that shit again?"

"You heard me. Whatever your problem is with her, man, it's bullshit. Get her out of your system and move the hell on."

Tiny's gravelly voice came over the speakers. "Our man of the hour is normally our DJ, so put your hands together for Mr. and Mrs. O'Halloran."

Finn crossed the dance floor before Mensa could say anything – or worse, punch him. He grabbed Riley's hand at the moment the piano notes started on Saint Motel's "Cold Cold Man."

Her infectious, beaming smile made him grin.

She wrapped her hands around his neck. "I love you, Finn."

"I love you, too, Riley O'Halloran."

"I know you probably want to get out of here, but this is the best day ever."

He smiled. "Damn right, baby. The first day of the rest of your life is always the best day ever."

Thank you for reading.
If you want more of Finn & Riley, sign up for my newsletter and you'll receive the Bonus Epilogue for Finn's Fury. Scan the QR code below using your smartphone to sign up.

The Riot continues with Mensa's Match.
Turn the page for a sneak peek.

Sneak Peek at Mensa's Match

Whitney

"**A**re you sure, Whitney?" Ben asked.

I resisted the urge to pull my cell phone from my ear and chuck it across the room. No amount of deep breathing could calm me down, but I tried again anyway. It gave me time to control my tone of voice. "Yes, Ben. I'm sure. My texts were rather clear."

"It's just a misunderstanding, baby."

My jaw shifted and I considered getting up from my seat inside Blue Moon Bayou Pizza. The lunch rush was in full swing, though, and seeing as how my order hadn't been called, if I stepped outside I'd never get my table back.

I firmed up my tone, but kept it from being bitchy.

Who was I kidding? When Ben didn't hear what he wanted to hear, he always called my firm tone bitchy.

"Agent Heston, we're done. You let it slip that we had been involved, and rather than both of us losing our jobs, only I did. I'm being as civil as I can, but hear this. I'm *very* sure that we are finished."

Ben said something else, probably more crap about how he didn't play the system or something about his good ol' boy charm, but I was distracted. The door had opened, the bells tinkled, and three Riot MC brothers sauntered inside wearing their colors.

Thank God, I sat in full view of the front door.

I ducked my head down in hopes they wouldn't notice me. Many would assume that my FBI training developed my habit of sitting with my back to the wall, but Langley didn't teach me that, Aunt Nadia did.

Aunt Nadia taught me a lot of things. Like not taking shit from anyone. Like living life to the fullest. And most recently, embracing life's curveballs and seeing the silver lining – though that lesson was still a struggle.

It was the only reason I wasn't appealing my termination. In many ways, Ben Heston owed Aunt Nadia a boatload of gratitude.

"Are you listening to me, Whitney?" Ben demanded.

"Can't say that I am. We're done. Stop calling me, Ben."

I ended the call, and my order was announced. My stomach growled as I sat down with my two slices of mushroom and pepperoni.

I heard the bells tinkle again, looked up, and sighed. This couldn't be happening. I specifically came to Blue Moon Bayou because it was a pizzeria. He wasn't supposed to be here, seeing as how he carried an EpiPen for his dairy allergy. Nevertheless, Kenneth "Mensa" Ragstone sauntered inside, and my heartrate accelerated.

Nothing about this was right. I gravitated to the good guys. I didn't go for the bad boys. I only wanted to see Mensa one way: him walking in front of me with his hands behind his back wearing handcuffs *I* put on him.

Yet, that wasn't to be. I hadn't been sent here to investigate him. I'd been ordered to befriend a judge's daughter. My orders turned into a genuine friendship – a definite silver lining.

The judge was suspected of fraud and other things. Over the course of the investigation, I'd come across Mensa's file. My superiors thought he might be in on the fraud, but we found no evidence to support that. In fact, aside from a drunk-and-disorderly when he turned twenty-one, it appeared that Mensa hadn't so much as jaywalked in the past fifteen years.

Rumor had it he came by his road name due to his brilliance at not getting caught doing anything. He wasn't a book-smart genius. He was a genius thanks to his street-smarts.

Thus the idea of bringing him in appealed to me. He hadn't been caught doing anything wrong, but my gut said he'd committed plenty of crimes.

That made my attraction to him all the more irritating and baffling.

My damned hormones were getting the best of me – had to be.

Nothing else explained my eyes seeking his whenever we were in the same room. The fact I went out of my way to do the opposite of whatever he wanted, like when he wanted me out of the Riot MC clubhouse back in November, but I'd stuck around until after midnight.

Now that I'd been terminated, I had no reason to give a damn about Mensa. Hell, I had no reason to stay in town... but I couldn't decide where I wanted to go. Or what I wanted to do.

You want to do Mensa, a little voice inside my head suggested.

I clenched my teeth.

I despised that I lusted over him. He wasn't my type and not just because he was an outlaw biker. My prior lovers had been over six feet tall, blue-eyed, clean-cut men. Sometimes they were built, other times they had the beginnings of the classic 'Dad bod.' I didn't care as long as a man was funny and friendly. The ability to take instruction or at least listen to what I wanted in the bedroom didn't hurt, either.

Mensa didn't qualify on most of those counts.

According to the dossier I had on him, he stood only two inches taller than my five-foot-eight-inches.

His brown eyes weren't soulful, no, they were so cold he could stare down the devil himself. When we argued, some foolish part of me craved the moment that I earned that stare-down.

He was built, but he didn't flaunt it.

He wasn't the least bit friendly to me, which meant I had no idea if he was funny.

And obviously, I had no idea about his behavior in the bedroom.

Hard to say what I hated more – the fact that I was attracted to him or the fact that he could be so freaking attractive with his messy hair and scruffy beard.

While I ate my pizza, I made note of where each Riot MC brother sat at their table. Mensa had his back to me. I had an excellent profile view of Gamble and Brute. Har faced me, but his focus was on the other men.

I had my head tilted down to read an article on my phone while I sipped my Dr. Pepper. Someone pulled the chair across from me out from under the table. I looked up to see Mensa sitting down. This was unexpected, but I kept myself from showing a reaction.

"I've been looking into you," he said.

I lifted my chin an inch.

His nostrils flared. "But I can't find anything."

Resisting the urge to smile almost overwhelmed me.

He narrowed one eye at me. "That tells me my gut is right."

I turned my head, and noticed Gamble and Har were watching us. My lips tipped up when I looked back to Mensa. "And what is your gut right about?"

He shifted the chair back. "That you're trouble. Do us all a favor, stay away from Riley."

That rankled.

"She's my friend. Or isn't she allowed to make those decisions for herself?"

"That's low," Mensa hissed.

I shrugged a shoulder. "You're part of the same family tree as her, for all I know you've got the same controlling ideas that her Daddy did."

His lip curled. "I don't operate that way, Blume."

I nodded once. "That's a relief – and I mean that."

"The fact I can't find out anything about you tells me you're not from here."

"Your point?" I asked when he lapsed into silence.

He shook his head. "When are you leaving town?"

I assumed an innocent expression. "What makes you think I'm leaving town?"

"Your brother left. Figured you won't be too far behind him."

If I were still employed, he'd be right – though not because I was following Wyatt, but because I'd be assigned to a new case by now.

The idea that Mensa wanted me gone bothered me.

It shouldn't, but it did. He wasn't the first person who didn't take a shine to me, and seeing as that feeling was mutual it spurred more confusion. Why did I care what he thought of me? Why did I want him to want me to stick around?

I couldn't contemplate that with his brown eyes boring into me.

I concentrated on putting my phone in my tiny purse before I looked up at him. "This might disappoint you, but I don't know that I will leave town. This isn't such a bad place. The weather's nice, there's a beach, and Aunt Nadia's cool as hell. I could see myself sticking around a while."

He twisted his head to the side and exhaled hard. He turned back, those eyes blazing. "You're full of shit and you're hiding something. I mean it, stay away from me, my brothers, and damn sure my cousin, Riley."

"Or what?" I asked, unable to stop myself.

He stood and looked down his nose at me. "Or there's gonna be hell to pay."

Available for Pre-order now

ACKNOWLEDGEMENTS

There are so many people to thank for this book. As always, thank you to you the reader. I'm honored that you want to spend your reading time with my characters and their stories.

Thank you to Cyndy with Engle & Völkers for answering my questions. Any real estate mistakes in this book are purely my own.

Thank you to the readers in the Romance Unraveled group for weighing in on cat names. Big kudos to Pegeen for giving me the name for Finn's cat, Baller is much happier with the name you came up with.

Thank you to the Target company for selling the perfect journal notebooks — no joke, most of this book was written by hand and retyped later.

The cover for this book would not exist without the talents of cover model, Shane MacKinnon, and photographer, Golden Czermak at Furious Fotog. Thank you for everything you do for the book community!

Thank you to Barbara J. Bailey for catching my lingual missteps.

Many thanks to Enticing Journey Book Promotions and the numerous bloggers and influencers who help get the word out about my books. I appreciate it more than you know!

Thank you to the ladies in my reader group. This book feels like it's taken forever, and to some extent it has — thanks to those of you who told me Melissa didn't need a book (you were all right!). If I'd gone that route years ago, Riley likely wouldn't have shown up for me the way she did.

    Thanks to my friends and family for your unwavering support. Much like being hangry, I'm sorry if I was snappish when desperately trying to finish this book!

OTHER BOOKS BY KAREN RENEE

Please visit your favorite retailer to discover other books by Karen Renee:

The Riot MC Series

Unforeseen Riot

Inciting a Riot

Into the Riot

Calming the Riot

Foolish Riot

Respectable Riot

Starting the Riot

A Friendsgiving Riot – a short story found in Romancing the Holidays

Rough Riot

Fighting a Riot

The Riot MC Box Set Series

The Riot MC Box Set #1 (Books 0.5, 1, 2, & 3)

The Riot MC Box Set #2 (Books 4, 5, & 6)

The Beta Series

Beta Test

The O-Town Series

Relentless Habit

Wild Forces

Abrupt Changes

Holiday Fixation (An O-Town short story) – found in Romancing the Holidays, Vol. Two

O-Town Series Complete Box Set

Riot MC Biloxi Chapter Series

Harm's Way

Brute's Strength

FINN'S FURY

Roman's War

Cynic's Stance

Gamble's Risk

Block's Road

Tiny Problem

Finn's Fury

Mensa's Match
The Riot MC Next Generation

Break Out

ABOUT KAREN RENEE

Karen Renee is the award-winning author of the Riot MC, Riot MC Biloxi, Beta, and O-Town series of books. She once crunched Nielsen ratings data but these days she brings her imagination to life by writing books. She has wanted to be a writer since she was very young, but it's taken the time for her to amass enough courage and overall life experience to bring that dream to life. Some of those life experiences came from the wonderful world of advertising, banking, and local television media research. She is a proud wife and mother, and a Jacksonville native. When she's not out and about with her family, you can find her at her local library, the grocery store, in her car jamming out to some tunes, or hibernating while she writes and/or reads books.

Made in United States
Orlando, FL
29 April 2024